Jack

Viking Warriors MC

Book One

By:

DEBBIE HYDE

Copyright©2025 Debbie Hyde

This book is a work of fiction. Names, characters, places, and incidents are the product of the author's imagination. Any resemblance to a real person, living or dead, events, or locals is entirely coincidental.

All Rights Reserved. No part of this book may be used or reproduced in any manner whatsoever without the author's written permission except in the case of brief quotations in critical articles and reviews.

Cover Design: Debbie Hyde
Front Cover Model: Ghostface_gulfcoast
Back Cover Model: Deposit Photo
ISBN: 979-8-3484-7147-7

In this series: Ariel's story is Kacy's story.

Honoring the memory of:
Kacy Magnolia Roberson, my daughter.
June 2, 1988 – January 18, 2011
You and your bright blue eyes, wonderful smile, funny, sarcastic attitude were ripped from us. Losing you wasn't fair. It's not right. It shouldn't have happened. You're missed. Oh, so missed. It hurts. It will always hurt. My world forever changed the moment you left. Even the air doesn't feel the same. My soul is gutted. Your babies are no longer 3 and 4. They're teens now and so amazing. She's sweet and creative. He has your attitude. If I could flip our world back to right, I would in a heartbeat. I miss you, so so much.
I love you, Katie Bug. Always will.
Mom

And to:

Angel Magnolia Roberson, my granddaughter
Due to this world June 24, 2011
Entered Heaven with her mother on January 18, 2011
Oh my sweet little girl. We didn't get to meet you or hold you. But you are deeply loved. I would have loved to have heard your laugh. Sadly, the only sound you got to make in this world was through a heart monitor in an ER a month before we lost you. Nanny will see you someday sweet girl. For now, you play big and fly high until we meet. It won't be easy, but keep your mom in line for us. I love you little angel.
Nanny

Trigger Warning

This series is meant to give a voice to victims of domestic violence. The subjects here may be harder to read than my recent novels. Please don't read if you are triggered by any of the following: domestic violence, mental, physical, and verbal abuse. Loss of a loved one, grief. Fighting, death. Some scenes won't be graphically detailed.

I lost my daughter and unborn granddaughter to this horrible crime. In this series, Ariel's story is Kacy's story.

This series is for every victim of Domestic Violence. Abuse is wrong, no matter the form it takes, physical, emotional, or verbal. You don't have to stay. You can go. You aren't meant to hurt like this. You are precious and should be loved, honored, and treated like the angel you are. Ariel's Angels in this series is a fictional group, but there are people to help. The Domestic Abuse Hotline number will be included below and in the back of every book in this series.

End the Silence – Stop the Violence.

National Domestic Violence Hotline
CALL 1-800-799-SAFE (7233)
CHAT www.thehotline.org
TEXT "START" to 88788

And for love is respect for youth, focusing on healthy dating relationships:
CALL 1-866-331-9474
CHAT www.loveisrespect.org
TEXT "LOVEIS" to 22522

1
Jack

This meeting is a joke. We don't belong here. Well, I don't. From the look my best friend is giving me from the corner of his eye, he knows he doesn't belong either.

Coty Michaels has been my best friend since we were toddlers. Our families are part of the same motorcycle club. An MC I'm proud to have been born into. No clue why I developed a wild hair and had to roam around the country for the past two years. Naturally, when I left Willow Creek, Tennessee, Coty went with me. To be honest, I probably would have gone home within six months if I had been out here alone.

"He's an idiot," Coty leans over and whispers.

I'm only half listening, but I nod anyway. My eyes roam around the room. We're in the main room of the Freedom Riders MC clubhouse. It's one of the smaller clubs south of Lexington, Kentucky. They're not a bad group. Far from it, in fact. From everything I've heard and witnessed over the last couple of months, the Freedom Riders are well on their way to transitioning into an all-Christian club. There's nothing wrong with that. I just highly doubt some of our guys will do well here.

"After much debate, we've decided that anyone who's not a blood relation to a member of the Freedom Riders has to join as a prospect like any new recruit." President Brant's eyes roam over the men sitting in the back row with me.

His decision doesn't surprise me. Within three days of arriving at this clubhouse, it was clear that most of our group wasn't wanted. Harry's blood relation. His little group of close-knit friends have blended in gracefully. No clue why they call him Harry. It's not his name.

"Jack." Coty nudges me with his arm. He feels the same bad vibes as I do.

"I know."

My eyes lock with President Brant's. He continues his little speech, but I tune him out. He's not a bad man. He just doesn't like strangers. Sadly, he's a sorry excuse for a leader. After tonight, he's not my problem.

Our group isn't technically a club anymore. They're nomads after leaving the Iron Rebels in Montana three months ago. When Buzz took over as President, the club started falling apart. Coty and I weren't members of the Iron Rebels. We met them on a run near Billings one day. We hit it off with Harry and just followed them around for a while.

Buzz began pulling the club into some dark, illegal business deals. Several members loudly voiced their disapproval. Fighting broke out among them daily. At the end of the last fight, which sent a few men to the Emergency Room, Buzz demanded that anyone not loyal to his rule leave. Harry convinced about half of the guys to follow him to Kentucky. Coty and I went with them. Buzz and I never got along anyway.

After President Brant ends the meeting, he and his club members shake Harry's hand. Harry's closest friends nod and accept the offer to join the Freedom Riders. I'm happy for them. Harry's a good man. He deserves a club that'll stand by him.

I motion toward the door with my head. Coty and three more ex-Iron Rebels follow me out to our bikes. I'm already a member of an MC. I've no desire to join this one or any other.

"That went south." Pip pulls his leather jacket from his saddle bags. The rest of us do the same.

It's the middle of Fall. The weather isn't too cold yet. Riding at night, even in the south, gets chilly.

"It was just a polite way of telling us to go," Taylor says.

"Knew it was coming," Coty adds.

Jack

Yep. We all knew it. The five of us shouldn't have stayed this long.

"Where's everybody heading?" Bobby asks.

My eyes lock with Coty's. "Home."

Coty grins and nods once. "Bout time."

Home started calling my name the moment we turned south in South Dakota. I only planned on roaming for a year. It's past time to go home.

"Where's home?" Taylor zips up his jacket.

"Hey, guys! Wait up!" Harry runs out of the clubhouse before I can answer. He motions over his shoulder with his thumb toward the door. "Sorry, bout that."

"Not a problem." I offer him my hand. "It's been great riding with you. We're going home."

"Home." Harry nods. "You mentioned your families were club members in Tennessee."

"Yep." I take off the plain leather cut and pull my real one from my saddlebag. Coty does the same. Sliding this cut on only makes the call from home louder.

"Oh, man." Bobby's mouth drops open when he sees the logo.

Pip gives a long whistle.

"Harry, if you ever need Coty and me, contact the Viking Warriors MC in Willow Creek."

"You're James Mcleod's grandson." Harry stares at me in awe.

I nod. Coty grins. Yeah, my grandfather is well known.

"Are you Jacob's or Jason's son?" Pip asks.

I turn to face him. "Jacob's. You guys are welcome to come with us."

"Thanks for the offer." Bobby sticks his hand out. I gladly take it. "The three of us have family in North Carolina. We're gonna head home, too."

"If you ever need us, just call." I make him the same offer.

The three men shake our hands, get on their bikes, and ride away into the night. It's kind of sad to see them go. I have a feeling it's not the last we'll see of them, though. I have their numbers. We'll stay in touch.

"You guys sure you don't want to stay the night and leave in the morning?" Harry asks.

"Nah, man." I climb on my bike and reach for my helmet. "We'll put a couple of hours behind us and get a room somewhere for the night."

"Sorry, bout your uncle." Harry drops his head. "And your sister." The last part was spoken so low. I'd have missed it if I didn't know it was coming.

"Yeah." My eyes meet Coty's. He drops his head and looks away.

My Uncle Jason died when I was ten. The cops said it was an accident. My family's not so sure. Losing Uncle Jason almost destroyed my family. His son, Jay, and I are more like brothers than cousins. We were born two weeks apart. We were inseparable until I left two years ago. Jay wanted to go with us, but he refused to leave his mom. And my sister? We're not talking about my sister.

"Can't believe we've had biker royalty with us all this time." Harry chuckles and shakes his head.

"I don't know about that." I've never liked being called royalty. Yeah, my grandfather is one of the founding members of the Viking Warriors and the first President.

"Well, check in once you get there." Harry holds up his fist.

"Will do." I bump his fist with mine and watch as he walks back inside.

"We gonna call our families?" Coty grabs his helmet.

I nod. "We'll ride a bit, get a room, and call them in the morning."

Just thinking of my family has me homesick. We'd ride through the night if Willow Creek weren't four hundred miles away. I can't wait to see everyone. Coty and I didn't leave on bad terms. We call home a couple of times a week. Our families and the entire club will happily welcome us home. My grandmother and our moms may have even begged us to return a few times. Yeah, they actually did.

"Maybe your sisters will be there when we pull up." Coty grins as he slides his helmet on.

I reach over and punch his arm hard. "Don't touch my sisters."

He laughs and starts his bike. I have two sisters, one older and one younger. Coty won't touch either of them. They're like sisters to him. His little sister is best friends with my little sister. Besides, Coty has his eye on someone else. Well, he did before we left. Hopefully, she hasn't wandered off and gotten involved with anyone. If Kayla had given him the time of day two years ago and asked him to stay, Coty never would have left Willow Creek. Without him, I doubt I would have left either.

Jack

"We're really going home." Coty's voice has a hint of excitement and unbelief, as if he never thought we'd do it.

"Yeah." The ties of home are pulling on my chest tonight.

Coty extends his left arm with his hand in a fist. "Till Valhalla." His excitement overtakes his unbelief.

It's been a long time since I've heard those words. Yep. Home's calling.

I extend my arm and bump fists with him. "Till Valhalla." I'm ready to get out of here. "Let's ride."

I start my bike and lead the way out of the parking lot. With any luck, by noon tomorrow, we'll be riding through the gates at the Viking's Den. It's time to go home and take my place in the Viking Warriors MC. When my dad steps down as President, it's already predicted that the position will be mine.

2
Jack

Usually, I'd sleep late on a Saturday morning, but not today. Coty and I checked out of the hotel early this morning and were having breakfast at a *Waffle House* by 8 am. We planned to ride easy today and be home by the middle of the afternoon.

We called our families while we waited for our food. Nana and Coty's mom were already at the clubhouse. They shouted the happy news that we were on our way home to everyone. Our families and club members shouted so loudly the customers sitting near us gave us dirty looks. One lady was seriously unhappy. She huffed, rolled her eyes, and grumbled under her breath. Maybe she wasn't a morning person. I ignored her. Tonight, we'll enjoy a home-cooked meal and sleep in our own beds. My stomach growls at the thought of a real meal. No one cooks as good as my mom and grandmother.

We pull up at the gate in front of the Viking's Den around four in the afternoon, just like we planned. The parking lot is packed with cars, trucks, and bikes. Wow. Mom and Nana have been busy today.

"Looks like we're having a party," Coty says through the radio in our helmets.

"Wonder what the occasion could be." I can't help but laugh. This is the biggest welcome home party I've ever seen.

"Well, well, well." Ross walks out of the guardhouse with a huge grin on his face. "Look what the cat dragged in."

Jack

Roscoe Barnett has been a Viking since before I was born. He's a big man, standing over six feet tall—all muscle. Of course, he has a full beard. Most of the older guys take the Viking image seriously.

I take off my helmet and clasp hands with him. "Ross, good to see you."

"I don't like cats," Coty grumbles as he takes off his helmet.

"Too bad. Deal with it." Ross stomps around my bike to Coty. He stares Coty down for a moment before grinning again and clasping his hand. "Welcome home, Rodeo."

"Thanks, man." Coty nods toward the clubhouse. "All that for us?"

Ross turns toward the clubhouse and nods. "Your moms and Jack's grandmother organized this after you boys called this morning."

Boys? We're almost thirty-year-old grown men. The old guys don't believe a man's grown until he's forty. Got a way to go for that status.

"Mom, Nana, and Mrs. Michaels did this?" I'm no fool. All three ladies are great, but they didn't put out a call this big.

Ross chuckles. "The moment your dad heard you were on the way, our Pres demanded the biggest party in history for his son's return."

I knew it. Mom and Nana may have all the ole ladies' numbers, but they don't have the entire club's numbers. From the looks of things, half the town is here too. Dad definitely had a hand in this.

"Well, let us in, old man. Let's get this party started." Coty has talked nonstop for the last two hours about everything he's missed about Willow Creek.

"Alright, alright," Ross grumbles as he heads back to the guardhouse to open the gate.

"Sorry, you're stuck out here." I feel bad for Ross. He loves a good party.

"I ain't stuck, boy." Ross hits the switch, and the gate rolls open. "Got a couple of prospects taking over at six. I ain't missing nothing."

"See ya later, Ross." I toss a couple of fingers up in a little salute.

The two front spaces near the door to the Den are waiting for us. I mean, literally waiting. Welcome home signs with our names are staked in the ground, reserving the spots for Coty and me.

"Our sisters did this." Coty stares at the signs covered in glitter.

"Yep." When I find my little sister, I'm dumping pink glitter in her hair.

Before we make it to the door, it flies open, and my little sister runs out. Maci launches herself into my arms. Seriously, I literally have to catch her.

"You're home," Maci squeals. "You're finally home."

"I am, Lil Bit." I squeeze her tightly. Oh, how I've missed her bouncy personality. She's still getting pink glitter dumped in her hair before tonight's over.

"Come on, Big Brother. Let's get inside." Maci grabs my hand and pulls me toward the door.

Squealing from behind us has me looking over my shoulder. Coty's twirling his little sister, Ember, around. Maci and Ember are the same age. Like Coty and me, they've been best friends practically from birth. These two girls are in their third year of college. We left Tennessee not long after settling them into their dorms for their freshman year. I should have been here to watch over her the last two years. College guys can be jerks. I was always a phone call away, though. If she needed me at any time, I would have been on her doorstep handling any problem she had.

The moment I step inside the door, one of the most important women in my life slams into me so hard we almost fall. Holding her in my arms fills a hole in my chest that I didn't realize was there. I was an idiot to stay away for so long.

"Oh, my sweet boy. You're here." My grandmother rocks us side to side. She hurt her back years ago and can't bounce around like she used to. It doesn't stop her from being loud, though. She steps out of my arms and faces the club. "Jack's home!"

The room erupts in shouts and whistles. I shake my head. Nana's the only woman I know who could command this room of rowdy bikers. Well, Mom does, too.

I drop an arm around her shoulders as we walk toward the bar. "I've missed you, Nana."

"Good." She slaps her hand against my stomach. "Maybe you won't leave again."

I laugh. "I'm not leaving again. Promise."

She smiles and nods. The tears in her eyes almost undo me. I never meant to cause her pain.

"Jack!" Granddad hops off his chosen stool on the right side of the bar and wraps his arms around me.

"Hey, Granddad."

"Bout time your tail came dragging in." Dad grabs my arm and pulls me away from Granddad. He wraps me in a bear hug.

"Glad to be home." I really am.

Dad narrows his eyes. "This for good?"

I chuckle. "Yeah, Dad. I'm home for good."

"Best news I've heard in two years." Dad slaps my shoulder and turns to face the club members staring at us. "My boy's home! Let's get this party started!"

Shouts and whistles go up around the room again. People start lining up at the buffet-style tables with food along the wall closest to the kitchen. Just the smell of the food has my mouth watering.

"Jack!" Mom shouts as she runs out of the back hallway.

I run to meet her. Oh, how I've missed her. She and I talked every day while I was gone.

"Hey, Mom."

"Don't you do this again."

"I won't, Mom."

Nana instructs the ole' ladies on what food to set where in the line. No one cares as long as they get what they want. Nana just likes order. Being the first ole' lady in the club and the former Queen, no one argues with my grandmother. Well, Granddad will. And trust me. The entire clubhouse will clear out when those two argue.

"Come on, boy. Let's get a beer." Granddad pulls me over to the bar and pats the stool next to his.

Two bottles of beer magically appear on the bar in front of us. It's how things are around here when you're a McLeod.

"Good to see you, Jack." Kayla twists the tops off the two beers. She nods to me but doesn't smile.

"Thanks." I nod back.

Kayla moves to the other end of the bar and pours a couple of shots for some members. When did Kayla Chambers start bartending at the clubhouse?

I look across the room to Coty. His mom and sister hover around him with drinks and plates of food. Has he noticed Kayla yet? I don't think so, but she's noticed him. Kayla glances at Coty when she thinks no one is watching. I'm watching. I watch until plates of food magically appear in front of Granddad and me.

For the next hour, I enjoy food and drinks with my family hovering around me. This kind of attention makes me nervous. I'll let them make a fuss over me tonight. I understand because I've missed them more than I thought I would.

Dad disappeared down the hallway half an hour ago. A couple of club officers followed him. That can't be a good sign. Club business doesn't care if we're celebrating. I watch the hallway until the man I've missed the most walks out. I was wondering where he was.

One side of Jay's mouth lifts when he sees me. Before I'm off the stool, he's standing in front of me.

"Glad you're home. Sorry, I couldn't go with you." Jay wraps me in a bear hug. The men in our family hug hard.

"Sorry, I stayed gone so long." I motion to the stool next to me. "Join us?"

Jay's lips form a tight smile. He nods once to our grandfather and meets my eyes. "Can't. Got some AA work."

Oh, man. I knew something was up.

"I'll go with you." I turn to say bye to Granddad.

"Nope, boy." Granddad pulls me onto my stool. "Jay's got it. You can't leave your own party."

"They may need help," I insist.

"Look." Granddad points his finger in my face. "I'm not fighting with your Nana or your mom for losing you tonight."

Oh, good grief. I drop my head back and groan. Nana appointed him my watchdog tonight.

Jay laughs and clamps his hand down on my shoulder. "Granddad's right. Don't make your mom and Nana mad. They worked hard on this party. You can ride with us next time."

Jack

"Next time," I agree.

I watch as my cousin leads about ten Vikings out the door. He has more than enough help tonight. I won't miss the next one. AA work is the most important thing we do here at the Den. But he's darn right. I'll be there next time. There's always a next time.

3
Lily

Weekend shifts are horrible. I've been here for four hours. Only eight more to go. It's midnight. My feet already hurt. Thankfully, it's time for one of my thirty-minute breaks. I hurry to the nurses' lounge and drop down on one of the sofas. Oh, if I could stay right here for a couple of hours.

"Girl, you need to eat." Nina Lowe pops two plates into the microwaves in the kitchenette.

"Too tired to eat," I mumble.

"I brought fancy spaghetti," she sing songs.

Of course, she did. She knows I love Italian food. Fancy spaghetti is what I've always called spaghetti where you put the noodles on the plate first. You top those with the sauce and meatballs. Parmesan cheese is sprinkled on next. Add garlic bread sticks and a side salad, and you've got a complete meal. My mom always mixed the noodles and sauce in the pot before serving it. When I was ten, I had fancy spaghetti for the first time at a friend's house. It was special, different, and tasted way better.

"I'm coming," I grumble and peel myself off the sofa. The smell of the sauce and garlic bread already has my mouth watering and my stomach growling. I want this more than I want to rest.

"Did you get any sleep today?" Nina sets the food on the table in the far corner.

Jack

"A little." And by a little, I mean less than two hours.

"You can go home with me in the morning. We can crash and get a good eight to ten hours before our next shift."

Her offer sounds wonderful. Too bad I can't take her up on it. I signed up for every three-day weekend shift I could get. Twelve-hour shifts are awful and should be outlawed, but it's better than being at home on the weekends. I've been doing this for the past four months. I'm not sure how much longer I can keep it up. I can pull the thirty-six-hour weekends with no problem. Joel's getting tired of it, though.

"Thanks, but I better go home." I turn her down, like always.

I'd love to go to Nina's apartment and get some actual rest. The consequences I'd face for doing so aren't worth it. Instead, I go home and listen to Joel fuss for hours. I nap when I can. It's the best I can hope for. I started doing these long shifts so I wouldn't have to spend so much time with him on the weekends. He's getting suspicious and meaner.

"Eat up, girl. You need your strength. No telling what craziness will burst through the doors tonight." Nina pushes a plate in front of me.

"Thanks." I twirl my fork into the sauce and noodles. "You don't have to keep bringing my dinner."

"Oh yes, I do." She gets four slices of garlic bread from the mini toaster oven and joins me. "You won't eat if I don't. Besides, I always have extra."

She's lying. Nobody makes this much food when they live alone. I'm grateful she's helping. There would be many nights I'd only get to eat junk food from the vending machines if it wasn't for her. I'd love to prepare my meals for work. I don't have the time. All I'm able to do is grab a bag of snacks and rush out the door. I usually clock in less than five minutes before my shift starts.

Nina sets the plate of garlic bread between us. She doesn't reach for her fork. Her eyes practically bore a hole into the side of my head. Tonight, we worked together with a couple of patients in the ER. I knew this moment was coming. I reach for my bottle of water and take a sip. Finally, I slowly lift my eyes to meet hers. Sure enough, she's staring at me.

She reaches toward the left side of my face but doesn't touch it. "How long are you going to put up with this?"

"It's nothing." I drop my head and glance around the lounge. Thankfully, we're alone.

"That's not nothing. Makeup doesn't hide it as well as you think."

Nina has been a nurse for over ten years. Half of that time, she's worked in the Emergency Room. She's seen a lot of horrors come through those doors. If this were a small town, maybe we wouldn't treat so many serious cases. As sad as it would be, a sick child in the middle of the night would be better than what we see. Every week, it's a never-ending cycle of car accidents, street fights, gunshots, stabbings, and abuse of every kind. I swear, Los Angeles doesn't sleep.

"It'll be okay." I break off a small piece of garlic bread.

"That's not true." Nina's voice lowers. "And it only gets worse."

"I can handle it." I close my eyes, knowing it's a lie.

"You shouldn't have to." Nina sighs. "Let me help you."

"There's nothing anyone can do." There's not, and I know it.

Joel's father is a cop. He's told me several times that there's no help for me.

"You're a nurse. You know we're in a position to report stuff like this." Nina watches the door. No one enters.

I grab her wrist. "No. Please don't do it. Please," I beg.

Nina's the only friend I have here. If Joel knew about her, he'd make me stop talking to her. All my friends from medical school have drifted away. They buy my excuse that I'm working or going out with my boyfriend.

"You know domestic abuse cases end badly if the woman doesn't get help." Nina's eyes plead with me to listen.

She's right. Most abuse cases end up here or worse. We treated a woman an hour ago. A fight with her husband brought her here with a broken arm. She needed surgery to reset it. The doctor on duty called the cops. Her husband was arrested when he showed up at the ER to check on her. She was already on the elevator heading to the operating room and missed his threats of finding her when he got out of jail. Hopefully, with the cops hearing him, he stays behind bars a little longer.

As a nurse, I've seen several domestic cases over the last three years. I know some women get away from their abusers. They always need help to escape. Most only make the break after being sent to the ER.

Some women don't make it out. Most that do go back to their boyfriends or husbands, and the cycle repeats. It's what I do. Only I don't seek medical help. It's better to treat myself in the bathroom and cover up the bruises with makeup. They're getting worse, and I know it. As Nina said, makeup isn't hiding them completely anymore.

My biggest fear about leaving is what will happen to me when he finds me. Joel works at a law firm. He's still in college and hasn't sat the bar yet. His dad's a police officer here in Los Angeles. He has me bound in every legal way possible. We've lived together for a year and a half. The first six months were great. The last year has been a nightmare.

"Nobody can help me. Please don't say anything?" I plead.

Nina is trained to notice the signs of abuse. She let it slip one night that she volunteers at a women's shelter. A shelter won't help me. I rarely work with the same nurses in the ER. It's one of the reasons I asked for this position. The ones I see more than a couple of times a month seem content with minding their business. Nina is in her late thirties. She's been around a while and doesn't often look the other way.

Nina reaches over and gently squeezes my hand as two nurses walk in. "If I could, would you let me?"

I squeeze back and whisper, "It's not possible."

"You're wrong, but I won't push tonight." Nina picks up her fork and twirls it in the noodles.

I drop my eyes to my plate. I'm too emotional to look up with other people in the room. The two nurses are caught up in their stories about going out next weekend with their friends. I miss those days. I have no one to hang out with except for Joel. Joel Clark only hangs out with his lawyer friends, college buddies, and his family. Sadly, that's the only places I get to go if I'm allowed out at all.

Could Nina be right? Is there help for someone like me? Can I hope? I don't dare. It's why I don't talk about my personal life with anyone. Hope's a dangerous thing. It can get you killed if you're not careful. No, there's no help or hope for me. Sadly, I've accepted my fate. I stay as quiet as I can and don't cause waves. Sadder yet, there's only one way out of this for me.

4
Lily

Lillian! Wake up!"

"Uh," I groan.

Pain shoots through my left side. What just happened?

"Lillian! Did you hear me?" The angry voice shouts louder this time.

My eyes pop open as the realization hits me. My work shoes, under the edge of the bed, lay inches from my face. Oh no. He's in a bad mood today.

"What?" I quickly scramble to sit up. "I'm up."

"Are you?" Joel snaps.

"Yes." I push to my feet and hiss from the pain in my left arm.

Oh my gosh. This idiot literally pushed me out of bed. I look across the bed at him and narrow my eyes. Big mistake.

"You were supposed to be up an hour ago." Joel storms around the bed and hovers with his face over mine.

"I'm sorry. I worked late. Three ambulances showed up before my shift ended. I had to stay over. I was just tired," I whisper the last part.

It's what happened and why I was two hours late getting home this morning. Joel won't care. He only cares about himself and his high society image.

"That doesn't explain why it's 7 pm and you're still asleep," he snaps.

"It's seven?" I gasp. "Oh, no. I'm going to be late for work."

"Late for work?" Joel grabs my left arm, sending pain shooting up it.

I grit my teeth to keep from crying out. "Yes. I have to be there at eight."

He knows this. Again, he doesn't care.

"That's it. I'm tired of you working all the time. Get on an eight-hour shift like a normal person or quit." He shoves me away.

The right side of my head hits the doorframe of the master bathroom. I stumble to my knees but quickly force myself to stand. If he sees me down for long, it just gets worse. The pain in my cheek is enough to know I'll have a bruise before I get to work. I'll have to take my makeup with me to keep covering it throughout the night.

"I'm not kidding, Lillian." He stomps to the bedroom door. "This is the last night you work weekend shifts. It's like you don't want to be around me."

Really? I hadn't noticed. Of course, it's why I work these shifts.

"No. It was what I was told to do," I lie.

"Well, I'm telling you, it ends today or else!" Joel storms down the hallway, leaving me alone.

One look in the bathroom mirror confirms my fears. Yep. My right eye and cheek will be black and blue within the hour. I don't have time to think about it or form a plan. I grab my scrubs from the closet and quickly put them on. After applying as much makeup as I have time for, I toss the containers into my purse. I slide my shoes on and grab a jacket. I need to get out of here fast before Joel decides we need to *talk* some more. He doesn't know how to talk calmly about anything when we're alone.

I release a long breath before stepping into the hallway. Maybe I can get out of here without him seeing me. The apartment is quiet. Maybe he left. A little hope blooms as I rush to the front door. What did I say about hope? Yeah. It's never a good thing.

Joel grabs my left arm as I step into the living room. I hiss from the pain. He digs his fingers in deeper and leans toward me.

"That hurt, Lillian?" His eyes practically dance. "Good. It'll be worse if you work another twelve-hour shift. End it tonight."

"I have to go." I jerk my arm.

He doesn't release me. His nails claw deeper into my skin. I jerk again and manage to pull free. My arm's bleeding. I know it is. I don't have time to treat it before work. I really have to get out of here. I run down the hall to the stairs and don't bother with the elevator. Like a crazy woman, I fly down the three flights to the parking garage. My car sits as a beacon of safety, even if it's for a few minutes. Thankfully, Joel doesn't come after me, and I make it to work with ten minutes to spare.

"Hold on there, Miss Harman." Doctor Thomas stops me on the way to the nurses' lounge. "You can't work in that condition."

He leads me to one of the Emergency Rooms at the end of the hall next to the stairs. It's the smallest room in the ER. We rarely use it.

"Sit there." He points to the bed. "I'll get someone to help us."

"It's okay." I'm protesting to a closed door.

Wow. That's the fastest I've seen him move. He just left me here. It's a good thing I'm a nurse. I can treat myself and bandage my arm before another nurse sees me like this.

Lifting my shirt sleeve, I see the deep scratch marks Joel's fingernails left behind. The bleeding has stopped. That's good. I wet some paper towels and begin cleaning the wound. There's no mirror in here, so I don't know how my face looks. Bad, I'm sure, from the pain. I'll have to slip into the women's bathroom and apply more makeup. Some ibuprofen will help the pain. I have a full bottle in my purse. The last thing I need is a prescription and a record of this.

The door flies open before I can properly bandage my arm. Oh no. Nina rushes in ahead of Doctor Thomas.

"Oh my," Nina gasps as her hand flies to her chest.

"I trust you to handle this," Doctor Thomas says.

"Yes, Doctor. I have this under control." Nina gives him a firm nod. He hands her a file and leaves.

"Nina." I try to turn away, too embarrassed for her to see me like this.

"No, ma'am." She opens a cabinet and pulls out a Polaroid camera. "I need to see that arm and your face."

"No, Nina. You can't report this. He'll kill me, " I cry.

She steps in front of me, forcing me to look her in the eye. There's no judgment in her eyes. She cares. She's the only friend I have left in the world.

"I'm not calling the cops, but I'm helping because if I don't, he *will* kill you. Now, show me the arm, Lily."

Jack

"What? You're not reporting it?"

She shakes her head. "Trust me, please."

Why I do it, I don't know. I hold my arm out, and she snaps a couple of pictures. Next, she gets three of my face. She slides the pictures and the file Doctor Thomas gave her into a manila envelope and seals it. What in the world is going on? Without a word, she treats and bandages my arm as fast as she can.

"Where's your phone?"

I take it from my pocket. She snatches it up and tosses it into a cabinet.

"Nina?"

"Shh. No talking. You listen." She opens one of the bottom cabinets and pulls out a black bag. It looks like a book bag or a small backpack.

"What are you doing?" Naturally, I don't stay quiet.

"We're getting you out of here before he hurts you again," she replies calmly, like this is an everyday thing.

"We?"

"Yes. We." Nina doesn't explain further. She opens the bag and shoves the envelope in before offering it to me. "Here."

"What is that?" I cross my arms. "I'm not taking it until you explain."

"We don't have time for me to explain everything." She peeps out the door. "Take the bag and follow me. We can talk while we walk."

Reluctantly, I take the black bag and walk with her to the door leading to the lower-level parking garage. Doctors use this level. None of this makes sense, and she doesn't talk while we walk.

"Nina?"

"Come on. Almost there." She doesn't slow our pace either.

Finally, she pushes the door open to the garage. A black pickup truck is parked near the door, not in a parking space. A man I've never seen holds the passenger door open—a huge, serious-looking man.

"Nina?" I take a step back.

She gently takes me by my wrists to keep from adding more pain to my left arm. Tears well up in her eyes.

"I've known for months what you're going through."

"I..." Oh my gosh. I'm going to cry. She knew but never said anything.

"Shh. It's going to be okay. Maybe not today or tomorrow, but someday." Nina sniffles. "I've been where you are. It's why I know there's help."

I shake my head as the first tears begin to fall, for me and for her. "I can't. You know I can't. He'll find me."

She doesn't listen. "This is Andrew. He's going to start you on this journey to freedom. You'll meet a couple more helpers along the way."

"I can't leave." I really should leave.

She continues, "You have nothing holding you here. You'll start over in a new town and a new state." She taps the black bag in my hands. "There's a few days worth of clothes in here and some cash."

"Nina? What have you done?"

"I'm saving my friend." She leans closer. "When you get to the final stop, ask for Jacob. Tell him I sent you and say Ariel."

"What? Who's Ariel?" I don't understand any of this.

"Lily, pay attention, please." She doesn't yell and scream at me like Joel does, so I listen. "Do you understand what I just said? It's important."

"Yeah. Ask for Jacob. Tell him you sent me. Say Ariel," I repeat the strange list.

"Good girl." She taps the bag again. "Give Jacob the envelope, but don't open it. It needs to be sealed when he gets it."

Fear rises. "I don't know."

"If you stay here, you'll die," Andrew says.

"Well, thanks, dude, for not sugarcoating things," I mumble.

Andrew shrugs. I can't fault him for being honest. He's not saying anything I don't already know. I don't know exactly what's happening, but they offer me hope. I already know how hope goes. Do I take it? I can stay and die, or I can die trying to get away.

"I wouldn't do this if there was another way." Nina gently wraps her arms around me. "I love you, my sweet friend."

That did it. That's where she broke through my fears. Well, I'm still scared, but maybe I can do this.

"I love you, too." I wipe the tears from my eyes. I look toward Andrew. "You trust him?"

Jack

Andrew shakes his head and rolls his eyes. A hint of a smile tugs at the corner of his lips.

Nina smiles at him. "With my life. They've been saving women like us for ten years or more."

Wow. I never knew something like this existed.

"We're wasting time," Andrew says.

"He's right." Nina smiles through her tears. "You have a long journey ahead of you."

I walk to the truck and turn to face her. "Will I see you again?"

Nina shrugs. "I don't know. You being safe and alive is more important to me."

"Thank you," I whisper and climb into the passenger seat before I change my mind.

I have no idea where I'm going or what's going to happen to me. I stare out the tinted window for hours. Andrew leaves me in my thoughts, only speaking when we stop for gas, restroom breaks, and food. Tomorrow, I'll meet a new helper and keep moving. Are these people risking their lives to save women? I don't know, but I'm glad they exist. Hope is a crazy, elusive thing. For the first time in my life, I allow it to bloom.

5
Lily

What am I doing? I've totally and completely lost my mind. This cannot be my life right now. Leaving was a mistake. I'm going to be in so much trouble. I drop my face into my hands and struggle not to fall apart. Well, any more than I already have. I'm a mental and emotional mess. I can't believe Nina did this to me.

"Breathe, girl. It's going to be okay." Gwen pats my back as she walks over to the window.

For her, everything is okay. For me, it's all kinds of ways wrong. Since Sunday night, I've been riding and sleeping in hotels. Not the big fancy kind either. We've been stuck here in Texas for two days. If I ever see Nina again, I'm giving her a piece of my mind.

"It's not okay," I cry. "Take me back."

Gwen lightly laughs. "No. No. No, girl. It doesn't work that way."

I slide off the bed and begin pacing. "If I go back now, I could apologize. Maybe I could come up with some story about rushing out of town for a family member." I nod several times. "It might work."

Gwen drops the edge of the curtain and plants herself in front of me. She roughly grabs my upper arms and gives me a little shake, snapping me out of yet another crazy moment.

"It won't work. Do you hear me?" She leans right in my face. "If you *ever* go back, you'll be dead within an hour."

"Dead?" My breath comes in quick gasps.

"Dead," she repeats firmly.

"I don't want to die."

"You won't." Gwen slowly shakes her head. "You're not going back. You're just scared. It's the fear talking. Your mind wants to go back to what's familiar. Fear has you trapped. We're setting you free."

Free. I latch onto the word. Oh, what I'd give to be free. Free from the pain, the fear, and free of Joel. Freedom is like hope. Both are fleeting and unreachable for me.

Gwen keeps her hands on my arms as I slowly lower myself to sit on the edge of the bed closest to the bathroom. Who knows. Maybe she guided me.

Sunday night, Nina started me on this insane journey. Tuesday afternoon, Andrew handed me over to Gwen. I have no idea where we were when I switched vehicles. All I remember is it was at a truck stop along the interstate. I'm not even sure which interstate.

A new helper was supposed to meet us late Wednesday night. They had a family emergency, causing my journey to halt longer than Gwen said should happen. My first thought flew to Joel. Had he somehow tracked me down and hurt the helper? Gwen didn't mention the helper's name. She assures me they had a genuine emergency, and a replacement is on the way. I'm not so sure I trust this system. All I know is that every minute we spend in this motel in the middle of Nowhere, Texas, causes me to go a little crazier.

For the next half an hour, I sit quietly on the edge of the bed and either pick or bite my fingernails. Gwen peeks around the curtain into the parking lot every few minutes. She's watchful yet calm. It's good that she is. I'm freaking out enough for both of us. She quickly checks her phone when it dings with a text.

She smiles at me. "Time to go."

Sensing I still need help, Gwen picks up the black backpack Nina gave me with one hand and takes my arm in her other. She leads me out the door to a dark blue pickup truck. I'm going to miss her minivan and calm voice.

The huge mountain of a man holding the passenger door open freezes me in my tracks. Andrew was a big man. This man is about the same height, maybe an inch or so taller. His muscles, however, make Andrew look like a child. Joel would be a ragdoll next to this man.

"Gwen?" I pull back slightly.

"It's okay," she assures me as she hands my backpack to the mountain. He puts it in the backseat. "This is Shepherd. He's taking you the rest of the way."

"The rest of the way?" I blink and stare at her like she's the crazy one.

"You're almost there, sweetie." Gwen pats my hand and nudges me toward the open truck door.

My eyes drift back to the mountain. "I don't know him."

He smiles and remains quiet.

Gwen laughs. "You didn't know me either." She taps Shepherd on the stomach. She probably broke her fingers. There's not an ounce of fat on this man. "He's a big guy, but he won't let anything happen to you."

Shepherd nods and patiently continues to hold the door open. I lock eyes with him. "Where are we going?"

His smile fades. He gives me a moment to understand that he's serious. "I'm taking you to Jacob."

"Jacob? Nina told me to ask for Jacob." I've repeated the things she told me to say at least a hundred times in my mind since leaving LA.

"Where is he?" No one has given me clear information about any of this.

"You'll meet him tonight." Shepherd motions to the passenger seat.

I cautiously take a step forward before spinning around to face Gwen. "Who is this Jacob? Why's he so important?"

Her eyes go to Shepherd for a moment. They have some sort of silent conversation before she turns back to me and smiles. "Jacob's story is his to tell when he chooses to tell it. He and his family started this organization."

"This is an organization?" My eyes dart between them. "An actual organization? With a name?"

They both laugh. And it hasn't gone unnoticed that they aren't clearly answering my questions. So far, all my *'helpers'* have done is given me more questions than answers.

"Yes, dear. This is a real organization." Gwen takes a deep breath and wraps her arms around me. Who knew she was a hugger? "It was nice meeting you, Lily. I wish it were for better reasons, though."

Gwen drops her arms and steps onto the sidewalk outside our motel room door. She was with me the longest on this journey. I'm going to miss her.

I climb up into the truck and fasten my seatbelt. I smile and wave goodbye to Gwen as we pull out of the parking lot. She didn't share much of her personal life with me. Well, not her present life, anyway. From the things in the back of her minivan, she has at least one child. She did tell me she grew up near the beach, but not which beach.

My other helpers didn't answer my questions. It's highly doubtful this one will either. Does it stop me from asking questions? Not at all.

"I'm Lily." I wait until we're on the interstate to introduce myself. I'm sure he already knows my name.

"Nice to meet you, Lily. Did you get breakfast?"

I drop my eyes to my stomach like it has the answer. It's only eight in the morning. Breakfast was the furthest thing on my mind. The only breakfast our motel included were muffins, coffee, and fruit. Gwen went across the street to a café for all our meals for the two days we were stuck there.

"No." I keep my eyes on my lap. "I was too nervous to eat."

"There's a travel center about thirty minutes away." He lifts a finger from the steering wheel to point ahead of us. "They have a little kitchen and make breakfast sandwiches. They have donuts, too. And I think you can get a hotdog and burritos twenty-four seven. We could get breakfast, top off the tank, and get road trip snacks."

"Sounds good." I also need to go to the restroom, but I'm not saying that out loud. I look Shepherd over from the corner of my eye. He, like Andrew, is wearing some type of leather vest. I can't get a good look at the emblem on it. He doesn't seem like the talkative type. I'll try asking a few questions anyway. "What's the name of your organization?"

Shepherd scratches the back of his head and scrunches up his face. "Jacob usually shares that."

"Uh." I toss my hands up. "Why's everyone so secretive?"

These people are crazy. They expect me to go along with them but won't explain things. I'm a deranged lunatic for following along so blindly. One teeny tiny glimpse of freedom let way too much hope bloom. I sniffle and wipe my cheek with my palm.

"Look." Shepherd holds up a hand and quickly wraps it back around the steering wheel. "I know this is scary for you. I promise you'll understand once you hear the whole story tonight."

I snap my head toward him. All of a sudden, every nerve in my body is on edge. "Tonight?"

"Yes, tonight." He glances at me and nods. "We'll be there in about eight hours."

Wow. Eight hours. It feels too soon. It's Friday. I left California five days ago. I should want this journey to end. Knowing it will in eight hours twists my stomach into knots.

Oh, please don't let me throw up in this truck.

"Relax, Lily. Slow, deep breaths. You're okay. You're safe. You're going to be fine. I can pull over if you need me to." Shepherd doesn't take his eyes off the road.

Oh my gosh. Did I say that out loud?

"I will tell you this much." He pauses and waits for me to calm down. I nod when I'm ready. "One reason this is so secretive is because every member has sworn to protect the organization. No matter what."

Well, that's not a big surprise. It's obvious none of the helpers I've met is going to share anything useful. Women have to be crazy or desperate to trust them. Like me. I'm crazy and desperate. Plus my friend didn't give me a choice.

"And the main reason it's so secretive is because thousands of women's lives depend on it being this way." He glances at me again. "Women just like you."

Women like me. He means abused women. Women who couldn't walk away on their own.

"Do you personally know Jacob?" So far, the man is a myth to me.

"I do," he admits.

"How do I know I can trust him?" I should have asked these questions five nights ago. Nina didn't answer the few questions I did ask that night.

"You don't know." Wow. Shepherd may be the most honest person I've met. "You trust the person who started you on this journey. They wouldn't have contacted us if you didn't need help."

"Yeah. Nina didn't give me any warnings. She just handed me off to Andrew with a hug and instructions about Jacob."

"Nina?" Shepherd sounds surprised and looks at me questionably. I nod. "Well, trust me. You're in good hands." He pauses for a moment. "And your friend saved your life."

Yeah, she probably did. Hopefully, I can thank her someday.

"What happens when we get there?" No one has explained the outcome to me yet.

"You'll meet Jacob. Maybe some of his family. He'll look over your folder and help you start your new life." He says it so casually that I can almost picture it.

Wait. I jolt up straight. "New life?"

Shepherd laughs. "Yeah. A new life. One where you'll be safe and happy."

I take a deep breath and lean back against the seat. "Safe. Happy. That sounds nice."

"Yeah," he says softly. "Just remember to say what Nina told you to."

"I will." I give him a tight smile as he pulls up to the gas pumps. "And thank you for telling me this much."

"Between you and me?" He grins.

For the first time in days, who knows how many, I laugh. "Yeah. Between you and me."

"Now, out. Food." Shepherd winks before opening his door.

I laugh again and follow him inside the travel center. In eight hours, I'll finally meet Jacob and discover what a safe, happy life could look like. There's that hope blooming a little more. At this rate, she'll be a full blossom soon.

6
Jack

Sure, coming home is a big deal. I don't think it calls for six days of partying, though. The entire Viking Warriors MC charter seems to disagree with me. I've told them every day for six days that I don't need another welcome home party. It's Friday night, and this one is just as big, if not bigger, than the first night I was home.

The first party was mainly family, friends, local townsfolks, and the brothers within a few hours' riding distance. Tonight, it's still family, friends, and everyone my family knows within riding distance. Tonight also brings in a hundred or more Viking Warriors from other chapters. At least six more states are represented here tonight. Needless to say, the Viking Den is a madhouse of activity tonight.

The Den has become suffocating. Every two steps I take, someone new welcomes me home. Most of those interactions have turned into thirty-minute conversations. I love seeing everybody and talking with them. I just need a few minutes to myself.

"Ross, you better win this pot." I nod to the pile of money in the center of the table. That's a nice size pot.

"Plan on it. You should join the next hand." Ross has been trying to get me to play poker with him all week.

He stopped me as I was walking by. Naturally, I had to speak with the other five men at his table. Two are local townsfolk. Three are out-of-state brothers. They're braver than I am. Ross has an unnatural way of winning. He swears it's lady luck. His wife walks by from time to time. She pats his shoulder, kisses his cheek, and walks away. Several men over the years have accused Ross of cheating. No one has ever proven it, though. The cameras can't even catch him if he is. Just know. I'll never play poker with Ross. I like keeping my money.

With a final nod to everyone at the table, I make a beeline for the bar. I need a drink and some fresh air. From the looks of things, my best friend needs saving.

I walk up to the bar and toss an arm over Coty's shoulders. "Crashing and burning again, I see."

"Shut up." Coty shoves my arm away.

The man next to Coty happily gives me his stool and heads out back. He has the right idea. I just need to tease my friend for a little bit first.

"Kayla!" I slap my hand on the bar. She turns at the sound of my voice. "Beer, sweetheart."

Coty growls and elbows me in the side. If looks could kill, his eyes would cut me in half. I can't help but laugh. He's an idiot sometimes.

Kayla twists the top off a bottle and sets it on the bar. She gives me a big smile. "Good to see ya, Jack."

She turns and walks away without so much as a glance at Coty. Oh, she knows he's there. He makes his presence known every chance he gets.

"Hey!" Coty calls out. Kayla finally glances at him over her shoulder. Coty lifts his empty beer bottle. "Can I get another?"

Kayla drops her head back and rolls her eyes. Sure, Coty could go outside and grab all the beer he wants from one of the coolers. However, my friend has parked himself right here on this very stool every night since he found out Kayla is now one of our bartenders.

Kayla grabs another beer. She walks right up in front of Coty, locks eyes with him, and sets the bottle on the bar. For a moment, they stare at each other. Coty opens his mouth. Before he can speak, Kayla snaps her head toward me.

"Can I get you anything else, Jack?" Her sweet smile is all for show.

Coty sits with his mouth hanging open. Kayla continues to ignore him and pretends she's happy waiting on me. These two need to work out whatever their issues are.

"No, ma'am." I nod and lift my beer. "Thanks. I'm heading outside."

"Great. Enjoy your night." Her eyes move to Coty, giving him a little hope. Her smile fades, along with his hope. I swear an icy feeling settles over us. "Take your friend with you." She spins on her heels and storms into the kitchen.

"Come on, Rodeo." I grab Coty's arm and pull him off the bar stool.

Reluctantly, he follows me. At the back door, he twists off the top of his beer and tosses it into the trash can.

"She didn't open mine," he grumbles.

I laugh so hard I have tears in my eyes. Coty shoves me ahead of him out the back door. The cool fall air is a welcomed change and just what I needed. The backyard of the Den is just as crowded as the inside. At least out here, I feel like I can breathe.

The firepit sits about halfway across the yard. A nice bonfire is already lit. A few people are even roasting marshmallows. Wooden benches surround the Pit. Those are full. Both sides of the yard are lined with picnic tables. The back side of the yard has a covered stage. Dad makes club announcements there during the summer. On nights like tonight, a live band performs. The group tonight is one I've never heard before. They aren't so bad.

The entire backyard is fenced in. Partygoers have to come through the clubhouse to get out here. Only the officers of the club have a key to the gates. Of course, my mom and grandmother do too. There's a reason for the fence. My grandmother insisted on it being built. Too many fights broke out by people we didn't know were here until it was too late. Nana actually started one of those back in her day.

"Uncle Jack!"

I hear her before I see her. I turn to the right just in time to catch my niece, Everly, as she launches herself at me.

"Hey, Twig." I wrap my arms around her and twirl her around. "Where's your brother?" I ask as I set her on her feet.

"Over with Uncle Jay." She points to my right. Ah. It's where she came flying in from.

Uncle Jay is actually Logan and Everly's cousin. They've called him uncle since they could talk. Jay's like a brother to me, so no one questioned it.

It's hard to believe she and her brother are teenagers now. I toss an arm over her shoulders. Her arm goes around my waist. I love this little girl. Everly will be seventeen in a couple of months. Logan turned eighteen back in July. He's in his senior year of high school and on the football team. He didn't have a game tonight. Next Friday night, I'll be in the stands with the rest of our family, cheering him on.

Jay and Logan sit on top of the picnic table with their feet on the bench. I join them. Everly stands next to the table and leans into my side. I happily keep an arm around her. This little lady is technically my house mouse. She's been cleaning and taking care of my house while I was away. Mom said Everly flat refused to let any of the club girls do it. My house is here on club property and in view of my parents' house. Mom had no problem letting Everly hang out during the day at my house. She's stayed with me a few nights this week. We've pigged out on pizza and ice cream.

"You okay?" Logan has me worried. He looks a little stressed.

"Yeah, Uncle Jack." Logan sighs and drops his head. "It's my last year. I need a scholarship."

My nephew loves football. He wants to play on a college team and dreams of going pro someday.

"You don't *need* a scholarship." My family has more than enough to pay for his tuition.

"I know." He slowly nods. "But if I get one, it would help." He shrugs. "It would also prove the coaches really want me."

Jay pats Logan's back. "Don't worry, kid. It's going to happen."

Jay and I lock eyes over Logan's head. If he were sitting up, we wouldn't be able to see each other. Logan's almost as tall as we are. My cousin and I nod. We'll be with him every step of the way.

Jay looks out into the crowd. He smiles and lifts two fingers. I turn to see who's approaching. I sit up straight and clasp arms with the big biker from Texas.

"Shep, good to see ya." Of all the visitors we've had this week, Shepherd is my favorite. He used to come hang out all summer with us when we were teens.

"You want a beer, man?" Coty clasps his arm next.

Shepherd rubs the back of his neck. "Yeah. That'd be great."

"Get it from one of the coolers!" I point to the cooler beside the table across the yard from us.

"Fine." Coty huffs and tosses his hands up. He was so going back inside.

My friend needs to lighten up. He's bothered Kayla enough this week. He doesn't realize pushing her too hard will eventually push her too far away. Thankfully, he listens and grabs Shepherd a beer from the outside cooler. The way Coty stomps across the yard and back is hilarious. It's all Jay and I can do not to laugh.

Coty hands Shepherd the beer and glances around. "How many more of your brothers rode with you?"

Shepherd takes a long swig and wipes his mouth with the back of his hand. "None."

Jay and I narrow our eyes at each other. That's odd.

"You rode from Texas alone?" Logan asks.

"That's not safe." Everly's eyes widen.

My niece and nephew have grown up listening to my parents and grandparents go over road safety every time we have a run. There's always someone new who hasn't a clue of what they're doing. Sometimes, we get a few riders who think they know everything. It's okay to ride locally alone, but not for long trips. The Viking Warriors is a relatively calm club. Even we have enemies. Shepherd knows all this. He was practically born on the back of a bike.

"Yes, ma'am. You're absolutely right." Shepherd ruffles Everly's hair. He's done it since she was little. My niece absolutely hates it. Shepherd is the only one who can get away with it. "But I didn't ride this time. I drove my truck."

That's odd, too. It's enough to relieve Everly's worry, though. Shepherd usually only drives his truck during the winter. It's a day's ride from here to Texas. Maybe he drove because no one in his chapter could ride with him today. Whatever the reason, I'm glad he came to welcome Coty and me home.

"It's too bad no one could ride with you. The weather was great today." Coty finishes his beer and tosses the bottle in the trash can beside the picnic table.

Jack

"Um. That's not what happened." Shepherd looks between my niece and nephew. His eyes settle on mine. "I delivered an angel."

The atmosphere around our table suddenly shifts. Everly's arm around me tightens. I return the gesture. Logan's back snaps straight. Jay places a hand on his shoulder. Coty sighs and waits for our next move.

"Where is she?" I ask.

"Your dad's office." Shepherd tosses his unfinished beer into the trash.

"She okay?" Everly's voice trembles.

Shepherd lowers his head to meet her eyes. "She will be."

Everly nods. She and her brother lock eyes. A flood of emotions overtakes them. They silently become each other's strength. It's always been this way between them. For a long time, one couldn't be in a room if the other wasn't there.

"Logan, why don't you take your sister to the kitchen to Nanny?" I suggest. My Mom's better at comforting Everly in moments like this.

Logan pushes off the table and takes his sister by the hand. "Come on, Evie. Let's go find Nanny."

Jay's phone dings. He reads the text and pockets his phone. "We're being summoned."

I stand. My eyes follow Logan and Everly walking toward the clubhouse. "Shep?"

"You guys go ahead. I'll follow them and make sure they get to your mom. I'll meet you in the office."

Shepherd doesn't just follow. He catches up and walks with them.

Shepherd's watchful eye is greatly appreciated. No one here would ever bother Everly. Logan would rip them apart if they touched her. Plus, she's wearing a Property of Viking Warriors cut. All our young girls wear them at parties. It lets newcomers and visitors know this is one of our daughters. Touching one of these girls would get a man killed.

Jay and Coty follow me inside. A few brothers in our chapter have a path cleared to the hallway leading to Dad's office. They stand side by side, creating a wall. They know an angel is here. I nod to each of them as I pass. This is the most important part of our charter. It's also the part no one knows about but our patched members and their ole ladies. Well, there are a few outsiders who help us. Each of those people has been vetted for loyalty and has sworn their life to the cause and its secrecy.

I pause outside the office door. It takes a moment to mentally and emotionally prepare myself for what we're about to walk in on. I haven't done this in a long time. This is the first angel I'll have seen in two years. Each one is different. Every single one of them is precious and deserves to be treated as such. When I'm prepared, I lightly knock on the door so the sound doesn't spook our angel.

Worley Bird eases the door open and nods when he sees me. I push the door open and step inside with Jay and Coty right behind me. One look at our angel, even from behind, causes me to stumble back into Jay. His hands quickly reach out to steady me. I was wrong. I wasn't prepared for her.

7
Lily

Whatever I was expecting, it sure wasn't this. Who would have thought a secret, mysterious organization helping abused women was possible? Sure, I came to terms with that after meeting my three helpers. After learning this was a real organization, my mind pictured a dark, hidden underground room as their base of operations. Never in a million years would I have guessed the secret organization to be bikers.

Our eight-hour ride turned into nearly twelve. Shepherd is not a drive-straight-through type of guy. After arriving here, I can definitely picture him as a biker who loves to ride for the beauty and enjoyment of it. He stopped about once an hour for snacks, restroom breaks, and just to stretch our legs. He got gas at every stop, whether we needed it or not. It was a good thing he did. A multi-car and truck pile-up on the interstate just outside of Memphis caused a two-hour delay.

The shock of realizing how wrong I was about all of this stunned me into silence when we pulled up to the fence around the building. Shepherd called ahead when we were about ten minutes away. He didn't speak to the young biker at the guardhouse. The man simply nodded to Shepherd, opened the gate, and stood at attention like a soldier until we were safely through the gate.

I'm not sure exactly where we are in Tennessee. The hundred bikes in front of the building assure me this is a motorcycle club. This entire journey has been insane. Nothing should surprise me at this point. I'm not even sure if I should be alarmed when Shepherd passes the front lot and drives around to a private one on the right side of the building.

The side door opens the moment we park. Whoa. Are there no small bikers in this club? Surely there are. This man is as big as Shepherd and Andrew. He's older but definitely not out of shape.

My door opens, causing me to jump and squeak. Shepherd lightly chuckles. I snap my head to the driver's seat. Empty. When did he get out?

"Come on, Lily. Let's get you inside." He opens the back door and gets my bag.

Numbly and quietly, I walk with him to the open door. Is this man in the doorway Jacob? Should I say hello? I have no idea what I'm supposed to do. Nina could have explained things better.

"Worley Bird." Shepherd nods to the man as we step inside.

Okay. He's not Jacob. What kind of name is Worley Bird, though?

"Shepherd." Worley Bird nods back. His eyes drop to me. "Hello, angel. Follow me."

Sounds from a very lively party come from somewhere in the building. I walk between the two huge bikers down an empty hallway. For the first time, I can study the emblem on the back of the man in front of me. I got glimpses of Shepherd's when we stopped. This one looks to be the same. Do all biker emblems have this much detail? The sounds of the party fade as I get lost in the details of the design.

A shield with a Viking sits in the center of a set of golden wings. The wings are outlined and shaded in places with red. What appears to be banners or ribbons adorn the top and bottom. The top one says Viking Warriors MC. The bottom one says Tennessee. Shepherd's bottom one says Texas. It's the only thing I caught during one of our stops. I was too afraid to ask him if I could get a closer look at the design. There seems to be a deep red or burgundy glow around the wings. It's absolutely beautiful.

The party must be around the corner. I don't get to see it. Strangely enough, I want to. I have no idea what's come over me. I've never been to a biker party. I'm led to a door on the right. Once again, what I was expecting the room to be isn't what I find inside.

Jack

The office is huge. Naturally, there's a wooden desk. Everything else takes me by surprise. The two chairs on this side look to be made of comfortable leather. A couch with a recliner on each side sits in both corners of the room closest to the door. The biggest surprise is the large window behind the desk. It becomes my focus point. Somehow, I find peace and comfort in the window. Yeah, my brain's just that warped. Why a window removes my anxiety is beyond me.

"Hello, angel." The deep voice has me snapping my gaze to the man behind the desk.

My anxiety amps right back up. No one has to tell me. Somehow, I just know. This is him. This is Jacob. Even with him sitting, I can tell he's as big as the rest of these men. He's strong and confident. He holds himself a little differently than the others. He's their leader. He's bold, brave, and a protector—or someone's destroyer. Your attitude determines which side of this man you get. No clue how I know all that just by looking into his eyes. I've never been able to do it before.

Oh, please let me be on his good side.

He smiles and motions to the chairs in front of the desk. "You definitely are, angel."

I groan as I sink into one of the leather chairs. I said that out loud. I'm going to have to get better control of myself than this.

"Shepherd, thanks for bringing her." The man behind the desk stands and clasps arms with my helper.

"Jacob, this is Lily. I'll let her tell you her story." Shepherd pauses and places a hand on my shoulder. "Stay brave, Lily. Tell him everything. Jacob's a good man. You can trust him. You remember?"

He means, do I remember what Nina told me to say? I nod. I may not remember what she said word for word, but I remember enough.

"You're leaving?" I glance over my shoulder at the door. I don't want him to go.

"Just for a moment. Your story is yours. You don't need me or anyone else hearing it. I'll come back in a bit if you want."

"Yeah." They seem to have a system for how things are done. Asking him to stay would probably be pointless, no matter how comforting his presence would make me.

Shepherd places my bag on my lap and leaves the room. I'm left alone with Jacob and Worley Bird. The big biker by the door isn't as scary. He smiles. His face holds no anger, only kindness and concern. I know the face of evil. I have nothing to fear here.

A light tap comes on the door. Worley Bird opens it just a crack at first. He quickly opens the door wide and lets a woman in. I follow her as she walks across the room to stand beside Jacob. She never takes her eyes off me.

"This is my ole' lady, Evelyn." His arm lovingly goes around her waist. The two share one of the sweetest smiles I've ever seen before looking back at me.

"Hello, angel. Do you have a message for us?" Evelyn asks.

Okay. At first, I thought it was just a coincidence. Maybe kindness because they don't know my name. It's not. There's a meaning to this. Why are they all calling me angel? My helpers called me by my real name. No one here has asked.

"Um." I swallow hard and think. Message? Oh, yeah. "I was told to ask for Jacob." I give the man a nervous smile. "And to say Ariel."

Jacob and Evelyn's small smiles completely fade as their eyes meet. She closes her eyes for a moment and takes a deep breath. An indescribable pain radiates from her. One of the reasons I became a nurse was because I sensed other people's pain and wanted to help heal it.

"Okay." Jacob clears his throat. "Can I get your envelope?"

"Oh, yeah." I quickly unzip my bag and hand him the sealed envelope Nina shoved inside.

The door behind me opens and closes. I don't turn around. My heart has latched onto the broken woman behind the desk. Embarrassment and shame fill me as I watch her go through my file with her husband. I'm assuming ole' lady means she's his wife. Whether these two are legally married or not, she definitely has the role of his wife.

Someone moves to stand beside me. I look up at Shepherd. He came back. Someone else moves behind me. I don't look to see who it is. My eyes remain on Evelyn. Finally, after what feels like an eternity, Jacob closes the file. He balls his hands into fists before laying them flat on top of the file.

Evelyn wipes a tear from the corner of her eye. Seeing her break almost breaks me. I didn't see everything Nina put in that folder. If the contents detail my life with Joel, why does it make Evelyn cry?

"Who sent you to us?" Jacob asks.

"Nina Lowe."

The couple look at each other again before turning to every person in the room. I know there are more than two people behind me. How many more? I'm not sure, but I feel their presence. Jacob nods to them.

Evelyn walks around the desk and offers me her hands. Without hesitation, I place mine into hers. She pulls me to my feet. We're about the same height. I don't flinch or protest when she reaches up to remove my sunglasses.

Jacob quickly stands. He fights to keep his hand flat on the desk. "Welcome to the Viking Warriors."

"And to Ariel's Angels," Evelyn adds.

Okay. I saw the club name on the back of Worley Bird's vest. Nina told me to ask for Jacob and say Ariel. Since arriving here, they've called me angel. It's all connected somehow.

"I don't understand."

"We've been rescuing women and children from domestic violence for going on twelve years," Jacob says.

Wow. That's impressive. I work in the medical field, but I've never heard of an organization like this. If I had known something like this existed, I could have shared it with so many women in LA.

My eyes meet Evelyn's. "Thank you for helping me, but why would you all do this?"

She glances over her shoulder at her husband. Her tears fall unchecked. The pain in her eyes when she looks back at me almost crumbles me to my knees.

"Because not everyone makes it out." She's unable to smile through her tears this time.

"Ariel," I whisper when it hits me.

She nods. "Our daughter."

"I'm sure you have more questions. We'll answer those the best we can in time." Jacob moves behind his wife and wraps his arms around her. She falls easily against his chest. "Just know, you're safe here. We'll protect you and help you start over."

"The party's a bit loud. There's more people here tonight than we expected. I don't think keeping her in the clubhouse is a good idea." Worley Bird moves to stand on my left.

"He's right." Evelyn glances up at her husband. "Lily should stay in the guest house. Evie and I will make sure she has everything she needs for a few days." Her head snaps toward someone behind me. "Where are the kids?"

Shepherd steps forward. "I walked them to the kitchen and left them with Nana since you were here."

Evelyn sighs with relief. "Thank you, Shepherd." She kisses Jacob's cheek. "I should go check on them."

"I can walk Lily to the guest house." The deep voice behind me wraps around me like a blanket.

"Really?" Evelyn raises an eyebrow.

The soothing voice chuckles. "Yes, Mom. Really."

Jacob looks around the room. His gaze finally settles over my head. "Okay then. Thanks, son."

Evelyn hands me back the sunglasses. "I'll meet you at the guest house shortly. We'll get a list together of what you need."

"Thank you." I slip the glasses on and turn to meet my escort. I'm at eye level with the man's throat and have to tilt my head back to see his face.

Wow.

His smile widens. Several others chuckle.

Oh no. I drop my head all the way back. I did it again.

"Come on, Lily." Mr. Wow takes my hand and pulls me toward the door. "I'll walk you to the guest house."

"Shepherd," I gasp and spin around to face my helper. I don't miss the deep growl from my escort. I ignore him. "What happens to you now?"

He grins. "Don't worry about me, darlin'." The escort growls deeper. Shepherd ignores him, too. "I'm going to enjoy this party tonight and head back to Texas tomorrow."

Jack

"Thank you for everything." He has no idea how much I mean those words.

"My pleasure, darlin'. But don't worry. I have a strange feeling you and I will see each other again soon." Shepherd bends over laughing when the escort steps between us.

"Bye, Shepherd," Mr. Wow snaps before turning to face me, keeping Shepherd completely blocked from my view.

"Bye, Jack. Welcome home," Shepherd says as we move toward the door.

Jack? His name is Jack. At the door, I lock eyes with another man who looks a lot like Jack.

I look between them several times. "Twins?"

"Nope." Jack takes my hand again and gently pulls me into the hall. "Cousins."

Cousins? I would have guessed they were brothers. Jack leads me to the same door Shepherd and I entered. We start down a path behind the building along a large wooden fence. The party is on the other side. It's nice to hear people laughing and having fun for a change. I squeeze the hand holding mine once we pass the fence. He pauses and turns to face me.

"Hi. I'm Lily Harman." Yeah, it's corny, but we weren't properly introduced. "Thank you for helping me."

"Hi, Lily. I'm Jack McLeod." His eyes seem to find mine through the sunglasses. I know it's not possible, though. "I will do whatever it takes to protect you forever."

"Forever?" I whisper.

He nods once, sealing his promise.

Oh wow.

He lightly chuckles again. Uh. I'm not able to control myself around him. I'm going to have to figure out how. I can't let my mind wander like this.

8
Jack

We walk in silence for a long time. Lily takes in everything around us. She reaches out with her left hand to touch the decorative bushes and trees along the path. If it weren't for the solar lights and lamp posts, she wouldn't be able to see much in the dark. My niece and nephew walk these paths at night sometimes. Mom insisted they be well-lit.

Lily doesn't pull her right hand from mine. Knowing she trusts me stokes my pride. Her trust in me is small and delicate at the moment. For now, I'll cherish and honor it. I'll deepen her trust in time.

We pause several times to allow her fingertips to gently roam over leaves and petals. Since it's fall, there aren't as many flowers in bloom as in spring and summer. Lily kneels beside a huge planter to smell the yellow flowers. I'm not sure what this plant is, but it's now my favorite. There are some burgundy and purplish ones just like it nearby. I can't wait to see which flowers along the paths are her favorites in the spring.

The women in my family have decorated all the paths between our houses. My mom and grandmother love flowers. My niece has added her little flare to the flower beds. Our homes and these paths aren't visible from the clubhouse.

My family owns two hundred acres in middle Tennessee. The clubhouse was the first thing built here. It sits on the front side of the property. It's the only thing visible to the public. Dad locked the clubhouse behind a fence over twenty years ago after an attack from a

Jack

rival club. A thick grove of trees and a second fence hide our houses. Only family members and our closest friends know where these paths are. Everyone else is stopped at the clubhouse or uses the long driveway. Lily didn't even notice when we walked through the gate on this path. Dad will close and lock it when he walks home.

The guest house sits a little farther back between my parents' house and mine. You can see it from our back porches. Dad built this little house here for a reason. He doesn't tell people why, though.

"It's beautiful, Jack." Lily stares at the house in awe. "Are you sure it's okay for me to stay here?"

I lightly laugh. "Mom said so. Trust me. It's more than okay." No one will argue with my mom or my grandmother.

With one hand, I pull out my keys and unlock the door. I hold onto her hand for as long as possible. I push the door open and let her enter first. Yeah, I noticed how she paused when she saw the porch swing. I can already picture her curled up on it with a warm blanket around her and a cup of coffee or hot chocolate in her hands. It's mesmerizing, and it's just a vision in my head.

"Oh, wow." She walks ahead, dropping my hand. I immediately miss her touch.

I follow her into the kitchen and go straight to the fridge. It's empty. That's not surprising. No one has stayed here for a long time. Mom and Everly keep this house clean, too.

"Feel free to wander around and tour the place." I motion toward the hall. She doesn't need me crowding her.

"Thanks." Lily disappears into one of the three bedrooms.

Mom's getting the things Lily will need tonight. What can I offer her now? I spy the coffee maker on the counter. Women love coffee. Let's hope Mom at least stocked the cabinets. I open the door above the coffee maker and smile. A bag of my favorite coffee is here, along with a box of little half-and-half creamers. I check the expiration before I get my hopes up, as well as Lily's. They're still good. The universe is moving in my favor tonight.

The coffee finishes brewing as Lily walks back into the kitchen. She's still wearing the sunglasses Mom handed her in the office. It's not fooling anyone. Those glasses are hiding at least one black eye.

Anger fills my chest. How could someone hurt her? A part of me wants to remove those glasses and see it. A bigger part of me wants his name so I can hunt him down and make him pay. A silent whisper in my head stops me. *She's an angel, broken and hurting.* She needs something more than my anger. She needs to feel safe, loved, and supported. She'll get all that and more from me.

"You want a cup?" I hold up a black coffee mug and a soft pink one with flowers.

"Yes, please." She eases around the table to lean against the counter a few feet away.

I fill the two mugs and set a spoon on the counter. "You can fix it how you like."

With shaky hands, she reaches for the spoon and sugar bowl. "Thank you."

Surprisingly, she prepares the black mug. For someone who stopped to smell flowers earlier to choose black now is a sign of how she's feeling on the inside. It's okay. I don't mind using a girlie mug if it helps her somehow.

With coffee in hand, I motion for her to follow me. "We can sit in the living room and wait for my mom. You probably want to relax after the ride from Texas."

She freezes at the edge of the couch. "I'm not from Texas."

Okay. That's good to know. She's been traveling for days, though. I didn't see her file to know where she's from. I'll ask Dad if I can see that tomorrow. For now, I need to ease her tension.

Smiling, I nod. "No, but it's where you met Shepherd."

Man, it hurts saying that. Shepherd spent the whole day with her. The jerk laughed at me for being protective over Lily. He's not really a jerk. Shepherd is one of the most loyal people I know. I'm just jealous of the bond he seems to have with her. That is something I will never admit out loud.

"Yeah," she says with a sigh. She relaxes and shrinks into one of the corners of the couch.

As much as I want to join her, I don't. Over the years, we've been trained on how to act around an angel. They have to be treated tenderly and with extra care. Giving them space to process trauma and emotions is very important. Even if they don't outwardly show signs of needing space or ask for it, the battle within them screams for it in their minds. It's why I sit in the recliner across from her.

She stares into her mug, still wearing the sunglasses. "I don't want to talk about it."

I settle back against the chair. "You don't have to."

"Are you sure?" She bravely lifts her head.

Are her eyes brown to match her long hair? Are they blue? Freaking gold, maybe? I want to know so badly.

"Yeah. I'm sure. It's okay."

It's absolutely not okay. Hurting her was a sin. Somebody needs to pay. Once again, it's not about me. It's about what she needs. I keep my true emotions and thoughts hidden. Trust me. It's a struggle.

"Thank you." She takes a sip of coffee and drops her head again.

We drink our coffee in silence. I want to talk to her so badly. I want to know everything about her, not just what happened to bring her here. Her voice seems to settle the anger inside me somehow. The counselors who work with us said to allow the silence and expect it to last longer than normal. Forcing her to talk wouldn't go well for me. Even small talk could create a wedge between us.

Mom and Everly walk through the door with several grocery bags on their arms. They're the reusable kind. Mom hates those flimsy little plastic ones at the store. I quickly set my mug on the end table and hurry to help them.

"Here, Mom. Let me get those." I reach out so she can slide the handles onto my arms.

Lily stands with both hands wrapped around her mug. Mom notices.

"Oh, good. You made coffee." She gently places a hand on Lily's arm.

"Um." Lily turns her head toward me. "Jack made it."

"Really?" Mom doesn't sound like she believes her. Her raised eyebrow has me rushing the grocery bags to the kitchen.

"Yes, ma'am." Lily follows Mom into the room.

Everly and I get busy putting the food away. Wow. These two raided the coolers and pantry at the clubhouse. Both are always overstocked. This didn't even put a dent in them.

"Jack, will you stay with the girls for a little bit?"

"Yeah, Mom."

Seriously? She literally just asked me to stay here? I had no intention of leaving just yet. I'm even willing to sleep on the front porch if Lily will let me.

"Sweetie, is there anything specific you need?" Mom asks Everly.

"No, ma'am. I'm fine with anything." Everly continues to put the food away.

Mom looks Lily over from head to toe. "You're about a size eight." She's not asking a question. She knows.

"What's happening?" Lily asks nervously. Fear finds its way into her voice. I swear she's about to bolt out of here.

"I'm going to the house for some things. Everly and I are going to stay with you tonight. I'll get you a few outfits."

"That's not necessary," Lily says quickly.

"It's okay, dear. I wouldn't dream of forcing you to stay alone in a strange place tonight." Mom looks over at the coffee maker. "I'll make us a fresh pot when I get back."

Mom doesn't wait for anyone to say no. She rushes out the front door and down the path to her house.

"I don't understand the problem." Everly puts a carton of ice cream in the freezer. "Uncle Jack makes the best coffee. He has all the flavors and toppings you could ever want at his house. This morning, he even made chocolate shavings for me to put on the whipped cream."

I give her a one-arm hug and kiss the top of her head. "Thanks, Evie. Love ya bunches, sweet girl." I ruffle her hair.

Naturally, she swats my hand away. "No, Uncle Jack."

If Shepherd had ruffled her hair, Everly would have laughed. Once again, bloody Shepherd. And once again, I remind myself he's my friend. I'm not used to fighting jealousy off like this. I don't like it.

Lily's mouth falls open as she watches Everly. Yeah, she figured it out. Enough was said in Dad's office for her to know Ariel was my sister. Everly and Logan are her children. They were three and four when we lost their mom. My parents got legal custody of them within two months. I was fifteen when it happened. It's still hard for me to talk about. So I usually don't.

Jack

Since Mom's making more coffee when she returns, I get my mug and finish off this pot. We're not letting good coffee go to waste. When I turn around, Everly takes the mug from my hands and takes a sip.

"Thanks, Uncle Jack." She sits down at the table with *my* cup of coffee.

I stare at my niece like she's grown horns. Hey, this is coffee we're talking about. Lily giggles, and my head snaps toward her. It's one of the sweetest sounds I've ever heard. And one I want to hear again. Every day.

"No one has to stay with me." Lily sits across from Everly.

"Nanny insists." Everly continues to sip *my* coffee.

It's okay. I'm still staring at the beautiful woman across from her, hoping she'll giggle again.

"Oh. You don't leave the women you rescue here alone." She nods like she understands. She doesn't.

Everly shakes her head. "None of the angels have ever stayed here."

Lily turns her head toward me. I really want to see her eyes. I shrug in reply to her unspoken questions. She's the only angel to stay in this house.

No more questions are asked. No stories are shared. I haven't learned much about the woman I'm destined to protect. When Mom comes through the door pulling two large suitcases, I know I've lost my chance tonight. Naturally, I get up and carry the suitcases to which bedroom Mom orders them to go. One holds the things she and Everly will need tonight. The one I placed in the master bedroom is for Lily. It was the heaviest. Mom definitely went a little overboard here.

"Now, go enjoy your party." Mom kisses my cheek. It's her way of lovingly dismissing me.

"But." My eyes seek Lily out at the table.

"Don't worry, Uncle Jack. We'll take good care of her." Everly doesn't look up from the puzzle she's putting together on the kitchen table.

Lily turns her head and quietly watches me. Mom doesn't rush the moment. I really don't want to leave. I sure don't want to go back to the party.

She finally speaks. "Goodnight, Jack."

That's it. That's all I'm getting tonight.

"I'll see you tomorrow?" I don't know why I asked it as a question. Of course, I'll see her tomorrow.

Lily simply nods. Mom takes that as her cue to lovingly push me out the door. I stare at the closed door for several minutes. I can't stand here all night. Mom will flog me in the morning if I sleep on the swing. Going back to the party really isn't an option. It doesn't feel right. Instead, I walk home. Grabbing a beer from the fridge, I drop down on a lounge chair on the back porch and stare at the lights in the guest house.

9
Lily

I wake in one of the softest beds on Earth. It's not my bed. I bolt upright the moment my eyes pop open. This is not my apartment in LA. This isn't a hotel room. This is someone's house.

As the fog from sleep fades, my breathing slowly returns to normal. I'm alone. No one is going to shove me out of bed today. Nina got me out of my horrible situation. The nightmare from it will haunt me forever. I can't call what I had a life. I had dreams in high school and college of what my life would be. I no longer know what a life is. Not a real one, anyway.

I spent five days traveling across the country with three strangers. Each of them holds a different meaning in my heart. I'm used to talking to strangers. As an ER nurse, seeing the people we meet again is rare. After a while, their faces faded away. As much as I care for each of my patients while they are in my care, I let them slip into just another medical case in my mind once they leave the hospital. Each of us in the ER had our own way of handling overwhelming shifts. Mine was letting everything disappear inside a foggy mist.

Taking a deep breath, I push the soft comforter aside and let my legs drop over the side of the bed. My thoughts go back to last night. If I weren't living this, I'd laugh and swear it was a dream or some kind of drama movie. Of all the places I could end up in, I'm at the weirdest on the list. It's so weird, in fact, that it shouldn't even be on the list.

"Thanks, Nina. A motorcycle club? Really?" I say to absolutely no one. Again, I'm alone, and Nina is on the other side of the country.

I raise my head and stare at the bedroom door. I'm not actually alone, though. On the other side of the door are two sweet ladies. Two strangers I met yesterday. They're trying so hard to help me. I need their help. I've needed every person I've met along this journey. At times, I struggle to accept their kindness.

It's different from this side. It feels wrong. I want to be the one helping. My need to help others is why I became a nurse. I'm not the helper here. My position in this is not okay. I was never supposed to need someone pulling me out of the darkness. Dignity, pride, and happiness have been ripped from me. I'm not sure either of those can ever be restored. I failed, plain and simple.

A young girl's laughter pulls me from my depressing thoughts. Everly is awake. Her laughter is so sweet and soothing. The sound is infectious. Hearing her has me laughing, too. I don't even know what she's laughing about. It doesn't matter. She's just one big ball of sunshine. The need to see her and be within the warmth surrounding her pulls me to my feet. I have to see her.

Thankfully, this room has an adjoining bathroom. I grab a pair of jeans and a long-sleeved black T-shirt from the suitcase Nanny brought last night. I was firmly told to call her Mom or Nanny, never Evelyn or Mrs. McLeod. Everly said nearly everyone here and in town calls her grandmother Nanny. It's the safest choice and the one I'm going with.

After getting dressed, I force myself to examine my face. The black eye and bruising on my right cheek are fading. It's not enough to forgo the sunglasses, though. I grab the glasses from the nightstand and slide them on. I'm no fool. The glasses hide the visual, but everyone knows I have a black eye.

Letting it all fade away, I leave the room, searching for the warmth calling me. I find Everly and Nanny in the kitchen right where I expected them to be. The scene before me is from a *Hallmark* or *Lifetime* movie. The two ladies happily move around the kitchen, preparing breakfast.

"Lily, you're up." Everly's smile widens when she sees me. She lifts a hand and twirls it like a queen or princess. "Coffee first."

Jack

I instantly smile. Sweet girl. Smart, too. Coffee is always first. Nanny beats me to the coffee maker and pours a cup. She sets it on the counter next to the sugar bowl and creamer.

"Good morning, dear." Nanny grabs two containers of flavored creamer from the fridge.

I sigh happily and take the caramel macchiato from her. "Thank you, Nanny, and good morning."

The smell of bacon gets stronger when Everly opens the oven door. I've never seen bacon cooked in the oven before. Everly's practically vibrating with excitement, trying to hold back her laughter.

"What's so funny?" I take a sip of coffee and close my eyes. A good cup of coffee is so underrated. I need to find out what brand they use.

"Uncle Jack's mad." Everly drops her head back and bursts out laughing.

That's alarming.

"What? Why?" What happened while I was sleeping?

"Oh, it's nothing to worry about, dear. He's fine." Nanny slides a pan of homemade biscuits into the oven after Everly removes the bacon.

"Why is he mad?" How can this be funny and fine? I don't ask the last part.

"Nanny wouldn't let him in the house." Everly has to sit down from laughing so hard.

"What?" This gets weirder by the minute.

Nanny flips her hand like it's no big deal. "Don't worry, hon. He really is fine. He's probably still sitting on the steps."

This is insane. I quickly set my mug on the counter and rush to the front door. I place my hands on the glass, too afraid to open the door and draw his attention. Jack isn't on the steps. He's stomping down the path away from the house. Everly and Nanny follow and watch over my shoulders. Even from here, it's clear he's fussing or complaining. Hopefully, the trees are listening because he's alone. I can't hear him without opening the door, which I'm not about to. I don't want him to know I'm watching. He tosses his arms up just before disappearing into the trees. It sends Everly to the floor in a fit of laughter.

"See." Nanny pats my arm. "He's fine."

"That's fine?" With eyes wide, I point toward the door.

"Yeah." Nanny shrugs. "Sometimes, he rants and raves, but he'll be back when he calms down."

I step over Everly, who's catching her breath, and follow Jack's mother into the kitchen. "Why couldn't he come inside?"

She turns and gives me a sympathetic look. "My son is one of the best men you'll ever meet." She sighs deeply. "He's also just like his father, overbearing at times. You don't need that today."

Fear creeps up my spine. "What's today?"

Except for the unexpected layover in Texas, I've been moving for six days. They still haven't explained how all this works to me. From the little meeting with Jacob last night, they obviously follow a set of rules and steps. They're an organization rescuing battered women. Of course, something would happen today. It's a lot to take in, and I'm not sure what to do. This seems to be my life now. Where do I go from here? Will I constantly have to keep moving to be free? That doesn't sound like a good life to me.

"Today, you rest. If you feel like it later, we can talk about your next step. If not, it can wait until tomorrow." Nanny turns to take the bread from the oven when the timer goes off.

A day of rest sounds amazing. The unknown terrifies me, though. Nanny plates up eggs, bacon, and biscuits for each of us and sets them on the table.

"What is my next step?"

"We help you start over." Everly joins us at the table. Fits of laughter are gone.

"How do I do that?" I push the scrambled eggs around on my plate with a fork.

"Well." Nanny glances at Everly. She doesn't want to have this conversation in front of her. "When you're ready, we'll go to the office and talk about where you'd like to go. Your training as a nurse will allow you to start over just about anywhere. Once you've decided, we'll help you get there."

Wow. She didn't explain things in detail, but I understand. It's a bit overwhelming, and I'm greatly relieved. They're really offering me a new life somewhere far away from Joel. But can I do it? Can I really start over and never live another day in fear?

Everly looks from me to her grandmother. "Can't she stay here? Uncle Jack…"

"Sweetie." Nanny lays her hand flat on the table, interrupting the young girl. "Don't you have to work on the website for the bakery today?"

"Oh, yeah." Everly springs to her feet. "I promised them it would be ready by Wednesday." She hurries around the table to hug her grandmother.

"You'll do a fine job, dear. Now, go straight home."

"Yes, ma'am." Everly surprisingly hugs me, too. "I'm sorry, Lily. I forgot about the website. Hopefully, I'll see you at the party later."

I release her with my mouth hanging open. "You go to club parties?"

She's a minor. That's not a good idea. The party I heard last night was way too lively for children.

"Yeah." She nods. "All the kids have to leave by nine. Grandpa makes them show their manners while we're there."

I snap my head toward Nanny. "Is that safe?"

"Don't worry. No one would touch us," Everly assures me. "They'd die in the middle of the clubhouse floor if they did. Grandpa would then string their bodies up out front as an example."

I choke on air. This can't be real. She's sixteen. She shouldn't be talking this way.

Nanny quickly stands and nudges Everly out the door. "Sweetie, hurry on home. Maybe you'll see Lily later."

"Bye," Everly calls out as she hurries out the front door.

Nanny cautiously returns to the table. It takes her a few minutes to compose herself. Trust me. I'm struggling to do so, too.

"Lily?"

I remove the sunglasses and slowly meet her eyes. "That wouldn't really happen. Would it?"

"It never has." She looks away and quickly back. "No one is stupid enough to test it."

"Would your family actually do it?"

She's quiet for a moment and chooses her words carefully.

"Let's hope no one ever becomes *that* stupid."

I cover my mouth with my hand and tremble a little. Oh, it most definitely would happen if someone tried to hurt one of their children.

"Look." Nanny reaches across the table and covers my hand with hers. "I know we're a lot to handle most days. Bad things happened to us, but we aren't bad people. You don't have to go to the party. Just stay here and rest. Let us help you. We'll figure out your next step tomorrow."

There's not really much else I can say. They've helped me for six days and haven't asked for anything in return. I've come too far to walk away now. I have no choice but to let them help me. I nod, easing her mind. Tomorrow, I'll decide where I want to go next. At least I get a say in my next step.

10
Jack

I woke up in the *Twilight Zone* today. It's the only way to explain what just happened. My mom wouldn't let me inside the guest house. You'd think she'd be happy to see me. But nooooooo. She stepped out, turned me right around on the porch, and told me to go find Dad. I'm not sure what good it will do, but I march straight to Dad's office.

Another sign I'm in the *Twilight Zone* is I actually find Dad in his office. Most of the time, I have to spend hours tracking him down somewhere on the property or in town. Surprisingly, Worley Bird, Jay, and Shepherd are here, too. I storm across the room right up to Dad's desk.

I jab my finger at him. "You need to do something with your wife."

The room goes deathly quiet and still.

Dad stands and crosses his arms. "My *wife* is *your* mother. You might want to rephrase that, *son*."

Oh, I most definitely want to rephrase that. I'm not afraid of many things. My father, when he's angry, is at the top of that list. I quickly regroup and do the only thing I can—apologize and change my words.

"I'm sorry, Dad." I hold a hand up between us in surrender. "I shouldn't talk to you that way or ever refer to Mom like that. It won't happen again."

He nods, sits back down, and motions toward me. "Proceed."

"Mom." I pause when he raises an eyebrow. How do I say this respectfully? "Will you please talk to Mom?"

"Son, your mother has her reasons for not letting you inside this morning. I suggest you try again later this evening."

The other three snicker. I can only stare at Dad in disbelief. He didn't even ask why. He holds up his phone and smiles.

"Uh." I swipe a hand over my mouth and beard. Of course, Mom called him.

"Have a seat, son." Dad motions to the chair next to Jay.

I ease down into the leather chair next to my cousin. I love him. We were raised more like brothers than cousins. Right now, I wanna smack the grin off his face.

"Can I see Lily's file?" Asking for it feels like an invasion of her privacy.

Thousands of angels have come through our doors. Seeing their files didn't spark these emotions in me. Naturally, I wanted to protect them all. I wanted all the details. If I ever found the monsters who hurt those angels, I'd make sure he felt what they did and more. This time is different. Lily isn't just another angel passing through.

I lean forward to take the file from Dad's hand. He doesn't release it and holds my gaze for a moment.

"What's your interest in this girl, Jack?"

He'd see through me if I lied. So, I don't. "I don't know, Dad. She's different. I just feel very protective of her."

One corner of Dad's mouth lifts. He glances over at Worley Bird. The two men share a silent conversation. Worley Bird grins and nods once. Dad and Darin Worley are second-generation Viking Warriors. They've been best friends practically since birth. It's why Darin is Dad's Vice President.

"If you're sure you really want to see it." Dad releases the file. "I'll go ahead and tell you. All you'll find in there are medical records. Lily didn't know most of it was being recorded. Nina Lowe had eyes on her for months. Every time Lily treated her own injuries, Nina documented it. She took pictures the best she could from a distance. She had a doctor sign off on it every time. Sunday night's incident is the only one with clear photos and full documentation. Nothing more is in there."

I nod and place the file on my lap. "She has a black eye."

"She show you?" Dad asks.

"No." I clear my throat and shake my head. We all know it's true.

Dad leans back in his chair. "I've spoken with Nina and Lily's three helpers. Andrew picked her up from the hospital parking garage where she worked with Nina. He delivered her to Gwen in Arizona. Dylan was supposed to meet them in Texas, but he had a family emergency. It was a full day before Shepherd was able to get there."

Shepherd's grin fades. All jokes and teasing aside now. "I was the third on the list Gwen called. I left the moment I hung up with her. Gwen needed to get home and was antsy because of the delay. I got there as fast as I could."

The rest of us nod in understanding. It's never good to stay more than one night in the same place with an angel. You never know if the abuser found a way to track her and follow them.

Shepherd turns to Dad. "We might want to suggest that our distant female drivers don't travel alone. It worked out this time, but Gwen has kids. I'd hate to see something happen, and she couldn't handle it."

"I'll reach out to Arizona. Our women are not supposed to travel alone." Dad taps his fingers on the desk.

This bit of news is unsettling. Dad implemented that rule years ago. It's rare for a woman to transport the angels. Gwen's husband should have been with her. And where were their guards? The guards usually go unseen, but at least two other vehicles should have been traveling with them.

Shepherd shifts in his chair to face me again. "There's no doubt she has a black eye, but she never took the sunglasses off with me. I can't give you any insights about her. We kept our conversations to random stuff or about the things we saw on the road. She has a kind heart, though. At one stop, she gave her lunch to a homeless man with a dog." He holds his hand up before I can speak. "Yes. I promise I got her another meal."

"Jay." Dad breaks the silence we fell into. "Why don't you take your cousin to the shop? Show him his job. Get out of here for a while."

"What?" I slide to the edge of my chair.

"You're home now. Everybody pulls their weight around here." Dad nods toward Jay but keeps his eyes on me. "Come Monday, you start working at the garage with Jay."

"Really?" I glare at Jay. "Nice of you to let me know."

Jay shrugs. "It was decided five minutes before you barged in the door."

"Don't be mad at your cousin." Dad stands, signaling our meeting is over. "This was my decision. Go to town. Give Lily some breathing room today. If she's going to break out of her shell, your mom or sisters will be the ones to help her get there."

There's no point in arguing with him. Dad has a rule for the younger generation. You either go to school or get a job. Lazy is not allowed around here. Our older guys who've put their time in have more leniency. It's okay. I've spent two years without a steady job. Besides, I like working with Jay. We worked at the garage together when we were teens.

Jay gets up and starts walking toward the door. "Come on, cuz. Let's go make some noise in town."

Shepherd is right behind him. "I'll go with you."

I stand and offer Dad Lily's unopened file. Like him, I don't let go when he reaches for it.

"Watch over her?"

Dad nods firmly. "Promise."

Reluctantly, I follow Jay and Shepherd outside to our bikes in the side parking lot. I don't want to leave, but Mom's not going to let me get anywhere near Lily right now.

Shepherd grabs the helmet off the bike between mine and Jay's. That's his helmet, but not his bike. He brought Lily here last night. I glance around the lot. Sure enough, Shepherd's Ford pickup is in the corner space.

"Whose bike did you steal?" I don't recognize this one.

"Jay loaned it to me."

Jay laughs as he gets on his bike. "I got it off a college kid who had no clue how to ride. His mom made him sell it before he got killed. He had no problem spending more of his daddy's money on a fancy sports car. Took me three weeks to get all the parts in to straighten her out. Got a couple of guys interested already."

Jay's the best mechanic in Willows Creek. It doesn't matter if it's a car, truck, or motorcycle. If it has a motor, Jay can fix it.

"I don't need a tour of the garage, man." I doubt Jay's drastically remodeled his place while I was gone.

"Didn't think so." Jay sends a text and slides his phone into his back pocket. "It's why we're not going there."

"Then where are we going?" This fool has had some crazy ideas over the years. He's got me scared now.

"Since your dad wants you out of here for a while, the guys are meeting us at the diner." Jay starts his bike and leads the way to town.

Okay. The diner isn't so bad. Angie's is a historical landmark in Willows Creek and has the best food in the state. The restaurant opened when my grandparents were in high school, giving the teens a place to hang out. The owners named the restaurant after their only daughter. Angie is a real person. She went to school with my mom. If I gotta kill time in town, I can't think of a better place.

11
Jack

We find four empty parking spaces across the lot when we get to Angie's. Normally, we park closer to the doors when we meet up. Angie's is a family restaurant. We leave the closer spaces for the kids and the elderly.

Coty, Bankz, and Hendrix pull up about the same time we do. We park all six bikes in the four spaces and walk inside. I wish I could say we're well received here. The Viking Warriors have been in Willows Creek for more than forty years. Half of this town still turns their noses up at us.

The only table available that is large enough for the six of us is in the front dining area, right in the middle of the room. It's fine. We don't hide when we're out in public, and we don't let snotty people get to us.

"Good morning, boys." Angie hurries around the counter to hug each of us. She's part of the half that likes us, and she doesn't care who knows it.

"Good to see you, Angie." I hug her tightly when it's my turn.

"Glad you came home. You're family sure missed you." She slaps her palm against my chest before leading us to the empty table.

The moment we're seated, a lady in a fancy pink pantsuit in the booth to my right huffs and lifts her chin. After thoroughly assessing the parking lot, she turns back to find all of us staring at her. Angie even has her hands on her hips. The lady snaps her gaze right back out the window.

Hendrix glances at his watch and lays his menu on the table. "You still serving breakfast?"

It's eleven. It's definitely lunchtime. And this fool wants breakfast? Geez.

Angie smiles sweetly at Hendrix. "For you, sweetie, all day long."

"Cool." Hendrix grins like a Cheshire cat. "Pancakes, eggs, and bacon for me."

The others order the same with soda to drink.

"Jay, you want a bacon cheeseburger?" Angie takes his menu.

"I'm not turning down your pancakes. I'll have the same with sweet tea, though." Jay isn't fond of soda.

"Jack?"

"Make it easy, Angie. I'll have the same as everyone else and the sweet tea."

After our drinks arrive, I glance over at the pink pantsuit lady. She's shifted to try and turn her back to us. I applaud her effort. That's kind of hard to do in a booth. Her young daughter sits across from her. She's not scared to look at us. Her eyes dart away every time her mother moves. Oh, she's not ashamed to look at us. She's just scared of getting caught looking at us.

I know the look in her eyes all too well. Young rich girl looking for a bad boy. These girls need to give up that fantasy. This girl isn't old enough to drink. She'll have to wait until some of our college-age brothers come to town. Our group has already been through our wild and wooly days. Well, for the most part, anyway.

"I hear some more of your brothers will be here tonight," Hendrix says to Shepherd.

Shep leans back and straightens one of his legs. It's not enough to block the aisle between the tables. It's enough to offend the pink pantsuit lady, though.

"Yeah. We gotta help welcome these prodigal brothers home," Shep teases.

Coty sets his soda on the table. "Hey, man. We weren't prodigals. We were just traveling around the country."

"Okay." Shep thinks for a moment. "Wayward brothers?"

"Better." Coty gives him a salute.

Shepherd is ex-military. A couple of the guys in our chapter are, too.

Applause from the party in the back has everyone looking to see what's going on. Pastor Rhodes makes some kind of announcement, earning another round of applause from his group. His oldest son stands next to him. The pastor and his wife have four children—two boys and two girls. Only two of them are with them today. A man I've never seen stands behind their youngest daughter.

The sound of a knife flicking open draws my attention to Jay's hand at his side. He, Bankz, and Hendrix watch the church group closely. I'm missing something here.

"What's that about?" I ask.

"The Pastor's son is following in his footsteps," Jay replies. No clue why it has him upset enough to open his knife in public.

I look back to the group. "Who's the dude with Finley?"

"Must be the new guy they're trying to marry her off to," Hendrix replies.

The church group continues to celebrate. Matthew Rhodes humbly accepts their congratulations. He pulls a dainty little blonde up to stand at his side. Guess the pastor will have a daughter-in-law soon, if I'm reading the situation right. Maybe they can have a double wedding. They can marry their oldest and youngest children off at the same time. It's not likely. Who knows? It could happen.

"She's a cutie." Shep narrows his eyes. "What's wrong with her? Why are they having trouble finding her a husband?"

"No clue." Hendrix shrugs.

"All we know is that Finley starts dating a new guy for a few weeks. About the time everyone thinks it's serious, the guy breaks it off, and we never see him again," Bankz adds.

"This one probably goes to college with her. He looks the type," Hendrix says.

"They let her go to college?" That really surprises me. Finley was sick a lot as a kid. Her parents are seriously overprotective of her.

"Yeah. Nursing school." Hendrix finishes his meal and pushes his plate away.

Jack

"She at the big one in Nashville? Vanderbilt?" Coty asks.

"Nah. She's over at Staten Medical College." Bankz finishes his food, too. "No clue why they're letting her go. We all know her family won't let her work at a hospital."

Staten Medical College is about forty-five minutes from here on the other side of Dades Creek. If the pastor didn't pay for Finley to go to Nashville, Bankz is right. She'll never work in a hospital. It's doubtful she'll ever put her degree to use.

"Sweetie." Angie places a hand on Jay's shoulder and leans between us. "I get it, but you might want to put that away in here."

My eyes drop to the knife he's still flicking open and closed. So far, Angie's the only one to notice. I take that back. Rich pink pantsuit lady notices. She jerks her daughter out of the booth and storms at the door.

"Sorry, Angie. I didn't mean to cost you a customer." Jay closes the knife and slips it into his pocket.

"Oh, I'm not worried about her. She gets mad about something all the time. Won't see her for a few weeks. One day, she'll wander back in like nothing happened. Besides, it'll take a lot more than losing one prissy customer to shut us down."

We all nod. It's true. People come from all over Middle Tennessee to eat at Angie's. Jay feels bad about it, though.

"I'm fine," he assures her.

Angie starts clearing our dirty dishes from the table. Jay's no longer playing with the knife, but he has me worried now, too. Something happened to my cousin while I was away.

"You sure you're okay?" I know he's not.

Jay nods. He wouldn't tell me in here, anyway. I'll ask him about it later tonight.

"I don't like him." Jay glares across the room.

Matthew Rhodes used to sneak into the clubhouse and party with us. It was fine for a while. But one day, Jay didn't like him for some reason. If he's going into the ministry, I guess his parents straightened him out.

"Maybe he changed." The way Matt's eyes dart at us every so often, he doesn't want anyone to know he knows us.

"Don't care," Jay grumbles.

"Come on, brothers. Let's go for a ride." Hendrix stands and leads the way to the parking lot.

Getting my cousin out of here is a good idea. I still wanna know what's going on with him. It'll have to wait, though. Jay's a very private person.

"I hear you brought an angel," Bankz says to Shepherd when we reach our bikes.

"Yeah." Shepherd tosses a leg over his bike.

"She's with Mom," I add.

"She's still here?" Bankz pauses before putting his helmet on.

"Yeah." Coty snickers and grins at me. "From what I hear, she may not leave."

Hendrix reads between the lines and snaps his head toward me. "Really?"

I don't say yes. I don't say no. I can't say anything. I can't get close enough to Lily to figure out what's going on. Thankfully, none of my brothers makes a joke right now.

Bankz nods once. "Let us know if there's anything we can do to help her."

"Thanks, guys." No more needs to be said. A ride would help clear my head, though. "Let's ride." I look over my shoulder at my cousin. "Lead the way."

For the next two hours, we roam the back roads of the county. I let the wind and pavement soothe my troubled spirit. Riding with Jay and our brothers is the best medicine I could hope for. Still, more times than not, my mind drifts to the beautiful angel I've silently sworn to protect.

12
Lily

After helping Nanny clean up the kitchen, we spend the rest of the day relaxing around the house. And when this woman relaxes, she relaxes. She suggested a few things I could do before she settled down in a comfy chair by the fireplace. There's no fire going. It's not that cold.

Nanny hasn't asked for my story or the details about what happened Sunday night. She can probably figure everything out from whatever Nina put in that file. I thought she would bring the subject up since it was just the two of us here. But nope. Not one word. She sat quietly in that chair, reading and answering emails and texts. The only thing she's gotten up to do is make coffee. The stuff has to run in her blood. I'm not complaining. It's in mine, too. I finally saw the yellow bag of *Gevalia* coffee when she made the last pot. I'm definitely investing in this brand.

"Did the clothes fit? If not, I can get you some more." Nanny closes her book and lays it on the table by her chair.

This is the first she's spoken in hours. Usually, when I get coffee, she just looks up and smiles. I've been sitting on the couch for half an hour reading a magazine I found in the kitchen.

"Yes, ma'am." I tried on everything in the suitcase like she asked. "You knew exactly my size. You didn't have to get me new clothes, though."

I tried to give her a few items back this morning when I noticed they still had the store sales tags on them. I was expecting her to just loan me a few things from her closet. Nearly every item in that suitcase is brand new.

She places her hand against her chest. "I may have picked some of the items up at the store, but I didn't actually buy them. Ariel's Angels has a private closet called Ariel's Attic. We do fundraisers throughout the year to help fund it, and some of our friends donate new and gently used items."

Friends? She means people who know what they secretly do. Some of the women they've helped have probably contributed to this closet. Now that I know about it, I'll be one of them once I'm on my feet again. I was grateful the panties and bras were new and still in their original packaging. Everything else, I wouldn't have minded if those were gently used.

"The suitcase and everything in it is yours," she adds.

Wow. That suitcase is huge. It's packed with clothes and way more accessories than I need to start over. It makes me wonder just how much is given to Ariel's Attic.

"Thank you." I'm not sure if I'm ready to talk about the serious stuff, but I take a chance anyway. "Why do you do all of this? It's more than just rescuing women."

She wraps one hand around the other on her lap and watches me for a moment. "We weren't able to save our daughter. We were all losing our minds. So, we gave our grief, anger, and our *'what do we do'* moments an outlet before they consumed us. In honor of Ariel, we save as many women as we can. Helping these women start over lets little pieces in us heal for a while."

"Ariel was like me." The pain in her eyes makes me feel horrible for asking.

She presses her lips together and nods. Finding strength and bravery, she pulls out of thin air, her eyes meet mine. "Yes, Ariel was a victim of domestic violence."

I drop my head when the first tear falls from my eyes. Domestic violence. Two words I haven't allowed myself to say or think. Those words shove me and every woman like me into an even darker hole. They drastically change things, and not for the better.

Jack

"You want my story?" They haven't asked. Nina didn't even ask. She just threw me on this journey without any warning.

"Only if you want to share it. It's not a requirement."

I'm sure every woman who's passed through here is grateful for that. I sure am.

"Not yet, but maybe soon." Keeping it bottled up inside is starting to take a toll on me.

"Okay." She points to my right cheek. "If you're still in pain, I can get you some ibuprofen and ice. After six days, though, we should probably have it x-rayed."

I gently touch my cheek with my fingertips. "I do have a headache, but this is getting better. My cheekbone isn't broken."

"That's good." She stands and walks toward the kitchen. "I'll get you some ibuprofen for the headache."

She returns with a glass of water and two pain pills. Her eyes drop to my cheek for a closer inspection.

"He didn't hit me in the face," I blurt out. It's what everyone thinks. "I'm really not sure if it came from when he shoved me out of bed or from when I hit the doorframe before I left." Yeah, that doesn't sound any better.

"Thank you for letting me know." Her phone dings with a text. After reading it, she taps a finger next to her eye. "My daughters are about to arrive if you want your glasses."

Oh my. She has more daughters.

"Yes, ma'am, and thank you." I jump to my feet and rush to the bedroom. I left the glasses on the nightstand while I tried on the clothes. Nanny is the only one who has seen my face.

I hear Jack's sisters long before I see them. This family is loud. At least they sound happy. Everly has the same bubbly personality I hear now. I'm surprised they can be so happy with what they've lost and the reason why. I shake the thought away, slide the sunglasses on, and head to the kitchen. Maybe their happiness will rub off on me. Hopefully, they won't treat me like I have the plague. I don't want anyone to pity or feel sorry for me.

For a moment, I stand in the doorway and watch the three women interact. Nanny's daughters are beautiful. All three women have the same long, brown, wavy hair. Nanny is a misleading name for Jack's mother. If I had met her and her oldest daughter on the street, I would have sworn she was her older sister. The youngest one is following right along in their young-looking family gene pool. She looks to be my age or a little younger.

The youngest notices me and gasps. "Wow. You're beautiful."

Nanny and her oldest daughter stop their conversation about the party at the clubhouse and smile.

"I was thinking the same thing about you three." I lightly laugh. It's awkward. Totally awkward.

"Lily, this is my daughter, Harley." Nanny smiles at the daughter standing next to her. She points to the youngest daughter, who's getting ice cream from the freezer. "The one about to ruin her dinner is Maci. Girls, this is Lily."

"Hello." Harley's the serious one.

"I won't ruin dinner with just one scoop." Maci takes the small bowl her mother is offering her and, surprisingly, only gets one scoop.

Who does that? I want the whole bowl.

Nanny comes to me and takes my hand. She's getting a little more comfortable with touching me. Maybe she was waiting until I was ready. She hugged Everly a lot last night. Yeah, the problem is me.

"I hope you don't mind if the girls stay with you for a while. I'll stay if you prefer. If you're okay with it, I need to help Nana oversee things for tonight's party."

"Nana?" There's a Nanny and a Nana? I'm going to mess this family all up.

"Yes." Nanny laughs. "Nana is my husband's mother."

"Everyone calls Mom Nanny because it's what Logan and Everly call her. It was just easier, and it stuck," Harley explains.

"Logan?" I think I've heard that name.

"Logan is Everly's brother," Nanny reminds me. "Next week is his first football game of the season."

All three women beam with pride. Okay. They're a football family. I liked watching football in high school. Medical college didn't offer any sports. I'd ask to go with them, but I don't know where I'll be next week.

Jack

"You go ahead. I'll be fine." She shouldn't have to put aside her family duties to babysit me. "Thank you for everything."

Nanny places her palm against my left cheek. "You're going to be fine, Lily. I promise."

I wish I felt as sure as she sounds. Nanny surprises me once again and wraps her arms around me. At first, my body and mind want to fight off the intrusion. Her presence surrounds me with warmth, banishing my fears if only for this moment.

13
Lily

Tonight's dinner wasn't what I expected. After five days of fast food restaurants and gas stations, I'm not complaining about heating up a frozen pizza. Nanny just has me spoiled already with her home-cooked meals.

"Sorry. That's it on my culinary skills tonight." Harley gets up to put her plate into the dishwasher.

I do the same. "It's okay. I'm not a great cook, either."

Maci laughs. "Oh, she can cook. She's just lazy and in a hurry tonight."

"Shut up." Harley wads up the paper towel she used as a napkin and throws it at Maci.

"I don't know why you're in such a hurry to get to the clubhouse. You know the party won't come alive until after nine." Maci grabs another slice of pizza from the platter in the center of the table.

"The guys from Texas got here a couple of hours ago." Harley shrugs. "I just wanna talk to them."

"Sure you do," Maci mumbles.

Harley ignores her sister. "If you need me, you know where to find me."

She waves without looking back and walks out the front door. Harley doesn't have a bubbly personality like I first thought. I'm not sure how to describe her yet. She's a mix of emotions and personalities. What I mistook for serious is better described as cautious, reserved, and untrustworthy. I don't think she likes me.

"Don't mind her." Maci finishes her slice of pizza and puts her plate in the dishwasher.

"Does she have a thing for one of the guys from Texas?" It's not my business. I shouldn't ask.

"Yeah, but I don't think he notices her. So, she flirts with the others to try and make him jealous." Maci sighs. Worry covers her face. "Her plan is stupid. She won't admit what she's doing, not even to herself."

Maci's concern for her sister changes the atmosphere in the house. I can feel her pain. It highlights my own. Harley's playing a dangerous game. It could get her hurt. The men she's flirting with may not physically hurt her, and that's more than likely because they know her family. Still, in the end, they could break her heart and make her feel bad about herself. Mental and emotional trauma is just as painful as the physical part. In some cases, it could be worse. Mental and emotional abuse can take months or even years to heal. Neither form of abuse is better than the other.

"If you want to go to the party, I'm fine with staying by myself." I feel bad she's stuck here with me.

Maci looks at her phone. The screen's black. She sighs and shakes her head.

"I don't really want to go. I went last week. I'll just text Jack and Jay. They'll watch her." She sends two quick texts before following me to the living room.

"Do you have parties every weekend?" I grab the remote and find one of the shows where they flip houses. For some reason, these things fascinate me.

Unlike the rest of her family, Maci joins me on the couch. After all the battered women they've helped, they know to be cautious around one. They're just giving me the space they feel I need. I appreciate it, but it makes me feel like something's wrong with me. Well, something is wrong with me. I'm broken and battered. I feel so alone. What about me makes me unlovable?

Maci waves a bottle of water in front of my face, bringing me back to reality. She smiles sweetly. I have to look like an idiot to her.

She points to my sunglasses. "You don't have to wear those around me. I won't ask about it or make you feel bad."

"Thank you."

Her personality is more like her mom's and Everly's. She's sweet, kind, and wants to genuinely help others. I'm comfortable around her. Slowly, I slide the sunglasses off and lay them on the end table. True to her word, Maci doesn't say a word. Somehow, she doesn't even react to seeing my bruise.

"To answer your question. People party and hang out every week. They go back and forth between the clubhouse and JB's." She pulls her feet up on the couch and crosses her legs. "But we only have parties at the clubhouse to celebrate something."

"Who's JB?" Me showing up threw a wrench in her family's plans tonight.

She quickly glances at a text and lays her phone on the couch between us. From her tight smile, I'm guessing Jack or Jay confirmed they're watching Harley.

"JB's Roadhouse is Banks' bar in town." She tosses her hand out toward the TV. "You really like these shows?"

"It surprised me, too." I laugh and lean against the arm of the couch. "Gwen and I watched them when we were stuck in Texas. She loved them."

Maci and I spend the next couple of hours watching house shows and sitcoms. It feels good to laugh. Maci's faking being happy. I've done it so often that it's easy to spot. Her sister has her worried. No matter how many times she looks at her phone, the screen stays black. Hopefully, it's a sign everything's okay.

"How about some coffee?" Maci tosses the blanket over the back of the couch.

"Sounds good." I follow her to the kitchen. "Would you like some ice cream?"

"Absolutely. The bowls are in there." Maci points to the cabinet door next to the fridge.

"What's your club celebrating tonight?" I set everything on the table and grab the ice cream scoop from the dish drainer.

Jack

"Jack and Rodeo came home last weekend." Maci huffs. "The guys have celebrated every night this week."

"Where were they?" Yeah, I'm being nosy. Hey. It helps keep my mind off my issues.

Her phone on the table rings before she can answer. Everly's face lights up on the screen, making us both smile. I glance at the clock on the microwave. It's almost nine.

"Hey, sweet girl," Maci answers and puts the phone on speaker while she adds coffee grounds to the maker.

"Aunt Maci." The fear in Everly's voice slams into both of us.

Maci abandons the coffee and snatches up her phone, immediately taking it off speaker. "Everly, are you okay? What's wrong?"

I forget the ice cream and move closer. Maci's eyebrows draw together, and her face turns red. I can still hear the sounds from the party, but not what Everly's saying.

"Where's Nanny and Grandpa?" Maci closes her eyes and takes a deep breath. I admire her for holding back her anger to keep Everly calm. "Okay, sweetie. Meet us at the back gate."

Oh my gosh. Everly is the sweetest. Why would anyone hurt her? Oh dear. What she said earlier now concerns me even more. Is one of these bikers about to die?

"Lily, I'm sorry, but we need to go to the gate behind the clubhouse. Everly needs to go home." Maci shoves her phone into her back pocket as she heads toward the front door.

"I can wait here." I have no desire to see someone die tonight. If some guy hurt Everly, he deserves what her family will do to him. But still, I don't want to see it.

Maci pauses and takes another deep breath. "I don't know how much Mom and Dad told you about the organization." She shakes her head. "We don't leave angels alone. It's not that we don't trust you. Sometimes, leaving the women we help alone does more harm than good to their mental state. And if your abuser found a way to track you, the last thing you need is to be alone and vulnerable."

Everly's more important than me. "Okay. Let's go get her."

Wow. I now understand why someone has been with me from the moment Nina took me to Andrew. I'd never ask Maci not to save her niece to stay with me. I can handle my situation. Well, not if I had to face Joel alone right now. Everly is young and doesn't have experience. She needs us.

Maci hurries down the path Jack used to bring me to the guest house. The same path he stormed away on this morning. I assume the paths on each side of the house go to their family homes.

"We're not going to the party. Just to the gate. It's in the fence around the backyard of the clubhouse. We won't even have to go inside." Maci doesn't slow down.

"What happened? Is she hurt? I'm a nurse if she needs medical attention." I almost have to run to keep up with her.

"Thank you for that. But no. She's not physically hurt." Maci growls. She literally growls. "Apparently, my older sister decided to have a little too much to drink before the kids left. Everly's tenderhearted. She can't stand to see anyone drunk." She glances over her shoulder but doesn't stop. "She's scared the same thing will happen to Harley like it did to her mom."

Oh, that poor, sweet girl. My heart breaks for Everly. Yeah. We need to get to her fast. I know they're all worried about Harley. I am, too, but her selfish actions tonight make me mad. If she was going to cut loose and get drunk, she could've waited another fifteen minutes.

Maci stops where the wooden privacy fence meets the backside of the clubhouse. The crowd and music are extremely loud. They must have a live band in there. Maci knocks loudly on the gate. She pulls a set of keys from her pocket and quickly unlocks the padlock. I can hear the same thing happening on the other side.

The gate opens with a forceful shove, almost knocking Maci down. I place my palms against her back to keep her from falling. Everly flies through the gate and throws her arms around Maci's neck.

"I wanna go home," she cries.

"Okay, sweetie. I got you." Maci wraps her arms around Everly and rubs her back until she calms down. "Where's Harley?"

Everly waves toward the far corner of the backyard. "On the other side of the Pit, but I wanna go home, Aunt Maci."

"Okay, but I have to lock the gate back."

Jack

It takes another few minutes before Everly releases her so she can lock the gate. I get a glimpse inside the backyard. People are gathered around in little groups. Most of them are drinking. A few are dancing and drinking. All of them are loud.

Maci leans her head inside the gate to look around for her sister. Her eyes widen, and she sucks in a breath.

"What?" I look over her shoulder.

Everly does, too. "Ugh. I hate her."

Jack sits on the top of one of the picnic tables with his feet on the bench. A bunch of bikers are sitting with him or standing around the table. A woman with wavy blonde hair stands beside the table with her arms around Jack's neck. He doesn't even look at her.

"Oh, this isn't happening." Maci takes two steps inside.

"No, Aunt Maci. I wanna go home. Please," Everly pleads.

Maci's eyes meet mine. "She doesn't mean anything to him."

"Not my problem." But I want to help Maci jerk this heifer off her brother.

14
Jack

This party is already getting out of hand. The kids don't leave for at least another forty-five minutes. I love a good party. However, these idiots need to settle down. My sister is one of those idiots. Some of our guests tonight are new and don't seem to understand our nine o'clock rule. If Dad sees this, he'll blow a gasket.

The clubhouse was too stuffy, so I retreated to the backyard. It's crowded out here, but at least the air is cool. Brothers from six or seven states are here again this weekend. Shep's chapter from Texas arrived this afternoon. It's great seeing them. It's not so great watching my sister make a fool of herself. Jay and I have been watching her since Maci texted to give us a heads-up.

"Hear you'll be working with us come Monday." Cloudy Daze joins our group around the picnic table.

This table is the one closest to the clubhouse on the right side of the yard. The grove of trees hiding our homes is on the other side of the fence behind me. I've looked over my shoulder several times to where I know the guest house sits. My heart isn't into partying tonight. If Maci hadn't texted, I'd have already left.

"Yep, I'll be there." Honestly, I haven't given much thought to my new job. My mind's elsewhere. Once again, I look over my shoulder, wishing I were on the other side of those trees.

Jack

"Got a '57 Chevy coming in needing an oil change and a tune-up. Figured you'd wanna help with that." Cloudy takes the beer Jay offers him.

"Thanks, Blade." Cloudy twists the top off and takes a long swig. His head bobs to the music.

"Yeah, man. Can't wait to see it." A '57 Chevy? Now, that's a dream. Monday might not be so bad.

Frank Thompson, better known by the entire world as Cloudy Daze, has worked at the shop with Jay for as long as I can remember. He's not an official member of the Viking Warriors. We proudly claim him, though.

Cloudy doesn't belong to any MC. He went to school with my parents and hardly ever meets a stranger. His fun-loving nature has him well-known by nearly everyone in Middle Tennessee and half the country. He has so many friends in different clubs that he won't choose one. Every club I know has made Cloudy an honorary member anyway.

Jay sits beside me on the table and puts his feet on the bench next to mine. His eyes roam over the crowd. He pauses on Harley for a moment. Yeah, she's already drunk. Jay looks toward the clubhouse. A huge grin almost splits his face.

Jay nudges me with his elbow and nods toward the clubhouse. "Look who's here."

"Well, I'll be darn." Cloudy snatches the kid as he's walking by.

"Geez, Cloudy." Miles swats Cloudy's hands away. "Personal space, dude."

"No such thing." Cloudy raises his beer high before taking another long swig.

"Miles, man. When did you get in?" I thought we'd run into him when Rodeo and I were traveling. We never did.

"Just did." Miles and I clasp arms just below our elbows. He's already dropped the black bandana from his face. The red one is still on top of his head. This skinny kid is a mess.

"How long are you staying?" Jay asks.

Miles shrugs. "Don't know yet. Couple days? Maybe a week."

Joe Milam is a wanderer. He's not a nomad. He's not looking for where he belongs. He's actually a patched member right here in Willow

Creek. He's young, only twenty-two, an emotional age for my family. From the moment he got his license, he began following in his father's footsteps. He's determined to put as many miles as he can under his wheels before he settles down. The man literally has an app on his phone where he logs his miles every day.

"Jack!" Dad's voice booms over the crowd. He walks up and clamps a hand on my shoulder. "Need you boys in the office in the morning. We're going to sit down and talk next steps."

He means Lily's next steps. The guests standing nearby aren't part of the club. They won't understand. Our patched members do. It's not common for an angel to stay long in one location until she's at the place she chose to start over. I'm hoping to spend some time with Lily later before she has to make her decision.

"Hey, Mac." Cloudy shakes Dad's hand. "If you need an escort, I can ride."

Cloudy has helped us transport hundreds of angels. As crazy as he is, he's dead serious until the angel is safely relocated. The ride home is always interesting with him along. We learned early on not to let Cloudy lead the way home. The one and only time we did, we ended up at some lake I've never heard of in Georgia. To him, everything was fine because he knew several clubs in the area. Naturally, it turned into a party at the lake Cloudy Daze style. Needless to say, we dragged our tails home three days later. Mom was furious.

"Thanks, Cloudy. We'll let you know tomorrow." Dad's eyes narrow when they land on Miles. He grabs Miles by the front of his cut and jerks the kid to his chest. "Look, you little runt. You need to settle down. Take your rightful place in this club like your dad."

"Sorry, Mac. I...I...I will one day," Miles stutters.

Dad releases the kid and shoves a finger in his face. "And stay away from my son. You're the reason he took off for two years."

"I didn't tell him to leave," Miles mumbles.

No, he didn't say a word to me about wandering across the country. Seeing him do it is what put the idea in my head, though.

Dad forgets Miles completely when he notices Harley on the other side of the firepit. He cuts his eyes at Shepherd. "Shep, those are your guys. Keep 'em in line." Shep nods once. Dad turns to Jay and me. "You two handle that if they cross a line."

"Yes, sir." No one has to tell me to protect my sister. I'll handle a man quick if he tries to hurt Harley, even if he is a brother.

Dad glares at Miles one more time before he goes back to the clubhouse. I swear this kid is going to shake right out of his skin.

"Y'all, don't let him kill me." Miles straightens his cut and releases a long breath. The rest of us laugh.

"You should listen to the Pres and drag your skinny self home," Cloudy says.

"When he comes home to stay, we need to take him to the shop and get him a real bike." Jay aimlessly pulls a knife from his pocket and starts flipping it open.

"And the gym," Rodeo adds. Miles ignores him.

"Blade, I have a Harley," Miles informs my cousin.

Jay laughs. "What you have, lil man, is a little gray bike with a Harley Davidson emblem. What you need is a custom build. I can hook you up."

Jay can build a bike from the ground up. Men have come from states away for his designs or to have him rebuild their existing bikes. None have been disappointed. No two of Jay's designs are the same.

"Well, I'm not ready." Miles looks over both shoulders to make sure Dad didn't slip back up on him.

While Cloudy and Rodeo continue to tease Miles, I glance toward my sister. My niece is hurrying across the center of the yard with her head down. That's not a good sign. Everly's headed toward the back gate that will take her home. Mom's probably meeting her there. With the way things are going tonight, it's best she leaves early. I look back to Harley. Her group's still loud, and she's still flirting. If Everly saw Harley like this, it explains why she's upset.

Before I can slide off the table, someone steps close to my left side, and arms go around my neck. It happens a lot at the clubhouse. The older I get, the more I hate these moments.

"Ghost, glad you're home. Where've you been hiding?" Jenny, one of the club girls, rubs up against my side.

"Why don't you run along?" Rodeo suggests. He's been a little quiet tonight.

"None of us are looking for company," Jay tells her.

Jenny ignores them. She shifts just enough for our eyes to meet. "Come on, Ghost. It's been a long time since you and I caught up."

Yes, it has. I groan inwardly. This is one of the reasons I don't get drunk at club parties anymore. The night before Rodeo and I left Willow Creek, the club threw us a going-away party. I let loose and got hammered that night. I woke up the next morning with Jenny in bed next to me in my room upstairs. I swore right then to never be in a situation where I didn't know what I was doing and who I was with. Jenny's time with us is almost over. I only have to avoid her for a few more months.

I remove her arms from my neck as I stand. "And it's going to stay that way."

Jenny jerks her head back like I slapped her. The guys snicker, which only fuels her anger. I don't care. She knows the rules. If a brother rejects her for any reason, she's supposed to walk away.

Movement at the back gate catches my eye. Everly's trying to pull my little sister and Lily through the gate. Both ladies look as though they're ready to commit murder.

"Ghost," Jenny whines and reaches for my arm.

"No," I snap at her. I turn to Jay and point to Harley. "Keep an eye on that. You and Shep handle it. I'm going to make sure Everly gets home."

Jay leans back and looks toward the three ladies at the gate. He grins and shakes his head. Yeah, there's more to my leaving. He knows. I've never been able to hide anything from him.

"Go. Take care of Everly." Jay motions toward the gate with his head. "I got the wild one."

"Rodeo." I tap my best friend on the arm. "Lock this side behind us."

Without question, Coty follows me to the back gate. I never have to question his friendship or loyalty. My sister, my niece, and my angel glare at me like they could kill me. Really? Just what did I do? No clue, but I'll find out what's going on once we're on the other side of this gate.

15
Jack

"Maci, what are we doing?" I gently nudge all three ladies out the gate and lock this side behind us.

"What are *you* doing?" My little sister crosses her arms and shoots daggers at me with her eyes.

"*I'm* making sure you three get home."

"Didn't look like it," Maci snaps.

Great—just great. They saw Jenny. I open my mouth to snap back. I freeze when my niece's arms circle my waist. Her frightful, tear-filled eyes gut me.

"Please, Uncle Jack. I just wanna go home." She sniffles and tries to blink back tears.

"Evie, sweetie. What happened?" My little sister and her big temper are instantly forgotten.

"Aunt Harley." She lays her head against my chest.

I wrap her tightly in my arms. "I know, sweetie. Uncle Jay's still watching over her."

"I tried to pull her away. She wouldn't listen." She leans back and wipes tears away with the back of her hand. "One of the guys told me to get lost and let the grownups have fun."

"What?" Maci and I ask at the same time.

I wrap my hands around Everly's upper arms and hold her slightly away so I can look her in the eye. This little girl has owned my heart from the moment she was born. Her feelings matter to me. I want to protect her heart with everything I have, but right now, I wanna kill somebody.

"Evie, which guy said that to you?" Nobody talks to my girl like that.

She shrugs and sniffles again. "I don't know. I didn't look. Aunt Harley told me to go home, so I called Aunt Maci."

Okay. It looks as though the entire group from Texas is about to die. Well, minus Shep, of course. My dear older sister needs to be brought down a notch or two as well. She knows how tenderhearted Everly is. Sometimes, it takes days to calm my niece down. Mom and Dad will go livid when they find out about this. Maybe Dad will finally put his foot down with Harley.

"Okay." I look over her head at Maci. "Get her home. I'll handle this."

Coty has already locked the other side of the gate. I'll have to go around to the side entrance and walk through the Den to get to the backyard. It'll be worth it. Someone's, a lot of someones, are going to regret this.

"No, Uncle Jack," Everly cries and pulls on my arm. "Please don't. I just wanna go home. Please."

Once again, her pleas stop me. Her big puppy dog tears slice through my soul. I cup her little face in my hands for a moment before wrapping her in my arms again.

"Okay, sweetie. We'll get you home." This little girl has me wrapped around her finger. She may be about to turn seventeen, but she'll always be my baby.

"Do you wanna come to the guest house with us? Uncle Jack can go find Grandpa. They'll make sure Aunt Harley is okay and take her home." Maci gently rubs Everly's back.

"No. I really just wanna go home. Please," Everly pleads again.

I glance past Maci to Lily. I didn't forget she was there. I've felt her presence the entire time. That's never happened with a woman before. One look at her causes my hands to shake. My niece is a nervous and emotional wreck. My older sister and some jerk were rude to her.

On top of that, the most beautiful woman I've ever met has a black eye and bruised cheek. I knew she did. Seeing it changes things.

"Okay, sweetie. Aunt Maci will take you home and stay with you until Nanny gets there." I walk Everly into my sister's waiting arms.

"Jack?" Maci's eyes dart to Lily and back to me.

Yeah, I know. We can't leave an angel alone. The counselors have told us how bad it could be. Past experience with the abusers has proven just how bad things can get. Maci has nothing to worry about.

"I'll stay with Lily until one of you can get to the guest house." My sister wants to argue. I don't let her. "The main thing is that Everly's taken care of and Lily's safe. Neither of us can do both right now."

"You're right." Maci sighs and turns to Lily. "Are you okay with this?"

"Yeah." Lily presses her lips together and nods.

Maci hesitates and looks toward the clubhouse. She wants to go get Mom. Maci's the youngest, but she has a better head on her shoulders than our older sister does.

"Look. Let Mom help Nana with the party. You and I can handle things for a few hours. If Lily becomes uncomfortable with my presence at any point, I'll step out on the porch and call one of the ole' ladies." I offer the only solution I can think of right now.

"Okay," Maci agrees.

The four of us walk together through the trees. When the guest house comes into view, Maci and Everly take the path to the right. It leads to the main house where my parents and grandparents live. The path to the left goes to my house, and beyond that is Jay's house. His mom lives with him. Their house in town was sold years ago.

Lily and I walk side by side up to the house. As badly as I want to, I don't reach for her hand this time. Lily walks ahead of me up the stairs and to the door. I reach into the pocket of my jeans for my keys just as she turns the handle and pushes the door open.

"Wait," I call out.

Lily jumps back and shrinks against the outside wall by the door. I mentally beat myself up. I didn't mean to scare her.

I hold up both hands. The keys dangle from one of my fingers. "Sorry. I didn't mean to shout."

"What's wrong?" Her voice shakes.

"Probably nothing." I motion toward the door with the hand holding the key. "Maci didn't lock the door."

Lily glances at the open door and shakes her head. "I guess not. We were in a hurry to get to Everly."

"Thank you for that. Everly gets very emotional when she's upset. It usually takes Mom to calm her down. If it's not too bad, Maci can handle it."

"She's a sweet girl." Lily drops her head.

"She's the best. Why don't you sit on the swing while I make sure the house is clear?"

Her head snaps toward the open door as she walks backward toward the steps. "You don't think? He couldn't."

I reach out and wrap my hand around her elbow to stop her from aimlessly falling down the steps. "No. I don't think he's here. The property is well protected. Even with all the security we have, we can still make a mistake. It's just a precaution."

She sighs with relief. It's not a hundred percent, but at least she's back in the moment and not stuck in her head.

"Okay. I'll wait on the swing." She sits with her hands clasped together on her lap. It's not how I imagined her sitting out here.

I reach inside with one hand and flip the living room light on. With my other hand, I reach under my cut and pull the gun from the back of my jeans. I hear Lily take a sharp breath, but I don't turn back.

Room by room and closet by closet, I check every nook and cranny of the house. I even checked the back porch and called Nick to watch the camera footage. The outside of the property and the common room of the Viking Den are under twenty-four-hour surveillance. Not everyone knows that.

After I clear the house, I stand in the front doorway with my back against the doorframe and my eyes on Lily. It took Nick a little over thirty minutes to watch the footage from the time Lily and Maci left until she and I returned.

"All clear." Lily doesn't move or acknowledge me. I walk over and hold my hand out. "Lily?" She slowly lifts her head. "We can go inside now."

Jack

She places her hand in mine, and I pull her to her feet. This was a setback for her. She's now hiding behind a mask of fear. I want so badly to remove every ounce of it from her life.

"Can I get you anything?" I close the door behind us.

Lily slowly turns to face me. "A new life."

"It'll take a little time, but we're working on it." That's one wish I can grant. "What can I get you in the meantime?"

She nervously laughs. "Coffee?"

"Oh, that's definitely something I can do. One fresh pot of coffee coming right up." I smile and wink at her as I walk by. "Come on, angel."

One wish easily granted. Another is in the making. I want to make more of her wishes come true. I have an idea. Hopefully, she'll be intrigued and give me a chance.

16
Lily

The big, bad biker with a gun turns out to be a better barista than the ones at my favorite coffee shop in LA. Everything's fine. It's a normal day in biker land. Who am I kidding? Nothing about this is normal, not that I know much about the biker world.

I carry my fancy caramel coffee with lots of whipped cream and chocolate shavings to the living room. I cautiously settle into one corner of the couch. Can't spill any of this caffeine goodness, after all. It looks almost too good to drink. Almost is the keyword here. There's no way I'm passing this up. I take a sip and moan. Oh my gosh. Everly wasn't kidding. Uncle Jack makes the best coffee.

Jack pauses as he's about to sit in the chair across from me. His eyebrows lift. His eyes drop to my lips and the mug. I take another sip and sigh this time. His eyes never waver.

"Um." I pat the middle cushion with my left hand. "Will you join me here, please?"

"Are you sure?"

I nod and drop my head. "Everyone avoids me so much, it makes me feel like a disease. It's weird, but it's true."

"Can't have that." Jack quickly moves to the other corner of the couch.

Instantly, I feel better. He's close enough to where I don't feel alone and just far away enough that I don't feel crowded. I take another sip.

Jack

Once again, his eyes are drawn to my lips. Why's this so fascinating to him?

"Will Everly be okay?"

"Yeah. When Mom gets home, she'll calm Everly down."

Everly and Nanny are very close. I'm not surprised it would be Jack's Mom who helps Everly the most. I really like Everly. I wish I could've done something more to help tonight. I'm nobody to his niece. I'm just a lady passing through their lives.

Jack takes a sip of coffee. He has the same drink as I do. His tongue darts out to wipe the whipped cream from his mustache. Wow. This is good. Yeah. It's normal. Happens every day.

Jack's lips turn up into a grin. "You okay over there, angel?"

My eyes snap to his, and my mouth closes. Oh my gosh. I quickly turn my head to stare at the wall. I was staring at him with my mouth open. Oh, please let me crawl under the couch cushions and disappear forever.

"Uh. Yeah." I face forward and take another sip. There's no way I can look at him again.

"Do you want to watch TV?"

No, I don't. I've watched so many TV shows this week. I'm tired of it. There's more to life than watching TV. Only my life doesn't allow for anything more. If I don't get settled somewhere soon, I'm going to lose my mind and die from boredom.

"If you want to, it's fine." It's not, but this is his house.

"I like watching movies, but I'm not in the mood." He takes another sip.

I close my eyes and take a deep breath through my nose. How is it possible to literally hear this man drink? I have a hard enough time trying not to look at his tattoos. Who knew I'd be fascinated by tattoos?

"Will Harley be okay?" It's really not my business.

Jack finishes his coffee and sets the mug on the end table. "Eventually. Probably not tonight."

I turn to face him. "What does that mean?"

If the Viking Warriors rescue women, why aren't they rescuing his sister? One of their own should be more important than strangers.

"Nothing will physically happen to her. Jay and Shep have eyes on her. Several more of our brothers have surrounded her. They'll move on Jay's signal."

"Shep? Is that Shepherd?" I haven't seen him at all today.

Jack nods. "Shep is his road name."

"Do you have a road name?"

"Ghost."

"And your cousin, Jay?"

"Blade."

"That's not creepy at all," I mumble.

Jack laughs. "My cousin just likes knives."

I set my empty mug on the end table. My sunglasses lay folded up next to the base of the lamp. I gasp and raise both hands to the sides of my face. Oh no. I forgot to grab my glasses when Maci and I rushed out the door.

"It's okay, Lily. We all know you have a black eye. If wearing sunglasses helps you through the day, we'd never ask you to take them off."

"You saw it. I didn't want you to see it." Oh, please don't let me cry in front of this man.

"I understand that, and I'm sorry my family's drama tonight caused you to forget them. I thank you for putting Everly first, though."

How can anyone not put Everly first? When she's happy, you feel loved and happy, too. Seeing her crying tonight made me want to stab people. Maybe Jay will loan me a knife. Since he likes them so much to be named after them, he's bound to have one, or a dozen, on him.

"Is there no way to help Harley?" She's irresponsible and selfish, but I don't want anything to happen to her.

Jack sighs and drops his head. "Mom and Dad have tried for years. Dad will probably put his foot down with her after tonight."

"If I can help." I pause. What can I do? They don't know me.

Jack sits up and pulls one leg up on the couch like I have. He has the same worried expression as Maci had earlier.

"Thank you for that. We'll let you know."

It's a sweet sentiment, but it's not real. I won't be here much longer. I'll never know what happens with his family. Why does that feel so wrong?

"What happens next?" I lift my eyes to his. "With me, I mean."

He releases a breath and runs a hand through his dark hair. "Dad wants to sit down with you in the morning and talk about your next steps."

"What exactly does that mean? What are my options? No one has really explained how all this works to me."

He watches me for a moment. He's quiet for so long that I assume he's letting the moment and my curiosity pass.

"Dad usually explains things as much as he can and still keeps all of us safe. Not all angels come to Willow Creek like you. Some know right away where they want to go. Nina's request was to get you as far from California as possible and for you to see my dad."

When she led me to the hospital parking garage, Nina insisted I ask for Jacob. She made me repeat it and say Ariel. How did she even know about Ariel's Angels? I suck in a breath. No. Not Nina. I meet Jack's eyes again.

"Nina was an angel." It's not a question. I know. It explains so much. She had the file ready without me knowing. The backpack had clothes that fit me perfectly, and she took my phone in the exam room. Nina has been through this.

"Yeah. She was one of the first women we rescued," Jack admits.

"Where do I go from here?"

"That's up to you. If you have distant family or friends on this side of the country that your abuser doesn't know about, we can help you get close to them. If there's a city you'd like to start over in, that's possible, too."

I bite my bottom lip and shake my head. If one of those were possible, I'd gladly go.

"I don't have any family here that I know of."

"A city you've wanted to visit?"

Is he trying to get rid of me? That hurts.

I shake my head again. "I never thought I'd leave California."

He rubs his hand over his mouth and beard. "There's a third option."

Our eyes lock. The energy between us is so thick it practically vibrates around us.

"What's my third option?" I'm afraid to ask, but I need to know.

"You could stick around for a while. I could show you Willow Creek if you'd like. Who knows? Maybe you'll like it here."

I swear his hazel eyes shift to light brown and back with each tilt of his head. I've never seen that happen before. It must be the lighting. Whatever's going on in those eyes, I can't look away. Is he asking me to stay? I'm not a strong person. I've never been bold a day in my life. Why not change that tonight?

"I like option three."

He smiles again. This time, it reaches his eyes. "Good. I'm glad. We'll let Dad know in the morning."

We sit quietly for a moment. Neither of us looks away. Sadly, the magical moment between us is broken when Jack's phone dings.

His eyes widen, and he lightly chuckles. "Well, angel. It looks like you're about to meet my grandmother. So, brace yourself."

"What? Why?" I look toward the door.

"Mom's with Everly. She's going to be fine, but Mom can't leave her tonight. Maci's gone to help Dad and Jay with Harley. Nana's the only woman left to stay with you. Well, we could call one of the ole' ladies, but Nana has volunteered."

"Who are the ole' ladies?"

"They're the wives or serious girlfriends of our patched members," he explains.

Oh, yeah. I read that somewhere. Okay. Nana is on her way. I quickly grab the sunglasses from the end table. Before I can slide them on, Jack cups my face in his hands.

"You don't have to wear those around anyone in my family unless you want to. I promise. No one will make you feel bad or ask questions." He slightly tilts my head. "It's healing nicely. It should be gone in a few days."

"He didn't punch me." I don't know why I'm telling him. Telling his mother was bad enough. "I don't know if it happened when I fell out of bed or when I hit the wall just before I left."

"Either way, I'm sorry it happened to you."

Jack

He leans forward and gently presses his lips to my forehead. It's the briefest touch, yet I feel it in my soul. No one has ever given me forehead kisses.

Jack slides back and stands seconds before the front door opens. His grandmother rushes in, bringing the bubbly atmosphere back into the house.

"Hey, Jackie Boy." She hurries to him and throws her arms around his waist.

"Nana," he scolds.

"Sorry, my dear boy." She pats his cheek a couple of times. "It's what you'll always be to me."

Jack groans and motions to me. "Nana, this is Lily. Lily, this is my grandmother." He leans down to where he's at eye level with her. "Can you behave yourself for one night?"

"Geez, boy." She swats his arm. "Of course I can."

"I'm not so sure," he mumbles.

"Jackie," she scolds right back.

He holds up both hands. "Okay, Nana, but please be good."

"Always am." She walks over and takes both of my hands in hers. "Hello, Lily. Call me Nana. Everyone else does."

"Yes, ma'am." I like this woman so much.

She doesn't flinch at my eye and turns back to Jack. "Now, my dear sweet grandson. Say goodnight to this lovely lady, and go help your dad."

Jack runs his hand through his hair again. He struggles to fight away something dark. "Yeah, I was afraid Dad would need help."

"It's not out of hand yet," Nana assures him.

This is about Harley. Jack looks torn on what to do. His family needs him. I feel comfortable and safe with Nana.

"Good night, Jack. Go help your dad." I smile, releasing him of his charge over me tonight.

"Good night, angel. If you need me, Nana will call."

"Darn right, I will." Nana pushes him out the door and locks it. She turns to me. "Let's get some coffee. I smell it, and I know Jack made it." She grins as she heads toward the kitchen. "And I hear there's ice cream in this house."

Thankfully, Jack and I got back before the ice cream melted on the table. I see where Maci gets her love of ice cream from. I follow Nana to the kitchen. We spend hours sitting around the table talking until the ice cream is almost gone. Jack's grandmother has a knack for storytelling. She had no problem sharing stories of when Jack and his sisters were kids. She even talked about Ariel. Through every story, she found a way to make me laugh. As I said, I really like Nana. I'm glad Jack asked me to stay.

17
Jack

I've never been so glad to see the sunrise in my life. My sister is getting worse by the month. I would say day or week, but those aren't accurate. Harley's drinking isn't an everyday thing. Well, not that we know of, anyway.

Throughout the week, she works and keeps to herself. She goes out nearly every weekend with her friends. They don't always go to parties and bars. She acts out more during parties at the clubhouse. We don't have those every week. Her worst moments are when the brothers from Texas are here. After the night we had, Shep led his guys out of here first thing this morning.

The meeting with Dad is off to a rocky start. We should probably postpone this. We're all functioning on less than two hours of sleep. Lily may be the only one who got more. Mom was home with Everly. After my niece fell asleep, she paced the floor until Dad got home.

"Okay, Miss Harman. We apologize for holding you here for two nights. That's not common for us. It's time to discuss your next step and for you to make some decisions." Dad sits behind his desk with Mom at his side.

"What exactly do I need to do?" Lily sits in the chair beside me in front of the desk.

Jay leans against the windowsill behind Dad. Rodeo and Worley Bird stand on either side of the door behind us. Meetings with angels in our care are kept as private as possible.

"Your next step is to decide where you wanna start over. If you have family or friends on the East Coast, we'll help you get there," Dad replies.

Mom rolls her eyes. It's a good thing Dad didn't see it. A fight between my parents is explosive. With the headache I have this morning, the last thing I need is these two arguing.

"Ariel's Angels doesn't just rescue women. We've mentioned that we help you find a safe place to start over. We give you a new identity and help you find a new job. But you can never contact anyone from your old life again," Mom explains a little better.

"Not even your parents," Dad adds.

"Not a problem," Lily mumbles. She raises her head and looks Dad in the eye. Brave girl. "My mother overdosed five years ago."

"And your dad?" Dad asks.

Lily shrugs one shoulder. "I don't know where or who he is. Mom would never tell me."

I rub my thumb and index fingers over my eyes. I'm an idiot. I should have asked these questions last night so she wouldn't have to share them for the first time in front of everyone. Mom and Dad look at each other. I reach over and take Lily's hand. She looks toward me but doesn't meet my eyes. She really is alone. It could explain how her abuser was able to get her into a vulnerable relationship with him.

"What about your mom's family?" Mom is softer-spoken than Dad.

Lily slightly shakes her head. She doesn't look directly at anyone. "Mom ended contact with her family before I was born. I don't know why. All I know is she mentioned growing up in North Carolina."

Again, my parents do that looking at each other thing. I swear, in these moments, they're telepathic.

I slide to the edge of my chair. "Actually, Lily and I talked last night. I offered to show her around Willow Creek."

Yep, my parents are telepathic. From their expressions, they're shocked, or maybe they're angry. It's hard to tell. The latter sounds more like them this morning. Both are very touchy today. Jay's interest is piqued. Rodeo and Worley Bird move around behind us, but neither speaks.

Mom recovers first. "Lily, do you wish to stay in Willow Creek for a while?"

Lily looks up at Mom and lightly squeezes my hand. "I would."

Dad clears his throat. "Okay. That changes things. We'll get you settled and find you a job. We'll hold off on finding one in the medical field until you make a final decision. The bar isn't a good idea."

"Waiting tables at the diner isn't either," Mom adds.

Dad looks over his shoulder at Jay. "You need a secretary?"

"Nope." Jay shakes his head.

That's a lie. Jay seriously needs a secretary. His office is a mess. I don't understand how he finds any of his paperwork.

"What about the bakery?" Worley Bird suggests.

"Good idea. I'll call Emily and see." Mom definitely approves of the bakery. She'll make this happen.

"Okay. That's it for today. Sweetheart, take Lily to the kitchen. You two help Mom make breakfast." Dad pulls Mom down and kisses her until everyone in the room is uncomfortable.

When he releases her, Mom walks around the desk. Her eyes settle behind Lily and me.

"Worley Bird, please take Lily to the kitchen. I think I need to be here for this conversation."

What conversation? I groan. My idea went over a little too easily. Of course, Dad had more to say.

"Mack?" Worley Bird will honor Mom. She is the club Queen, after all. However, Dad's word is law around here. Dad dips his chin. Worley Bird walks up to Lily's chair. "Come on, Miss Lily. Let's get you to the kitchen."

Lily slowly lifts from the chair. "Don't I get a say in this?"

I stand, never letting go of her hand.

"You had a say. You chose to stay." Dad lifts one eyebrow. "Or have you changed your mind?"

"No, sir," Lily replies softly.

I gently nudge her toward the door. "I'll see you in a bit. Worley Bird will take you to Nana." It's best we get her out of here now.

She reluctantly follows Worley Bird. The room erupts after the door closes behind them.

"Jacob," Mom scolds.

"What was that?" I ask at the same time.

Dad stands and places his palms on the desk. "That was me doing my job as club President and the head of this family."

"The counselor said we have to speak gently to angels." It's why I've chosen my words carefully and controlled my actions around Lily.

"Well, she kinda stepped a little outside the role of angel, didn't she?" Dad snaps.

"She's still under our protection." It's never good to argue with him.

"Yeah, she is. But we don't keep them, Jack. We rescue them. We help them move on. They don't stay." Dad doesn't back down.

"Just because one hasn't doesn't mean one can't." I don't back down, either. This won't end well.

"What are you doing, son? What are your intentions with this woman?" Dad demands.

Mom steps between us to defuse things like the desk wasn't enough. "Jack, you really like this woman?"

"I do," I admit. "I just haven't had a chance to figure things out."

"She's attracted to you, too." Mom sighs. "We'll get her settled with a temporary job for now and let you get to know her. If it's more than just attraction, we'll do even more for her."

"Where's she gonna stay?" Dad asks.

"I was hoping she could stay on club property. She can have my room in the clubhouse." It's a bad idea, but it's all I have at the moment.

Mom shakes her head. "She can keep staying in the guest house."

Dad, Jay, and I snap our heads toward her.

"Are you sure?" Dad's temper softens for a moment.

"If our son is falling in love with her, she can't stay in the clubhouse." Mom shudders at the thought.

"Fine." Dad snatches his phone off the desk. "Nick, I need a full search on Lily Harman. Bring me everything you find by the end of the day." He ends the call and tosses his phone down.

"Are you insane? That's invading her privacy. You've insisted for years that we don't ask them questions. They only tell us their story if they want to." I just crossed a line, and there's no coming back now.

"She's in our home, Jack. A part of our lives. If she means something to you, great. Figure it out. Claim her, and make her your ole' lady. For now, I have to do my job and protect everyone."

"Your job? How's breaking one of your own rules doing your job?"

He jabs his finger at me. "When you're President, you'll have to learn how to protect everyone."

"I won't do this."

"Until you have to make these types of decisions, you can't say that. This job isn't as easy as it looks." Mom has a point.

"Call Nick off. Let me have today with her. Give her a chance to tell me her story first."

"If I thought she'd talk, I would. You can try to get her to talk, but I won't stop Nick."

"It's wrong, Dad."

"It is, but it's what I have to do. Every woman who comes to us, whether we meet them or not, comes with medical records. Some have police reports. All of them have bruises or broken bones and are emotionally broken.

"Somewhere out there is some lowlife piece of crap. He hurt Lily. He's probably looking for her. We know they do. If he finds her here, and she's on club property, he'll find my wife, my mother, my daughters, and my granddaughter."

I quiet down and back off with each word he yells. He's right.

"I lost my brother."

Jay flinches. Losing his dad almost destroyed my family.

"I lost my daughter, my firstborn, and an unborn granddaughter at the same time."

Losing my sister and her baby completely destroyed our family. No matter how many ways we find to honor Ariel and fight for justice, we're never coming back from this one. On the outside, everyone believes we have it together. On the inside, we silently destroy ourselves, and in moments like this, we do it very loudly. Our enemies don't have to come for us. We'll end ourselves eventually.

"I can't lose anyone else!"

My fight's gone. Those words slice through my soul.

Mom rushes around the desk and slams into Dad's chest. "Jacob, come on, hon."

"I can't, Ev. I can't bury anyone else."

"I know. We won't. You're protecting us all, Lily included." With her arms around his waist, she eases Dad into his chair. She doesn't take her eyes off of him. "Jay, you and Rodeo take Jack to the kitchen. Send Worley Bird back."

"Got it, Aunt Ev." Jay pushes off the window sill and motions for me to walk ahead of him.

"Mom? I didn't mean…"

She looks over her shoulder. Her tears send another dagger through my heart. "Please, Jack. We just need some rest. Go take care of Lily."

I say no more and follow Rodeo out the door. This has officially gone to pot.

"Everybody's exhausted." Rodeo falls in step next to me.

"Yeah," Jay agrees. "Lily isn't why he's upset. Your sister said some horrible things to him before you showed up."

Harley said some horrible things to everybody. I was only there for thirty minutes. I'd hate to imagine what was said and done before I arrived. Finally, she collapsed into Maci and Ember's arms. Rodeo and I put her to bed. We left our younger sisters to watch over her. They're still at Harley's house, waiting for her to wake up.

"Why don't you let Lily stay with Nana for a few hours and get some rest?" Jay suggests.

"What about you? You ok?" My cousin worries me. He keeps everything bottled up.

"Nope. Going for a ride." Jay walks across the Den and out the front door.

"He shouldn't be alone." I go to follow him.

Rodeo grabs my arm. "I'll call Bankz and Cloudy. They'll watch over him. Your mom has your dad. Go have breakfast with Lily. She'll be fine with Nana. I'll have the entire club watching today. Go get a nap, man. I sure need one." Rodeo has things handled. He's going to make a great VP one day.

"Thanks, man." I slap him on the back and head to the kitchen.

18
Lily

Helping Nana in the clubhouse kitchen wasn't as bad as it first sounded. No, I'm not a good cook. Far from it. Jack's grandmother has made it her personal mission to help me learn. Cooking for such a large crew takes a lot of planning and preparation. Pancakes were my job today. It was the only thing I couldn't really mess up.

The meeting with Jack's father wasn't comfortable. In fact, the entire clubhouse has been on edge all morning. Jack was quiet during breakfast. He left me with Nana and disappeared. It's lunchtime. Hopefully, things will be better soon.

Nana knows what's going on. As outgoing as she is, she's also tight-lipped when it comes to serious matters about her family. She's also kept me in the kitchen all morning and all the guys out.

"Hey, Nana." A woman with sandy blonde hair walks into the kitchen. "Pops wants a cheeseburger and fries. You cooking lunch today?"

"Might as well. Got nothing else to do." Nana gets a package of ground chuck from the fridge and sets it on the preparation table in front of me. "This is an easy one. Make us a hamburger patty."

I'm not a total idiot in the kitchen. I can make a burger. Mine never seem to have the best flavor, though. Pops is going to be very disappointed. While I make the patty, Nana drops a basket of fries into the fryer.

"Lily, this is Kayla. She bartends for us sometimes." Nana pulls spices from the cabinet and sprinkles them on the patty I just made. Okay. That's what I was missing.

"Hi. Nice to meet you." I offer Kayla my hand.

"Likewise." Kayla's handshake is firm. I've read that you can tell a lot from a handshake. "I also work at JB's. It pays more," she adds with a grin.

"The bar in town?" I think Maci mentioned it.

"Hello, ladies." Jack walks in with his friend Rodeo right behind him.

"Hey, Jackie." Nana flips the burger as Jack kisses her cheek.

He looks better than he did this morning. He's still dressed all in black, black boots, black jeans and a black t-shirt. The man just loves black, I guess. The only thing he wears with color is his vest. No, wait. He called it a cut. Rodeo's eyes instantly lock onto Kayla and never leave.

"See ya around, Lily." Kayla holds her head high and goes back through the door to the bar. Rodeo follows behind her. Something's going on with them.

"Hello, angel." Jack leans on the counter next to me. "Wanna get out of here for a while?"

"Really? Can we?" I'm so tired of sitting around.

He lightly laughs. "Well, I did promise to show you the town." He takes my hand and pulls me toward the side door. "Let's go, angel."

"What about Nana?"

"I'm fine, dear." Nana waves and continues cooking.

He leads me to a side parking lot. This isn't the same one Shepherd and I went to. Just how big is this place? We stop beside a motorcycle. It's all black, too. It matches its owner's perfectly.

"Uh, Jack. I've never ridden on a motorcycle."

"Never?"

I shake my head. He leans close. His eyes practically dance as they bounce between mine. I haven't seen this side of him. I'm instantly pulled in.

"What do you say, angel? Wanna live on the edge today?" His deep voice sends shivers all the way to my toes. His eyes move to the black Chevy truck a few feet away. "Or we can play it safe."

"Safe," I barely whisper the word.

Going anywhere with this man, no matter what vehicle we take, isn't safe. I've never been interested in the bad boy type, and bad boy is written all over him. My attraction was for business suits. Suits turned out to be a huge mistake. Bad boys can't be my thing, either. I need to break whatever's pulling me to this man. I'm just not sure I want to yet. One day with him couldn't hurt. Right?

He opens the passenger door. "In you go, angel. Maybe we can live dangerously tomorrow."

I place my foot on the running board and climb inside. No need to wait for tomorrow. Today's already dangerous, so so dangerous.

"Where are we going?" I ask as we drive through the front gate.

"We're going to the bakery. Mom talked to Emily. You start work in the morning. Thought you might like to meet her first."

How does someone find a job in just a few hours with no experience in the field? These people are insane. I'm a nurse, not a baker.

"I'm going to work at a bakery?"

"Yep. I work at the shop with Jay, so I can drive you to work." He's perfectly fine with this.

The drive to town takes fifteen minutes. Jack talks about all the places we pass along the way, which seemed few and far between to me. Willow Creek isn't as small as it sounds. It's a really charming town. Jack pulls into the parking lot of the bakery downtown. The gray building with the pink cupcake sign is adorable.

"I work at The Cupcake Cottage?" This can't be real.

He laughs and points to a side street across from the bakery. "I work at Jay's Garage around the corner."

"That's simple enough. I like it."

"Jay is simple and easygoing most of the time. His work, however, is amazing. I'll show you sometime." He sounds really proud of his cousin.

He's out of the truck and at my door before my foot touches the running board. He offers me his hand. "Always wait for me."

"I can get out of cars and open doors for myself. No one has ever helped me before."

He doesn't move, and there's no way I can step around him. His eyes seem to pin me in place. "Then they were doing it wrong."

He has no idea just how wrong things have been in the past. I just got out of the worst relationship in my life. Everything about the man in front of me should instill fear. Nothing about his appearance says sweet. Yet, here he is, showing me kindness. And surprisingly, his bad-boy qualities draw me to him. My mind's so messed up.

He steps back and walks beside me to the front door. The bakery has another parking lot on the other side. Four bikes sit in two of the spaces closest to the door.

"Friends of yours?"

"No."

We look through the huge front window. A biker glares at us from the other side of the glass. Another leans on the front counter near the cash register. He either knows the lady behind the counter very well, or he's harassing her. Two more bikers wander around the shop. Jack moves me behind him and reaches for the door.

I grab hold of the back of his cut. "You don't have to do this."

"I most certainly do."

Jack opens the door and walks up to the counter like he owns the place. "Emily, how's it going?"

Emily glances at the four bikers one by one before replying, "Seen better days. Can't remember when."

Is that some kind of encrypted code? I already need a biker's manual. Might as well add a bakery one to the list.

Jack leans on the counter and faces the other biker. "Trace, what brings you to town?"

"Passing through, McLeod. Won't be here long, so don't get your panties in a wad."

Jack doesn't take his eyes off Trace. "Emily, are these guys bothering you?"

"Not exactly bothering. Not helping either." Emily doesn't flinch.

I feel the other three men move closer. Two behind me, one on my left side. I turn to face them and walk backward to the glass display case. There's another on the other side of Jack and the fourth biker.

Jack

Jack looks at the three over his shoulder. "I wouldn't take another step toward her if I were you." He turns back to Trace. "It's time for you to leave."

Trace straightens. He looks around Jack and grins at me. "So this is the woman to get you off your ride."

"Should we call the cops?" I ask.

Everyone looks at me like I'm insane, Jack included. Yeah, I kind of am, but okay. I get it. No cops.

Trace drops his head back and laughs. "Look at you, McLeod. Stooped so low you got a cop lover in your bed. I was going to say she was gorgeous, but I've changed my mind."

Jack straightens and places a palm on the counter. "Emily, you wanna call Nathan?"

"Not if they buy something or leave peacefully." Emily reaches for a set of tongs next to the other display case.

Trace huffs. "Think I'd rather have ice cream."

Jack crosses his arms. "Good. Get that on the other side of the mountain in your time zone."

"Come on, Trace. Let's go." The biggest man pushes the door open. The other two follow him out. Trace is the last to leave. He pauses at the door and places a finger on the side of his forehead.

"Next time, Ghost." He gives an odd one-finger salute before walking out.

The tension in the bakery slowly fades. Two young girls come from the backroom. I have no idea what just happened. The only thing I know is I don't belong in this world.

19
Jack

Work doesn't bother me. I don't mind getting my hands dirty. I'm not as comfortable as Jay and Cloudy are, though. They do this every day. I won't lie. After two years of wandering, I've gotten lazy. I love Jay and want to help out, but I'm tired. My first day felt more like three. Seeing the '57 Chevy was worth my time.

Thank goodness I only have to do this three days a week. I can choose any three days I want from Monday to Thursday unless Jay needs me. Since I'm expected to be the next club president, Dad wants me with him or out doing club business from Friday to Sunday. Club business is every day, all day, and it comes first. Dad has his work or school rule, so here I am.

The tension at the clubhouse was still on edge. Maci and Ember come home from college every weekend. Mom's running ragged between Dad and Harley. My older sister is dead set on destroying herself and the entire family. Everly, Logan, and Granddad are helping as much as they can. Nana's overseeing the kitchen at The Den. Everybody's spread thin.

Dad and I haven't spoken since things exploded between us. It wouldn't have happened if it weren't for the rough night with Harley. My family has a lot to deal with, and none of us seems to know how to navigate through any of it. Changes are definitely coming, though. We can't keep going like this.

Jack

For three weeks, I've worked at the shop with Jay. Lily's doing okay at the bakery, not great but okay. She and Emily have become good friends, but she doesn't enjoy working there. Emily keeps her in the back doing prep work and teaching her to bake. Lily's passion is being a nurse. This job is slowly draining her. A little piece of her seems to die every day. I'm struggling, too.

For three weeks, I've followed the advice from Mom, Nana, and the counselors we secretly employ for Ariel's Angels. I've been gentle and soft-spoken with Lily. For every step I make forward with her, a memory hits, and things are thrown ten steps back.

Mom insists Lily needs gentleness and time. The pull I feel with Lily is more than attraction. I haven't admitted it, but my family and brothers see it. Jay thinks it's downright funny. I may have to hurt my cousin.

Lily's slipping into depression. Mom mentioned our counselors to her, but she refuses to speak to one of them. I may need to, though. This soft, sweet, gentle side I have to show around Lily is driving me insane. I care about her, so I do it. I feel like a caged bear ready to explode at any moment. I definitely have a split personality now.

The thundering sounds of bikes on Main Street fill the air. Hearing them has me itching to ride. I drove my truck again today. Lily's still not ready to live dangerously enough to get on the back of my bike. She wants to. Her eyes fill with excitement for a moment every time I mention going for a ride. Fear pushes her excitement away too quickly. Eventually, I'll get her behind me.

"We might get some work done if everybody wasn't coming to see you. It's not like they all haven't seen you already." Cloudy throws a shop towel at me and walks toward the street to see who's coming this time.

"Those aren't ours." Jay steps beside me in the open bay door.

How he knows those bikes aren't our members just from the sound is a mystery to me. Sure, I can recognize a few of our guys' bikes, but most of those are custom designs. The sounds of the engines get louder, sending an eerie cold feeling up my spine. If Jay's right, does it mean we have trouble coming?

I glance at my cousin. There's not a doubt in his mind those aren't our brothers. He's never been wrong on this before. He and I walk across the drive to where Cloudy's watching Main Street.

A few weeks ago at The Cupcake Cottage flashes in my mind. My eyes dart toward the bakery. If Willow Creek Market weren't on the corner, I could see the front of the bakery. Surely, Trace went home after our little run-in. My first thought is to run across Main Street. Lily's safe. Emily knows what to do if trouble starts.

The three of us watch as four bikes, and not our brothers, travel east on Main Street toward the center of town. Every bone in my body stiffens, and my hands ball into fists. The only reason I'm not running across the street now is because they kept going.

"Well, I be darn." Cloudy's eyes harden. "Midnight Mavericks."

Trace didn't listen. He should've gone home and stayed there. Chattanooga is about three hours away. What's got him hanging out in Willow Creek?

"That's not good." Jay pops the top on a soda.

"Why? The Mavericks up to something?" I take a step closer to the street, straining to hear their engines.

"Sounds like they stopped at Angie's." Cloudy's listening, too.

Jay leans against the side of my truck on the edge of the drive. "Rumor in the vine says Trace's family's pissed about something. No word on why or who at."

"I had a run-in with him at the bakery a few weeks ago. Told him to go home." I look toward the direction of the bakery again. The Mavericks aren't there. They've stopped, but they haven't killed their engines yet.

"Trace is here?" Jay asks.

"Yeah. Brock, Diesel, and Buck were with him." I should've had one of our brothers follow them out of town.

"If Trace is here, guess that means they're pissed at us." Cloudy joins Jay against the truck.

"What have we done?" I've only been home for a month. Whatever it is, it happened before that.

Jay shakes his head. "No clue. We haven't done anything major in months."

I turn to face him. "What was the last thing you did?"

My cousin knows an enemy can take months, sometimes years, to plot revenge. If you want to do it right, you want to serve it up cold. The colder the better.

"Concerning the Mavericks?" Jay thinks for a moment. "Just racing in The Valley."

The Valley is an open field that the owner turned into a racing track over sixty years ago. He and his buddies started the races during their high school days. It's not an official race track by any means. It's about fifty miles south of us and Dades Creek. The Valley gets raided ever so often. The staged raids let the locals believe the cops are monitoring it. They aren't. The cops are paid to look the other way.

"What did they lose?"

"Just cash. Nobody put up slips or anything else against them." Jay finishes his soda and tosses the can into the back of my truck.

I point my finger at him. "That's not a trash can." With my thumb, I point to the shop. He's got plenty of trash cans in there.

Jay rolls his eyes and laughs. He gets that can out of my truck bed, though.

"Bring me a soda," Cloudy calls out.

Jay comes back with two sodas. Cloudy walks to the middle of the drive with his. I don't want a soda, but my hands need something to do before my mind goes crazy.

"Losing a couple thousand dollars isn't enough to make them come after us," Jay says.

It's not. Everyone who goes to The Valley knows it. The rules at The Valley are straightforward. Whatever happens at The Valley stays in that field. Cash doesn't usually cause problems. It's when they bet slips and other things that cause fights. A few guys have been so wasted that they bet their women. That's against the rules. In fact, it's rule number two. However, side bets happen without the people running the races knowing about them.

"They're moving," Cloudy calls out.

Jay and I walk out to the middle of the drive, not as close to the street as Cloudy. The roar of the engines gets louder. The sounds bounce off the buildings.

"They aren't on Main Street." Jay points to our right. "They're using the back streets and coming this way."

I glance at him from the corner of my eye. "You armed?" Stupid question.

"Absolutely."

"I mean more than just knives." Still stupid.

"Absolutely." Jay grins, and his eyes dance. My insane cousin lives for moments like this.

It's beyond bold, cocky, and stupid for Trace to come to Jay's shop, no matter how mad he is. Everybody knows Jay can come unhinged in the blink of an eye. Sadly, for a lot of men, they didn't realize it until it was too late.

There's no time to call for backup. It's just the three of us today. We're more than enough to handle four Mavericks.

Four bikes come around the curve two blocks down the street. The lead rider, without a doubt, is Trace. I'd know that low-life piece of crap and his bike anywhere. Tracy Coombs and I were born hating each other. Our families' clubs have been rivals long before we were born. We'll die hating each other, too.

Jay, Cloudy, and I stand firm, waiting for their arrival. Jay already has a knife hidden in his palm. I should have known he'd go for a knife first. The Mavericks slow but don't pull into the drive. Jay and I keep our eyes on Trace as he rolls by.

"Hit the deck!" Cloudy shouts.

I snap my head toward our brother. Cloudy throws his soda toward the street and dives into the grass between two cars on the other side of the drive. The last rider throws something toward us. The ball of smoke sends Jay and me scrambling to the other side of my truck. Was that a bomb? The sounds of gunfire echo through the streets. Customers at the market scream and run for their cars or back inside.

"That's not gunfire." Jay's on his feet and heads to the center of the smoke.

"Jay, wait!"

He doesn't listen. He's not wrong, either. The last couple of pops come, leaving only a cloud of smoke. Cloudy walks through the smoke, waving his arms. It's not that bad. The wind's already carrying it across the street.

Jay meets me at the back of my truck. He places a brick in my hands. "They had at least two or three strands of firecrackers around this."

"That's a lot of smoke for firecrackers." Cloudy glares down the street. Trace is long gone.

"From the ashes on the pavement, I think they had paper wrapped around the brick." Jay leans back against the truck and shakes his head.

"What does this mean?" Cloudy takes the brick and looks it over. "Why are the M&Ms messing with us?"

"It means they're toying with us." I rub the back of my neck. This is a childish prank.

"It means we call Uncle Jacob and have church. I'm closing the shop." Jay storms away.

"Guess this confirms we're who they're pissed at." Cloudy places the brick back in my hands and follows Jay.

Once again, my cousin isn't wrong. I haven't apologized to my father yet. As much as I don't want to do this, I pull my phone from my back pocket and make the call. Within seconds of ending the call, a text demanding church went out to every member in Willow Creek.

20
Jack

While Jay closed the shop, I picked Lily up. Emily had no problem letting her leave early. All it took was a quick call saying there was trouble and Church. Emily doesn't have a family member in the club. She's not dating one of my brothers, either. She's ours, though.

Emily grew up in Willow Creek and went to school with Maci. Unlike her parents, she's been a loyal friend to us and knows how the club operates. I trust her with my life. Of all the jobs Mom could have gotten for Lily around town, the bakery was the best choice.

The Viking Den's already packed by the time we arrive. Brothers are making their way toward Church. Ole' ladies and a few kids are scattered around the commons room. Prospects are playing pool in the corner. Jenny steps away from one when I walk in. I groan. Of course, club bunnies would come running when they noticed a lot of activity at the Den. I ignore the bunny and guide Lily toward the bar and kitchen area.

"What's going on? Why's there a party on a Monday?" Lily scans the room several times.

"Not a party, angel. It's Church."

She looks up at me over her shoulder with her eyebrows pulled together. "You go to church? Most people have that on Sundays, by the way."

Jack

I laugh. "Not that kind of church, angel. It's a club meeting. We have them once a week and for important matters."

Her steps slow. "Is this a weekly meeting or an important matter?"

"Um." I swallow hard.

"That wasn't firecrackers earlier," she says softly.

I place my hands on her shoulders, bringing us to a stop in the middle of the room. I stay behind her and lean forward so she can see my eyes. "It was really firecrackers. There was just a little something attached to them." Her body stiffens. "Relax, angel. It had nothing to do with you. Club business. Promise."

She nods, and we start walking through the crowd again. I intend to take her to the kitchen. Mom and Nana are here. We don't make it that far, though.

"Lily!" Kayla calls out and waves from behind the bar.

Lily hurries over and climbs up on one of the stools. "I'm glad you're here."

I'm glad she's made a friend in the club and one that I trust.

"Can I get you a drink?"

"Just water, please." Lily folds her hands together on the bar. She turns her head toward the old timer on her right.

He grins. "Hello, princess."

I step behind her until her back touches my chest. Not the best idea I've had today. Now, I want to wrap my arms around her.

"Lily, this is Pops." I glare at him, warning him to act right.

She gasps. "Your grandfather."

Pops looks mortified. Kayla and I burst out laughing.

"No, angel." I point to the old timer at the end of the bar. "That's Granddad."

Granddad smiles and waves. He gives me a nod of approval and a thumbs up.

"Pops is Worley Bird's father." Kayla sets a bottle of water in front of Lily. "He was our first club treasurer."

"Yeah, thought my son would follow in my footsteps. He traded up for VP," Pops grumbles. He's not really upset. He's proud of his son.

"Vikings!" Worley Bird shouts from outside the double wooden doors. "Church! Now!"

I lean down, allowing my cheek to touch her hair. The sweet scent of coconut hits me. It's her shampoo. I saw the bottle in her bathroom when I searched the guest house.

"Stay here, angel. If the crowd gets too much, go to the kitchen. Mom and Nana are in there."

She looks up at me and slightly nods. Kayla dips her chin once, assuring me she'll watch over Lily.

"Pops, you behave yourself." I slap him on the back and walk away.

"Can't. Got a pretty girl next to me." The old man props his elbow on the bar and grins at Lily.

I turn around to scold the old-timer.

"Jack! Let's go!" Worley Bird shouts, saving his old man.

Pops is harmless, so I leave him be and go to Church. Worley Bird closes the double doors behind us. He takes his place next to Dad at the officers' table down front. Jay and Cloudy stand against the wall on the right side of the room. My cousin motions for me to join them.

"Vikings! Settle down!" Dad stands and slams the gavel down. Church has officially begun.

The room goes quiet, and everyone finds a seat. The only ones left standing are the three of us and Dad.

Dad tosses the brick on the table and points at it. "This was stupid. It shouldn't have happened. It also can't be ignored." He turns to the three of us. "Cloudy Daze isn't an official patched member, but he's one of us. Cloudy was there, and you need to hear what he saw. Boys, tell 'em what happened."

Cloudy steps forward first. One by one, each of us shares what happened. Jay tells them about the races in The Valley back in the summer. I include the run-in with Trace at the bakery three weeks ago. Someone in the rows near me growls at the mention of Emily Powell. Everybody's mad, so I don't know who it was. Several members are on their feet complaining. The entire club likes Emily. I'm not sure what that growl was about, though. Does someone not like Emily?

"Settle down, brothers." Worley Bird's voice booms above the noise. Once again, the room goes quiet. "Of course, we'll protect Emily and the bakery. We'll set up a security detail for her until we know what's going on. Rodeo will put a sign-up sheet for volunteers at the bar. If there's not enough volunteers, we'll recruit you."

From the amount of heads nodding, we'll have enough volunteers to watch the bakery. It eases my mind a little, knowing eyes will be on Lily, too, while she's working.

"Alright, brothers. I agree with my son. There's more to this than losing some cash. Have any of you had a run-in with a Maverick that we don't know about?"

Everyone looks around. A few whisper. Several shake their heads, but no one stands. I study as many faces as I can. Without looking at him, I know Jay's doing it, too. There's no odd behavior that I can pinpoint. A guilty man always shows something to give himself away. You just have to catch it. But I see nothing that alarms me.

"Does anybody have any theories?" Dad asks.

Hendrix stands. "Pres, I don't know what sparked it, but whatever caused it is personal. Tracy Coombs isn't coming across the mountain to give a warning and possibly declare war on another club unless it involves his family somehow. Yeah, his method is beyond ridiculous, but I think it's personal to him."

"He's got a point," Bankz adds. "The Midnight Mavericks' President wouldn't be doing a job he normally sends others to do unless it was personal."

"Alright." Dad nods. "That's possible. Can anyone confirm it? If you crossed the Coombs somehow, we need to know. Tell us now so we can prepare, and there won't be any repercussions for you."

Once again, no one speaks up. Dad looks at his officers before turning to me. I see the question in his eyes.

"The day at the bakery was the first time I've seen Trace in probably four years."

"Alright, brothers. Keep your eyes open. If you see these guys hanging around, report back. Worley Bird and Rodeo will have the volunteer protection sheet at the bar tonight. If you're interested, sign it before you leave." Dad slams the gavel down again.

After most of the guys leave, Dad makes his way over to me. He's upset and worried. At least he looks rested now.

"Son, I don't think this is because of what happened at the bakery." He looks away. "About the other day."

"Dad, I shouldn't have pushed."

"Yeah." He runs a hand through his hair. "I wasn't really listening and thinking straight. I…"

"You were worried about Harley. We all are. We don't want her to end up in a position like Ariel did."

He takes a deep breath. "I…"

"Hey." I place my hand on his shoulder. "I understand, and I have a lot to learn about leading this club. But if you're good, I'm good. We're good. I promise."

"We're good," he repeats. This is the closest he and I get to an actual apology. It's fine. We both understand what it means. He tosses an arm over my shoulders as we walk toward the door. "Any progress with Lily?"

"Not really. Did Nick find anything?" I'm not trying to start an argument with them.

"Yeah, but I haven't read the file yet. He's still looking, too." We stop at the door, and he meets my eyes. "Jack, if you really like this woman, make it happen. She'll have better protection as family. If it's not what you were hoping, we need to move her to her new life."

"Okay, Dad. I understand."

I do understand. I just need to figure out how to move forward with Lily and be gentle at the same time. I'm not sure I can do both.

My heart rate speeds up the moment I step into the Den. Lily's bar stool is empty. Kayla points toward the kitchen. Her eyes glare at something across the common room. I follow her gaze. Jenny has her arms around Skip's neck. He's a skinny kid and our newest prospect. Jenny notices me and grins slyly. I look back at Kayla. She nods. I drop my head back and groan. I may have to kill a bunny tonight. First, I have an angel to see.

21
Lily

The clubhouse quietened down drastically after most of the men went into the other room. The loudest sounds now are children playing and pool balls clicking. The women with children sit around the tables closest to the doors where the men are having Church. I don't understand why they call their club meetings Church. It's another example of why I need a biker's manual, or handbook, or something. Maybe if I weren't hiding out between the bakery and the guest house, I might learn what stuff around here means.

"Why didn't everybody go to Church?" I ask Kayla.

This area of the clubhouse is huge. The bar and kitchen are together on the left side. Nana said the doors past the kitchen go to the backyard. Six couches have four pool tables boxed off in the far right corner of the room. Four men are playing pool. Two more are making out with their girlfriends on the couches. Note to self. Never sit on those couches. That's disgusting, and there are children in here. The blonde, who was hanging on Jack a few weeks ago, sits on a wooden stool next to one of the pool tables. I really hate her.

"Only patched members are allowed in Church." Kayla sets a mug of beer in front of Pops.

"You and Granddad aren't patched?" There are patches all over Pops' cut. I'm not sure which one means they're a patched member.

"Pops and Granddad consider themselves retired." Kayla lays her arms on the bar in front of me.

"We go to the weekly meetings." Pops tosses a hand toward the wooden doors. "We leave this stuff to the younger generation."

"Women don't go to Church?"

Kayla shakes her head.

"They can if they're part of the problem." Pop takes a sip of his beer.

I study the women in the room. The ones with children wear cuts with patches on them. The three around the pool tables don't have cuts.

"But some women wear cuts. Are they not patched?" Look at me using biker language.

"Ole' ladies and members' kids wear them. It shows they belong to the club, and nobody will touch them. They aren't patched members, though," Kayla explains.

"You don't wear a cut," I point out.

"Don't want one," she mumbles.

Pops laughs. "That's a lie."

Kayla points to the mug in his hand. "And that's your last beer tonight."

There's definitely a story between her and Rodeo. They don't talk, but he follows her around. Since Rodeo was gone for two years, maybe she likes someone else, and his being back is a problem. My heart hurts for her. Hopefully, she figures things out soon. She's not ready to face her problems yet. I get it. I'm not ready to face mine, either. Kayla fakes a smile as she sets three sodas and four small cartons of apple juice on a tray. One of the ole' ladies carries the tray to her group by the Church doors.

A woman's hand slaps down on the bar between Pops and me. Pops rolls his eyes. I jump, and Kayla's back stiffens. She slowly turns around and glares. I look up at the blonde I seriously hate.

"Can I have a martini?" She taps the professionally red-manicured nails on the bar.

"Does this look like a cocktail bar to you?" Kayla snaps.

"What? A martini beyond your bartending capabilities?" The blonde huffs.

Jack

I slowly ease over to the next bar stool. Pops should do the same before these two come to blows over the bar. Pops doesn't move. He and Granddad sit quietly and watch with interest.

"It is tonight. How about a wine cooler?" Kayla snatches a *Seagram's Strawberry Daiquiri* from the cooler and firmly sets it on the bar.

The blonde slides onto the stool I abandoned. "You're an idiot."

"And you're a piece of trash." Kayla spins around and storms off to the kitchen.

The blonde turns to me and grins slyly. "You must be the new girl."

"New girl?" Only patched members know about Ariel's Angels. Does this woman somehow know why I'm here?

"I heard we were getting a new girl. That must be you. Has Nana given you all the rules?" She flips her hand. "Don't worry. The girls and I will explain everything."

"Go away, bunny." Pops demands.

She laughs and lays her hand on his shoulder. "Awe, Pops. You want some company?"

Pops slaps her hand away. "I don't do crazy." He points toward the pool tables. "Go back to the prospects where you belong. And watch how you speak to your future Queen."

"What?" Bunny slaps a hand to her chest.

"Leave now before I have you escorted out the front gate." Pops looks past her and smiles at me. "This is Lily. Jack's girl. So show her some respect."

Bunny spins so fast toward me that she almost falls off the stool. "Jack doesn't have a girl."

"He does now. So, as Pops said, show her some respect." Kayla returns. Her temper is still fully intact.

Bunny looks me over with disgust. She needs to look in the mirror. Her two sizes too small cropped top and short shorts scream trashy. She's perfected the perfect devious smile. It might be the only thing she's accomplished in her life.

"You must like it rough. Might be what he sees in you." Her smile widens.

I spew water into my hand. "What?"

She points a long red fingernail at my face. "Women only wear sunglasses inside when they're hiding a black eye."

"Leave now," Kayla demands.

Bunny ignores her. She twirls her bottled-blonde hair around her fingers. "Jack give you that?"

I gape at her. This woman is insane. Slowly, I take my sunglasses off and lay them on the counter. My black eye and bruised cheek have healed. The sunglasses have become a safety net and a crutch. They let me hide. I only wear them when I'm out in public.

"You haven't been in his bed." She drops her head back and laughs like a maniac. She straightens up and turns serious just as fast. "That makes one of us."

Oh my gosh. She's Jack's lover. If he has a girlfriend, why is he helping me so much? Wait. She can't be Jack's girlfriend. She was hanging all over one of the men at the pool tables a few minutes ago. What does that make her? Oh no. My back stiffens, and my eyes meet hers.

"Leave now, bunny, or I'll have you escorted out the gate." Granddad stands behind Pops with his arms crossed. "This is Jack's girl. You treat her as such."

Bunny slides off the stool. Her laugh is pure evil. "You're not made for this world. You're too soft. You bruise easily. He'll chew you up and spit you out in a week. I'll be here when he does."

"That's enough." Granddad grabs Bunny by the arm. "Talk to her like that again, and my ole' lady will end your contract." He practically drags her over to the pool tables.

The ole' ladies at the tables watch with their lips pressed together. Pops wants to say something but doesn't. Kayla has turned three shades of red and is ready to kill.

"She's a club girl."

"She's a piece of trash," Kayla corrects.

"She's been with Jack." I shouldn't care. He's not mine. I don't want a biker.

Kayla sighs but doesn't deny it. Does everyone know? Of course, they do.

Jack

"I can't do this." I slide off the stool and rush to the kitchen. I'm not sure if I'm mad, hurt, or disgusted. Why choose? I can be all three.

22
Jack

Lily leans back against the counter with her arms crossed. She doesn't look up when I enter the kitchen. She stares at absolutely nothing on the floor. Mom and Nana shrug and shake their heads. They don't know what's going on, but I do.

"Angel?" I take a cautious step toward her.

"Don't call me that," she snaps and turns her back to me.

Oh, somebody has a little spunk today. Where's that been hiding? Trust me. I don't mind. I can handle attitudes like this.

"Jack, why don't you take Lily home?" Mom suggests. Her tone is warning me to be gentle.

"I can find it myself." She pushes off the counter and takes two steps toward the door to the Den.

"Yeah. Still not happening." I slide an arm around her waist and turn her toward the back door of the kitchen. "See ya later, Mom, Nana."

"Bye," they say at the same time.

This door opens at the lower end of the front parking lot. I walk her across the lot to my truck and open the passenger door.

"The path behind the building goes straight to the guest house. I can find it."

I point to the road at the edge of the lot. "So does the driveway." I motion to the passenger seat. "I know you're mad. We'll sort it out when we get to the house."

Jack

"Fine." She steps on the running board and drops down onto the seat.

I get in and start the engine. My day's gone from bad to worse and beyond. My oldest enemy has reverted to childish pranks. We pulled enough of that crap when we were kids. I have a club bunny we need to cut loose. Thanks to the bunny, I have to figure out how to talk to the woman beside me without upsetting her even more. I don't know, though. I love this fiery attitude. Sweet and gentle won't handle things today.

If Lily hadn't come to us as an angel, I'd handle things like my parents do. Those two love each other like crazy and aren't ashamed to show it, and they don't care who's watching. Watching your dad kiss your mom senseless is beyond uncomfortable. If you get on to him about it, he'll just do it again for good measure.

My parents will also go toe-to-toe with each other quite often. I can't be like that, though. The counselors have given us a long list of guidelines on how to handle abused women. With as crazy as things are right now, it's getting hard to remember them all. Every rule means delicate. I'm trying. I really am.

When we pull up at the guest house, Lily hops out without waiting for me. I'll honor her little demand for independence for a bit. She marches up the steps and waits by the door for me to unlock it. Naturally, I let her enter first. I leave her to herself and head to the kitchen. Coffee is a magical substance for the women in my family. Lily seems to enjoy a good cup. Maybe it'll defuse things between us tonight. Then again, maybe not. She didn't follow me to the kitchen.

With two cups of coffee in hand, I find her curled into one corner of the couch. I set a cup on the end table beside her and settle into the other corner. She asked me to sit with her on the couch a few weeks ago. I'm not giving that right up just because she's mad.

"You wanna talk about it?" Asking is risky, but the silence has become deafening.

"Not really."

"It won't solve anything if we don't." I'm trying to show patience, but I don't like putting things off.

"I know." She stares into her mug.

"What happened?" I have a pretty good idea. I'd like to hear it from her, though.

She's quiet for so long that I fear she's shut down for the night.

"She's your mistress," she finally replies softly.

"Absolutely not. I don't have a mistress," I inform her.

"You slept with her."

"Yeah, once. I think," I admit.

She snaps her head in my direction. "You don't know how many times you've slept with her?"

"It's not like that. I don't know if anything actually happened with her. If it did, it was only once." I didn't explain that well at all.

"How's that possible?"

"The night before Rodeo and I left, there was a party. I woke up the next morning with Jenny next to me." I'm not painting myself in a good light here.

"A man should never be that drunk."

No, they shouldn't. I don't like the look on her face. I may have just knocked myself back ten feet with her.

"It's the only time it's ever happened." I glance at her from the corner of my eye. She doesn't believe me.

"I thought her name was Bunny."

I press my lips together and struggle not to laugh.

"Bunnies is what we call club girls," I explain.

Lily shudders. "Why do they have to be real?"

That's a loaded question and one I'm not answering. No explanation I could come up with wouldn't sound right to a good woman. I glance at her again. Lily Harman is, without a doubt, a good woman. A good woman that bad things happened to.

I turn to the side and face her. "My question, angel, is why are *you* so upset over a club bunny and something that may or may not have happened over two years ago?"

Her eyes slowly roam over me, not settling on a particular feature. Once again, her coffee quickly becomes the most interesting thing in the room. Well, well, well. One corner of my mouth lifts. This attraction isn't just one-sided. Good to know. I can work with this.

Jack

I set my mug on the end table, slide to the center cushion, and rest my arm on the back of the couch.

"What do you want, angel?"

She shakes her head. "I don't know."

"You do know. You're just scared to ask for it." My words hit a mark I wasn't aiming for.

"I'm not scared." She springs from the couch and begins to pace.

"It's okay to feel, even if it is fear." I push rather than defuse as we've been trained to do.

"I'm. Not. Scared." She glares at me for a moment before tossing her hands above her head. "Maybe I am. And I hate it. What do I want? I want a normal life. I want the job I love doing. I'm no baker. I want to go home at the end of the day and not worry about what I'm walking into. Has he found me today? Will he come for me? Joel has taken so much, and it's like he's still taking.

"I want to go to sleep and not worry if I'll wake up back in my apartment. I don't want to be shoved out of bed because I overslept. I don't understand my life. My only friend took me to a parking garage. She handed me over to a man I didn't know and expected me to trust him on her word. I spent five days traveling with him and two more people I'd never met. I end up in Tennessee in the middle of a motorcycle club." She stops pacing and faces me. "A motorcycle club, Jack."

I nod because it's all true. Well, I didn't know she was afraid to go home every day or was shoved out of bed. The black eye. She didn't fall out of bed. He pushed her. I knew there was more to it. Her ex better never show up in Tennessee. If our paths ever cross, he'll regret every time he hurt her. I'll make sure of it.

"I still don't understand everything that's happening. No one fully explains anything to me. I don't have a phone. I can never contact my friends again. Well, Nina. She was the only friend I had left. I don't understand how your club works. Things are just different and weird. I've been here for three weeks, and people think I'm your girl and some future Queen. That makes no sense."

It makes perfect sense. If she gives me a chance, I'll prove it and answer all her questions. She's on a roll right now, so I let her continue.

She tosses her arms up again. "And club girls are real. Nasty, but real." She shudders again. "Then there's you."

Me? Now we're getting somewhere. Everything she just said is important. Hopefully, I'll remember it all later. We're going in this direction now.

I spring from the couch and plant myself in front of her. "What about me?"

Her eyes lift to mine, and her lips slightly part. *Yes, ma'am. You sure went there.*

"You're … you," she stutters.

It's cute, but she's not backpedaling here.

"I am, and you're you." I lean down with my lips close to her ear. "What do you want, angel?"

"I…" She takes a step backward and swallows hard. "All of it."

That was a long list. Her little rant was a bit chaotic. It's okay. Eventually, she'll have it all and more. I'm not letting her deflect on me here. For each step I take, she takes one backward until her back hits the wall.

"What's the one thing you want the most today?" I ask.

"Today?"

Maybe taking things in smaller steps will work better with her.

"Today. Tomorrow, we'll work on something else."

She thinks for a moment and lifts her chin. "Stop treating me like I'm glass."

"What?"

"You and everybody else treat me like I'll break. I'm hurt and scared, but I'm not fragile. I appreciate you all being kind, but you're overly kind. It's not normal. People don't act this way all the time. I want to feel some sense of normal."

"I treat you how we're trained to treat an angel."

She bravely meets my eyes again. "Maybe I don't want to be an angel anymore."

"What are you saying, Lily?"

"Stop babying me and handling me with soft gloves."

My eyebrows lift. "*I* handle you with soft gloves?" I do. I didn't think she realized it, though.

Jack

"You're the worst."

She's not wrong.

"Are you sure? Because if I take the soft gloves off, they won't go back on."

"I'm sure," she replies softly.

I lean closer to her ear again. "You know I'm attracted to you, right?"

She nods. Well, now. This day isn't ending so badly after all.

Against her request, I softly press my lips to her forehead and linger there for a long moment before stepping back. I wasn't expecting this tonight. My phone vibrates in my pocket. Club business never stops.

"Tonight, you sleep on that. Imagine everything it could mean. And I mean *everything*, angel. Tomorrow, it all changes." I hold up my hands and wiggle my fingers. "The soft gloves are already gone."

Before I change my mind, I turn and leave. Plus, I'm being summoned by someone. I'll give her tonight to process what she asked for. Tomorrow, she'll see the real me. There'll be no turning back and no way out for either of us. Tomorrow's going to be an interesting day.

23
Lily

Fully dressed and ready for work. Check. A to-go cup of coffee in hand. Check. Breakfast. Nope. My nerves are too shot for food. Is this what having butterflies feels like? I place a hand on my stomach. It doesn't settle. My hand moves to my chest. I can feel my own heartbeat. No, this feeling isn't butterflies in your stomach. The bad-boy biker set off a volcano of emotions within me last night. Whatever he did runs through my blood. No part of my body goes untouched, which is virtually impossible because he didn't even kiss me.

My lack of sleep last night wasn't from nightmares. I have plenty of those. Joel's degrading words and punches didn't cross my mind all night. I awoke for reasons just as dangerous. This danger could own me, consume me, burn me alive, and, in a way, heal me. My mind's so warped. Maybe I should make an appointment with the counselor Nanny keeps mentioning.

His words are on repeat in my head. The soft gloves are gone. Everything changes today. And like he requested, I thought of *everything*. Some of those everythings kept me awake for hours, but from a different kind of fear.

I've thought about the members with their ole' ladies. Like bunnies, it's a term I'm uneasy with. Jack's parents' relationship is intense. I'm not sure his dad likes me very much. Still, there's no doubt that these men love their wives and children. From what I've witnessed, their love is all-consuming. Nothing stops it. Nothing gets in its way.

I lightly laugh. What am I thinking? Jack didn't ask me to marry him. He didn't even ask me on a date. Do bikers date? Still, everything means *everything*. Right?

When I close my eyes, I can still feel his lips on my forehead, soft, sweet, tender. I've imagined and even dreamed of those lips moving across my body.

"Nope." I jerk myself from those thoughts.

Those kinds of thoughts kept me awake most of the night. I can't think like this right now. I have to go to work.

Three hard, distinctive knocks pound on the front door, causing me to nearly jump out of my skin. Geez. Even the way he knocks on the door is different today. *Girl, get it together. It's just a knock.* My imagination has seriously run away with me.

The three hard knocks come again, jolting me from where I planted myself. This is ridiculous. I'm going to feel like a fool when I open the door. Nobody, or situations, can be that different overnight. Not even Jack McLeod.

"Lily!" Jack shouts as I reach the door.

A set of keys jingle. Oh no. I jerk the door open before he barges through it.

"Geez, Jack. Settle down. I'm fine."

I'm far from fine. Because of him, I'll never be fine again. And I was wrong, so very wrong.

He's wearing the same black boots and T-shirt as always. His jeans are dark blue today. He's worn them before, but it's rare. Of course, he has his cut on and a black leather belt. I've no clue why he wears the belt. His jeans fit so well that the belt isn't needed. There's a black bandana tied loosely around his neck. Now, that's new.

His mustache and beard are neatly trimmed. He has a little more than the five o'clock shadow most women swoon over. The long strands of his dark hair fall to the side when he tilts his head. I see nothing drastically different about him. Leave it to me to work myself up over a fantasy.

Mentally laughing at myself, I look into his eyes. Everything, including the air around me, shifts. Those are different. His eyes are dark hazel today. When the brief flash of worry leaves his eyes, it happens. I feel the moment those eyes lock onto my soul. Did he feel it, too? His cocky grin says he senses something. I sense I'm in serious trouble. Trouble I won't be able to save myself from.

"Morning, angel. Ready to go?" He offers me his hand.

And just like that. Mood and fantasy ruined. I step past him without taking his hand.

"I don't want to be treated like an angel anymore." I shouldn't have to remind him.

"You won't be." He locks the door, grabs my hand, and pulls me down the steps.

His truck isn't in the front yard. We take the path toward the clubhouse. Okay. Really? Just because I don't want to be treated like glass means I'm no longer being picked up at the front door? Geez. That's kind of harsh.

He answers a call as he opens one of the doors at the back of the building. Am I working here now? I mean, it's fine, but what will Emily think if I don't give her a notice? Not doing so is very unprofessional. Hold on a second. I slightly hang back. Jack pulls me right along behind him.

"Jack, wait."

He doesn't stop or slow his pace. Jenny thought I was the new girl last night. If I'm no longer a part of Ariel's Angels, does it mean I have to work for the club? As a bunny? Oh no. No. No. No. No way am I doing it.

"Jack, I'm not doing this."

We walk through the middle of the clubhouse with him still on the phone. Surprisingly, there are a lot of people here for a Tuesday morning. The same group of guys play pool but minus the bunnies. Three older members sit at the bar with Pops and Granddad. All of them call out good morning to Jack. He lifts the hand, still holding mine, and keeps walking. We walk right out the front door into the parking lot.

"What was that?" I look back at the clubhouse over my shoulder.

"That was the Den. You've been there several times." He continues to pull me along like I'm a ragdoll.

Ha ha. Very funny. I swat his left shoulder. He abruptly stops and pulls me to him. The left side of his lips twitch.

"So, we're doing this today, are we?"

"You're insane." I shove against him. No, he doesn't budge an inch.

"A twelve on a scale of one to ten." He gives a firm nod, proud of his assessment of himself, and starts walking again.

"Where are we going?"

"To work, angel," he replies over his shoulder.

He stops behind a row of motorcycles parked in front of the clubhouse. "Now, just what is it you're not doing?"

"Um." I release a shaky breath. "Where am I working?"

"The bakery." He narrows his eyes and tilts his head. "You alright, angel? Did something happen last night after I left? You hit your head? Maybe eat something you're allergic to?"

That's a really weird question. If I ate something I was allergic to, I'd break out in a rash, or it would affect my breathing. It wouldn't affect my mind. Wait a minute. He's calling me crazy.

"No." I don't say what I'm really thinking. "This is just different."

"As I promised," he reminds me.

I don't want to talk about last night. Instead, I slowly scan the lot. "Where's your truck?"

"At home."

He takes a black helmet from the motorcycle seat in front of us and hands it to me. I stare at the shiny object in my hands. The front, back, and one side are just black with no markings. The design and shape of the helmet make plain black look pretty. I gasp when I turn it to the right. This side has a set of gold wings, and my name is printed in a fancy red font. This makes the helmet beautiful.

"Jack, I can't ride your motorcycle."

He throws a leg over the bike and settles on the seat. Wow. That was hot. If I asked, would he do it again? Nope. Not happening.

"It's not up for debate." He taps the helmet. "Put this on. Safety first."

"Jack," I plead.

He leans close, balancing the bike between his legs, and wraps an arm around my waist. This *is* different. Better. Please don't let it be a dream.

"Come on, angel. Live dangerously with me today."

My eyes drop to his lips. Dangerous with this man has nothing to do with getting on a motorcycle. He pulls me closer to where our noses almost touch. His eyes seem to darken while I watch.

"Oh, we're definitely going there today, angel." He holds my gaze just long enough for me to forget my own name before pulling back. "But we gotta go. We're going to be late. Put your helmet on. Then step on the peg." He taps my thigh. "Swing one of these babies over and wrap them around me."

I suck in a breath and lean back. He's beyond insane. Twelve my foot. He's at least a fifteen.

"Helmet." He taps it again.

I turn the helmet over. I've never worn one, but it's obvious which way it goes. Jack pops the strap and takes it from me. He tucks loose strands of hair behind my ear. Yeah, I understand now why that's a swoon-worthy move. He carefully slides the helmet on my head and adjusts the fit.

He fastens the strap and smiles. "Perfect."

"I can do this," I whisper, mostly to myself.

"One foot on the peg. Leg over," he reminds me.

"And wrap them around you," I add.

His cocky grin is back. "Absolutely, angel."

I would say I abandoned my fear. I didn't. While still clinging to it, I step onto the peg and swing my leg over the bike.

"Happy?"

"Nope." He places a hand behind my knee and pulls me forward until my chest is against his back. He grins over his shoulder. "This'll do for now."

Oh my gosh. I may die right here. We don't have to move, and I already understand why women enjoy this. Jack puts his helmet on and starts the bike. The vibrations intensify what I'm feeling. Please don't let him ask if I'm okay.

"Wrap your arms around my waist," he says through the speaker in my helmet.

"We can talk to each other?"

"Technology is wonderful." He eases the bike through the gate and stops at the end of the drive. He leans back against me slightly and glances at me over his shoulder. "Hold on tight, angel. It's time to fly."

My body vibrates just as much as the bike does. I've never felt a high like this. The moment the tires touch the road, we fly.

24
Lily

I have never felt so free in my life. When I first got on Jack's bike, I was beyond scared. I'll admit, I was a little excited, too. I swore I'd never get on a motorcycle. Look at me now.

At least once a week, we treated patients from motorcycle accidents in the ER. During the summer, it was almost daily. I was the attending nurse for a few of those patients. Seeing the damage and the devastation it caused for their families was heartbreaking. Sadly, some of the accidents were so bad that the rider didn't survive. Others needed surgery and months of physical therapy. On really good days, the riders walked out with cuts, bruises, broken bones, and limps. Their pain and loss made me hate motorcycles without ever touching one.

For the first few miles, fear was winning my inner battle. The thrill of riding exploded like fireworks the moment I stopped fighting. And like fireworks, this ride is beautiful. The scenery comes alive without the body of a car around me. The trees, fields, houses, people raking leaves in their yards, and the farm animals seem to jump out at me. Until today, they were boring figures that were part of the backdrop in my mind.

We pass a pasture with horses and cows. I extend my right arm and slowly move my fingers, letting the wind flow through them. It's the feeling you get as a child when watching the clouds and pretending to reach up to touch them. Instead of clouds, it's horses, cows, and trees today. I'm a city girl in the middle of farm country, hiding inside a motorcycle club. My life is so comical.

I'll never be the same after this ride. Freedom feels wonderful, and I hope it never ends. I know it can. It's happened so many times before. Rather than slipping into the corners I was shamefully pushed into, I'll fight to hold onto this. This ride has opened a floodgate of emotions, all good and exciting. Hopefully, more good things will follow this.

I lean closer to Jack and rest my helmet against his back. As beautiful and thoughtful as this gift is, I wish it wasn't here, and his leather cut was gone. His shirt could go, too. Does he have tattoos on his back? I sneak peeks at the ones on his arms when he's not watching me. I sigh happily and tighten my arms around his waist. He laughs but doesn't speak. This moment is perfect without words.

He places his right hand on my knee and rubs up and down my calf. More emotions and fireworks explode. I wouldn't have believed riding could be intimate until now. It's a whole new level of intimacy. Is this why biker couples have a bond the rest of the world doesn't understand?

We pull into the bakery's parking lot, and Jack kills the engine. The ride to town is way too short today. A strange feeling of loss overtakes me. How's that possible? It was just a ride. Only it wasn't. It was something more. I cling tighter to Jack's back, not wanting this to end. Who needs cupcakes and donuts today? We should go for another ride.

"You okay back there, angel?" His hand moves up and down my calf again.

"Yeah," I whisper.

"Time to go to work." He taps my hand just above my knee. "Put your left foot down and swing this leg over."

I don't want to, but I do as he asks when he leans the bike slightly to the left. I unsnap the chin strap and slide the helmet off. He gets off, removes his helmet, and sets it on the seat.

I offer him mine back. "Thank you for this. It's beautiful."

"That's yours. Keep it. You'll need it for the ride home."

"Thank you." I'll put it in the breakroom with my bag. I'm using the backpack Nina gave me as a purse. "And thank you for the ride." I bounce on my toes like a kid. "Can we do it again without having to go to work?"

He pulls his phone out and glances at the screen before shoving it back into his pocket. He doesn't smile. Hopefully, that message wasn't bad news.

"Absolutely, angel." He tosses an arm over my shoulders and turns us toward the front door. "I knew you'd love it."

"I did. So much. I wish the ride to town were longer."

He laughs and opens the door. "We'll take the long way home today."

Great. Now, today's going to drag by. If taking the long way home means getting lost with him for a few hours, I'm all for it.

The bakery has its normal stream of customers today. Emily's at the register, taking an order. Ava and Melody are filling boxes with the pastries and breads customers point to in the display cases. My job is in the back. It's fine. I have no desire to be on the frontline here. I'm great at meeting people in the hospital, but I'm no saleswoman.

Jack walks me to the opening in the counter next to the wall. The weight of his arm around my shoulders has me leaning into his side. I feel safe and protected under his arm. The rare hugs I got from Joel never felt like this. As much as I want to put my arm around Jack's waist, I keep mine locked around my helmet.

When we reach the counter, I turn to tell him goodbye like I always do. Only this time, I don't want him to leave. After the ride we just shared, I feel like I'm losing a part of me, even though he'll be just a couple of blocks away. I lose all train of thought when his palm cups my cheek. A different day indeed. A much better day.

"Have a good day, angel. I gotta go. Jay needs help with a tow."

"You have a good day, too. And be careful."

His cocky grin returns. "Yes, ma'am."

"Jack!" Emily waves from the front register.

"Good morning, Emily." He walks toward her as I do the same on the backside of the counter.

"Did you send these to Lily?"

Her question has us both hurrying to the register. A long, narrow gold box with three long-stemmed red roses with a matching bow sits on the counter. He sent me roses. Oh, my goodness. That's so sweet. I reach to touch the satin fabric they lay on.

Jack

Jack's hand quickly covers the box, stopping me. "Don't touch it." Every ounce of happiness drains from his face. He turns to Emily. "Where did you get these?"

Wait. He didn't send them? Happiness and my newfound freedom are sucked from my body. I stumble backward until I feel the wall behind me.

"They were delivered an hour ago," Emily replies.

"The card?" He already knows there isn't one.

Emily shakes her head.

"Who delivered them?" A darkness I've never seen fills his eyes.

"My cousin, Chrissy. She works at Blooms and Bows," Ava replies.

Jack walks over to the display case in front of Ava. "What did she tell you about them?"

"Uh. She just said they were for the bakery, and we talked about our family's Thanksgiving plans." Ava grits her teeth. "Sorry, Jack. I didn't think more of it."

He points to the roses. "So, these could be for any of you, not Lily specifically?"

My three co-workers look dumbfounded. It's a rare look for Emily. We should probably mark this day on a calendar.

"None of us are dating, Jack." There's my sassy boss. Whew. We couldn't lose her.

He pulls his phone out and makes a call. "Hey, Sandy. It's Jack McLeod. Who does the delivery to the bakery this morning go to?" He's quiet for a moment and nods his head a few times. "Okay. Thanks, Sandy."

Without saying a word, he carefully removes everything from the gold box and lays it on the counter. After a thorough inspection, he puts it all back.

"Well?" Emily Powell is not a patient person.

"It was an anonymous online order. Not all the questions and details were filled in. There was supposed to be a card inside saying *thinking of you*. Sandy answered a call and missed adding it before Chrissy left. The card is still lying on the counter. There was no personal name on the form, just The Cupcake Cottage."

"What does it mean?" Melody asks.

"It probably means one of you three have a secret admirer. Until you figure it out, keep 'em here in the shop, or each of you takes one," Jack replies.

"I'm fine with each of us having one." Emily lifts one of the roses to her nose and sniffs. The other two happily reach for one, too.

Jay pulls up out front in a rollback truck. Jack goes to the front window and holds up a finger. He comes around the counter to where I've become a wall fixture. He lifts my chin until our eyes meet.

"Bake some cookies, angel." His thumb slides just below my bottom lip. "We'll grab something to eat after work and take a ride."

He doesn't say anything about my ex. We were both thinking that's where the roses came from. I'm happy for whoever the flowers are intended for. Looks like I panicked for nothing.

"I'd like that."

He presses his lips to my forehead before walking away. Cloudy meets him at the door for the key to his bike. Jack jogs around to the passenger side and jumps in. It's fine. I'm fine. It's a normal day in a small town.

Emily steps in front of me. "You okay?"

I take a deep breath and fake a smile. "Yep, but one of you three has an interesting life. Who do you think those are from?"

"You're the one with the interesting life," Ava says.

"What?" Does she know my story? Since Jack's mom got me this job, I'm sure Emily knows something, but do the other two know, too?

Melody points to the front door. "Girl! Have you taken a good look at that man? The black leather, motorcycle, muscles, tattoos. Jack McLeod is beyond hot and one of the sexiest men in the state." She waves the rose in her hand. "Whoever sent one of us these is nowhere as interesting as the man who just walked out of here."

"And just so you know." Ava smiles slyly. "You're the only woman Jack McLeod has ever chased."

"He's not chasing me." I narrow my eyes. Or is he? Do bikers chase? I don't think so.

"Trust me." Emily pats my arm. "He is. Now, back to work, ladies. Willow Creek needs its sugar fix for the day."

Jack

    Jack's chasing me? Do I want to be chased? Better yet, do I want to be caught? After the things Joel did, I shouldn't want another relationship, especially one so soon. I glance toward the front windows. Cars pass by like normal. Jack's gone. Just thinking of him makes me smile. No. He's not chasing. After all, you can't chase what's not actually running.

25
Jack

Those roses almost ruined the best morning I've had in a long time. Lily's excitement over riding was like a kid on Christmas morning. I love Christmas, and I knew she'd be hooked once she got on my bike. The roses caused a setback for us. Things will be back on track by the end of the day. I'll make the ride home as magical as possible for her. We'll get an order from Angie's and ride out to the river for a picnic. I wanna hold her in my arms as we watch the sunset. It sounds romantic. I glance at Jay from the corner of my eye. Thank goodness he can't hear my thoughts. I'd never live this down.

"What we got?"

"A wreck between here and Dades Creek. A truck, motorcycle, and a car. The truck's already been picked up by Dades Creek. A family member for the car asked me to get it. The Sheriff's Office asked if we'd get the bike, too."

A multi-car accident with a motorcycle involved. The day's going further off track. Jay keeps his eyes on the road. He's not okay. His back is too straight, and his hands grip the steering wheel tightly. I'll ask Dad to call the Sheriff's Office and remind them not to send Jay to accidents like this. He owns a garage, so he's going to see plenty of accidents. It's the ones involving motorcycles that get to him.

"Everybody okay? The rider? He anybody we know?"

"The guy in the truck is okay, but his family convinced him to get checked out. The Dodge is totaled, though." Jay makes a left onto the main road to Dades Creek.

Of the three vehicles, the truck was the safest unless it was one of the smaller models. Jay rolls one shoulder, still keeping his eyes on the road.

"Who owns the car?" If the family called Jay, they may live in Willow Creek.

"Laura Westbrook. She was taken by ambulance to the hospital. Her son called."

"Grayson?"

Jay nods.

The Westbrooks live in Dades Creek. I've met their whole family. Grayson and I hung out for a while until he ran off to California to make it big. When he did, he moved right back to Tennessee. His family lived in Alabama for a while when he was younger. I don't know that story. Gray never talked much about it.

Now, for the question I hate asking the most. "And the biker?"

Jay snaps his head in my direction. His eyes are dark, and his lips are pressed together. This isn't good. He quickly faces forward again.

"Don't know the biker's condition. Mrs. Westbrook and the guy in the truck said a car pulled up shortly after the accident. The biker limped his way to the backseat. The cops are watching the hospitals and clinics to see if he shows up."

That's weird. So weird, in fact, the hairs on the back of my neck stand up. Maybe the accident was his fault and he's running. That doesn't feel right. There's more to it. I feel it.

"Cops run the plates and VIN number?" If the guy caused the accident, both of those would lead the cops straight to his door.

"No plates." He glances at me from the corner of his eye. "And the bike was reported stolen from Murfreesboro yesterday."

I want to believe this was just a punk kid who stole a motorcycle and took a joy ride. Maybe that's what it'll turn out to be, but this weird feeling won't go away. With the Mavericks showing up and strange flower deliveries at the bakery, we can't overlook this. Nick's gonna be a happy man later. He loves surfing the internet for information. Nick does more than just surf the web. He's one of the best hackers in the business.

By the time we get to the accident, it's mostly cleared up, and everyone's gone. The only things here are the car and motorcycle. The accident is closer to us than Dades Creek. Jay backs the rollback up to the car. We step out and inspect the car before loading her up. I let Jay handle hooking up Mrs. Westbrook's Ford Taurus while I get some photos of the skid marks and the bike.

Once the car's loaded, I step between Jay and the bike in the ditch. "You get in. I'll load up the bike."

"Stop it." He shoves me aside. "I can handle seeing a wrecked motorcycle."

No, he can't. It messes him up every time. I rub the back of my neck and let him proceed. I want to save him from the pain and torment that will follow soon, but I don't want to fight my cousin. We've come to blows a few times when he's off the deep end. Jay's not easy to take down.

He stares at the broken, twisted pieces that were once a nice bike. It's not a custom design as Jay prefers, but there are enough accessories to know the owner wasn't a beginner. Jay looks at every wrecked vehicle that comes through the shop for ways to restore them. The bike might have some used parts he can salvage, but that's it.

Jay runs a hand over his face and motions for me to follow him into the ditch. "Let's load it up."

It takes both of us to load the Harley onto the rollback behind the car. I would have seriously struggled to do it by myself. We cover it with a tarp and strap it down.

Jay's quieter than normal on the ride back to town. Not that he's a big talker when others are around, but with me, he will. I send a quick message to Cloudy and a few more brothers. We need eyes on Jay all night. I also messaged Nick and have him looking into the accident.

"I really am fine," Jay says when we get back to the garage.

"Good." Calling him a liar would cause an outright brawl right here in the truck. We've been sitting here for five minutes and haven't opened the doors.

"What was the hold up at the bakery earlier?" Really? He waits until now to ask?

"Strange flower delivery. There was no card."

"That's odd. The flower shop wouldn't tell you anything?" He finally opens the door and steps out. He just needed a distraction to snap him back to the present.

"It was an anonymous online order." After this accident, the flowers feel off, too.

"Nothing's too anonymous for Nick." Jay leaves the wrecked vehicles on the rollback and walks into the shop.

"I think Emily may have a secret admirer." I hope she does. The alternatives I have about those roses cause my skin to crawl.

"You heard it too?"

I should have known he heard the growl during Church. It's hard to believe one of us didn't catch who it was.

Jay walks over to our bikes in the last bay. "So, you finally got Lily to ride."

"Yep."

"And?"

The memory brings a smile to my face. "She loved it."

"Knew she would." He slaps my shoulder. "It's always the ones who say they'd never get on a bike who love the ride the most."

That sounds a bit personal. How does he know that? I'm on his heels before he can get to the office and close the door.

"Who've you been riding, Jay?"

He laughs. "Nobody."

"Why? Because she says she'll never get on a motorcycle?" Finally, I have a reason to tease him. He's been dogging me from the moment Lily arrived.

He totally ignores me. "You know what you should do? When Lily gets off work, have a picnic by the river. Show her a Tennessee sunset." He insanely wiggles his eyebrows. "And maybe a few other things once it gets dark."

"Shut up!" I grab a pen off the desk and throw it at him.

"That's what you're planning on doing anyway." He laughs so hard he almost falls out of his chair.

That's it. I can't deal with this fool today. "Cloudy and I'll unload the rollback."

"And have Nick look into the flower delivery. Too many coincidences happening," Jay calls out when I'm halfway across the shop. Of course, he's still laughing at me.

On the way outside, I call Nick. Hopefully, the wreck and flowers are actually coincidences. The wreck feels like something more, though. Still, I can't ignore the eerie feeling about the flowers. Hopefully, the worst-case scenario with them is finding out one of my brothers likes Emily Powell as more than just a friend.

26
Lily

This was the longest work day of my life. It was worse than pulling double shifts at the hospital. It was a hundred times worse than my three-day weekends with twelve-hour shifts. Those served a purpose, and I was thankful for them.

The highlight of the workday was listening to Emily, Ava, and Melody tease each other about the roses. Those three came up with some seriously off-the-wall ideas about who the flowers were from and to which of them they were meant for. Of course, I teased right along with them. We even started voting on the ideas.

The one I voted no to immediately was Jay. Ava and Melody have a seriously unhealthy thing for the Viking Warriors, especially for the McLeod men. They said they couldn't swoon over Jack anymore now that he was taken. Emily didn't help matters when she told them messing with a taken biker could get a woman killed. My co-workers are insane. Jack isn't mine, and I'd never stab them in the neck with a decorating spatula like they think. They don't know weapons. A decorating spatula doesn't have any sharp edges. I pause and try to imagine it. That would seriously hurt. It would be more along the lines of torture. If Jack were mine, and Jenny touched him, yeah, I could do it.

At four o'clock, the end of my shift, the person I want to see the most walks into the bakery. Every motorcycle I heard today had me looking out the windows. Two hours ago, Emily refused to let me out of the kitchen. Those two hours felt like eight. Emily doesn't stop me when I step into the doorway this time.

Jack smiles at me over the display case. "Hello, angel. Ready to go?"

"Yes," I reply with a sigh.

"Yes, pleeease take her. She's gotten on my nerves checking the door for you every time a motorcycle rode by today." Emily should try doing theater. She has a flair for being dramatic.

Without breaking eye contact with my wonderful dramatic boss, I grab a decorating spatula off the counter and wave it at her. Ava and Melody burst out into a fit of laughter. Jack knows there's an inside joke. Thankfully, he doesn't ask.

I quickly grab my bag and helmet from my locker in the breakroom. My helmet. That's such a strange statement coming from me. And my locker? It's really a fancy cubby because Emily is a major do-it-yourself person. She decorates everything in her life, not just cakes and cupcakes.

When I return to the front, Emily's handing Jack a small pastry box. He hands her some cash and refuses the change. Emily just smiles. Ava and Melody are about to vibrate out of their skin. We need to get out of here. These three have no problem with openly embarrassing you in public. They've done it all day, and even with customers present.

Jack, once again, tosses an arm over my shoulders. "You ready to take the long way home, angel?"

The sighs and swoons behind us are loud. I swear two customers are part of it. I ignore them and nod. Jack doesn't ignore them. He grins and winks at me.

At the door, he pauses and looks over his shoulder at Emily. "You ladies, have a good day. Lily might be late in the morning."

My mouth drops open. Emily claps. Ava swoons and literally drops to the floor. I rush past the front windows and to his bike without checking to see Melody's reaction.

Jack strolls across the parking lot, happy as a lark. It's just a normal day in the life of Jack McLeod. Women everywhere swoon over him. No, really, they do. There's a lady in a minivan driving by right now, staring at him with her mouth open. I cut my eyes at her. Finally, she notices me when Jack's a couple of feet away. She snaps her head forward. I'm going to have to invest in a few cases of spatulas from the looks of it. A knife from Jay would work so much better.

Jack puts the box Emily gave him into one of the saddlebags and taps my helmet. "Put this on. We're losing daylight."

Geez. Causally taking our time is gone. Now, we're in a hurry. I don't understand how a man can go from happy and fun-loving to snappy and mean so quickly. Joel did it every day. I knew better than to ask him what was wrong. Now, Jack's doing it, too. No. Jack is nothing like Joel. Jack hasn't degraded me, hit me, or hurt me in any way. Comparing him even slightly to Joel is wrong.

"Angel, you okay?" He's already on the bike waiting for me.

"Yeah. Sorry." I put my helmet on and fasten the strap.

"Foot on the peg and swing your leg over," he instructs and offers me his hand for support.

"And wrap my thighs around you." It's a repeat of our conversation this morning.

Jack releases a long breath. "Yeah, that."

He doesn't mean riding a motorcycle. If another man, Joel included, implied something like that to me, I'd smack them. Yeah, Joel would make me pay for it later, but I'd do it. Not with this man, though. I sit behind him and slide as close to his back as possible. My thighs lay against his. His thighs are muscular. Mine are fat. Movies and novels call what I have thick thighs. It's not a romantic term to me at all. My hands slide around to his stomach. I shift slightly, causing my thighs to move against his.

He moans. "Angel, you're killing me."

No, he wasn't referring to riding a motorcycle a few minutes ago. Before I can slide against him again to test my theory, Jack starts the bike and pulls out of the parking lot. The same wonderful free feeling settles over me again.

We definitely take a longer ride than this morning. We're on the same side of Willow Creek as the clubhouse. This road has more houses and small businesses. Of course, there are pastures and fields out here, too. What I wasn't expecting was to stop at a park by a river.

We park at the lower side of the lot. The playground is more toward the center. Picnic tables are scattered all around. Naturally, most of them are near the playground. There's only one where we are.

I need no instructions on how to get off the bike this time. Jack hangs our helmets on the bike before handing me the box from The Cupcake Cottage. Cupcakes by the river with a biker. I've never heard of such a thing. This is definitely a first. He pulls a to-go bag of food from Angie's from the other saddlebag. Oh my gosh. Not just cupcakes. We're having a picnic. The biggest surprise is the red checkered blanket he pulls out. Wow. All of a sudden, I feel special. That's the biggest new thing yet.

We pass the picnic table and stop at a grassy area under a tree. I don't know what kind it is. Growing up in LA was fast-paced. We had trees and nature classes in school, but I didn't bother to memorize tree types. I did learn more about flowers, though. We had a neighbor when I was little who grew some of the prettiest flowers. It was more fun to help her with her flower beds rather than being at home.

The park and river are beautiful. The picnic is such a sweet gesture. I really want to enjoy every part of this. Jack's grown quieter than usual, and it concerns me. He hands me the bag of food and sets two bottles of water on the ground so he can spread the blanket out.

We sit down, and I try to put the food between us. He moves it all to his other side. His arm slides around my waist and pulls me against his side.

"Sit with me here for a few minutes, angel." He rests his forehead against mine.

"Are you okay?" I ask softly.

"Jay and I picked up two vehicles from a wreck this morning."

I slide my arm around him and lean closer to his side. "I'm sorry. Did you know them?"

Willow Creek is a small town. He grew up here and probably knows everybody. It has to be bad going to an accident and finding it's someone you know.

"The lady driving the car lives in Dades Creek. We know her and her family. She was taken to the hospital, but I don't know her condition."

"I'm sorry." My heart hurts for him.

"After lunch, Dad called. We had to close the shop early."

Jack

"More firecrackers and bricks?" I knew those bikers were trouble when we ran into them at the bakery.

"No." He's quiet for a long moment. "Harley got into it with Mom today."

I raise my head and lean back slightly. "Jack, if you need to be there, we can go."

He lays his palm against the side of my neck and lifts my chin with his thumb. "No, angel. I wanna sit here, eat this food, and watch the sunset with you."

"You're so sweet."

He slowly shakes his head. "I'm not sweet, angel. I carry darkness everywhere I go. Sometimes, like now, it lays in wait."

"You're not a bad man, Jack. You've shown me nothing but kindness. I know what a bad man is," I whisper the last part.

"When the darkness douses out the light, please remember this moment."

"Just because you think you're bad and live in darkness doesn't mean it's true."

He places a finger on my lips. "Shh, angel. We'll talk about it another time. I made you a promise this morning. I fully intend on keeping it."

Promise? I quickly run through this morning. I don't remember a promise.

"Jack?"

"There's no turning back," he whispers.

He closes the few inches between us and brushes his lips over mine. Our kiss is slow, sweet, and tender. Soon, it turns into need. It's not the need with desire. This is deeper and more meaningful. It's the need to feel and belong. My arms circle his neck, pulling him closer. He's right. There's no turning back for either of us.

27
Jack

The past week and a half has been chaotic and ridiculous. Oh, and nerve-racking. Can't leave out the fact that everyone's about to lose it. Our nerves are beyond shot. There are way too many things happening around here. I can't sort any of it out.

The Midnight Mavericks are still pulling stupid childish pranks around town. At random times throughout the day and night, firecrackers pop off. Not as many or with bricks like the first one at the garage. It's just enough to be bothersome and annoying to the entire town. We wouldn't know it was them if Jay, Cloudy, and I hadn't witnessed Trace and his guys throwing the first one.

The senior citizens in Willow Creek are freaking out. Naturally, half of them believed it was us and called the Sheriff's Office. Our wonderful sheriff, Nathan Bowers, showed up at the Den yesterday. His beloved law-abiding citizens fear a biker uprising is coming. It's one of the dumbest things I've ever heard.

That's not all. It gets better. Exactly a week ago, red paint splatters started showing up around town in driveways, parking lots, and on the sidewalks. We haven't figured out what the paint means, and no one has claimed responsibility.

Nick believes the two are the same group but can't prove it yet. When both pranks happen, the traffic cameras blink in and out. When they're thrown from cars, the license plates are missing, so Nick can't run those.

Jack

When they're thrown by people running through town on foot, the person is always dressed fully in black and wearing a ski mask. We don't have faces to ID.

The only reason Nick isn't a hundred percent sure it's the same group is because the cars throwing the firecrackers aren't the same makes and models as the ones throwing the paint. And from their shapes and height, it's different people on foot.

The last paint splatter was found yesterday morning in Angie's parking lot. Jay's garage was the night before. The last firecrackers went off yesterday around lunchtime, two days before Thanksgiving. The sound bounced off the buildings, preventing us from getting an exact location. When our wonderful citizens' holiday shopping was interrupted, they called the Sheriff again. It's when Nathan came to see us to get everyone off his back.

We've had two emergency Church meetings this week. The alert for this one went out ten minutes ago. It's been quiet today. No paint. No firecrackers. I'm not sure what this meeting is about. Jay's the last Viking to walk in before Worley Bird closes the doors.

"Settle down, Vikings." Dad stands and slams the gavel. "Time for Church."

Jay hurries down the aisle between the chairs and the wall to stand beside me. He's carrying a small cardboard box. Jay has the same faraway look in his eyes as he does when he wants to stab somebody. My cousin is a bigger problem than the Mavericks and their little firecrackers could ever be.

"You bring a bomb or something," I tease. Hoping he'll relax.

"Something like that." Jay's eyes are darker than normal. When he does this, I look for him to shift into some crazed animal from a paranormal movie.

"Sorry to call you all in on such short notice again and the night before Thanksgiving. Jay just found something that might be important." Dad turns toward us. "What did you find, son?"

Jay moves to the front of the room. "Uncle Jacob, I was mad when I called. Church might not be necessary, but we do need Nick."

Our computer genius joins Jay down front. We're working Nick overtime this week. He's living off energy drinks, protein bars, and beef jerky.

"What did you find?" Nick keeps his eyes on the box in Jay's hands.

"I've been taking the bike from the wreck apart to see if anything's salvageable. This was hidden and attached to the speedometer." Jay reaches into the box and lifts a small device up for Dad and Nick to see but doesn't take it all the way out.

Nick snatches the device from Jay's hand. He turns it face down on the table. He quickly disassembled the device with a small tool he had in his jacket.

"Was that a camera?" Dad points to the tiny pieces on the table.

"Yep, and an active one." Nick puts the pieces back into the box. "I'll take it to the lab and see what I can find."

That wreck wasn't an accident. Someone has had eyes inside the garage for over a week. Chills run up my spine. Are the Mavericks after Jay? My family can't lose another member. No, we're not losing Jay. I'll destroy every Maverick I can find if they even try to touch my cousin.

Bankz stands. "Pres, if I may?"

"If you've got anything right now, we'll take it." Dad motions for Bankz to continue.

"Just a thought here." Bankz clears his throat. "We all know how stupid the firecrackers and paint are. Could they just be a distraction for whatever that camera has coming?"

Dad slowly turns his head toward Worley Bird. "He's got a point."

"If he's right, and since Coombs himself was involved in the first prank, we may have a war coming." Worley Bird's words rip through the hearts of every Viking in the room.

We haven't had an open declaration of a club war in over twenty years. I was just a kid then. We've had a few fights and battles over the years, but not a war.

My phone's on silent. It vibrates in my pocket from an incoming call. I don't answer it. If we have a war coming, Dad needs every member's full attention, mine included. My phone goes off three more times while Dad's giving instructions on the things we need to do to be ready. The safety of our families is at the top of the list. A loud pounding comes on the Church doors as my phone rings for the fifth time. Everyone turns and watches Worley Bird rush to the doors. The moment the doors are barely open, Mom pushes in and ducks under Worley Bird's arm.

Mom stays just inside the door and points at me. "You need to answer that, Jack. Now!" That is all she says before she ducks back out again.

"Lily." I frantically dig my phone from my pocket.

Jay and Rodeo are instantly at my sides. I feel like an idiot for not at least looking to see who was calling. Lily only has a flip-style burner phone, but it's not her number on my screen. It's Emily.

I quickly answer the call. "Emily, is Lily alright?"

"Uh. I think so." She doesn't sound sure or like Lily's the reason she called.

"Put it on speaker," Dad orders. I quickly hit the button.

"Emily, what's wrong?" The Mavericks have been quiet all day. If they hit the bakery while we were in Church, I'm riding straight to Chattanooga tonight.

"Jack, I don't think these flower deliveries are from a secret admirer."

Dad walks over and glares at my phone screen. "Emily Powell, did you really just interrupt Church to talk about flower deliveries?"

"Sorry, Pres, but I did." Emily's voice is heavy with worry. She wouldn't call like this if it weren't important.

"Miss Powell, we don't have time for nonsense. I expect to see you in my office after you close the bakery today." Dad is furious.

"Dad, wait. I don't believe this is nonsense." I also don't think Emily should be in trouble. "Emily, you need to explain and clearly."

"Okay. Flowers and their colors have different meanings. They've been used for centuries to deliver messages. At first, the deliveries were sweet. I didn't think anything of it. I thought you might be right and one of us three had a secret admirer."

Dad tosses his hands in the air. "For crying out loud."

"Dad, please. Let her finish. Go on, Emily."

"Well, the types of flowers started changing. I haven't looked all of them and their meanings up yet, but they aren't what you'd send in a typical bouquet. The ones today definitely deliver a message and it's not a good one."

"Is this true?" Dad looks around Church. A few members shrug. Most sit with blank expressions on their faces.

"It is," Jay confirms. "Mom used to talk about flowers and their meanings."

Jay's mom doesn't talk much anymore. After losing Jay's dad, she withdrew from everyone but Jay for a while. She still helps out during holidays at the Den. In fact, she's in the kitchen right now with Mom and Nana, preparing Thanksgiving dinner for tomorrow.

"How many deliveries have you gotten?" At least Dad's listening now.

"We get one every day or two. I have them in the back. I'll look their meanings up after we close."

"What was today's delivery?" I ask. It's the reason she called, after all.

"Jack." Emily's voice shakes. "I think they're for Lily."

"What?" Panic flies through me. "Why do you think they're for her?"

Every brother in the room sits forward. No one whispers a word. They know Lily came to us through Ariel's Angels.

"There are three types of flowers in this box. They don't go together at all. I think they're for Lily because one is a white Calla Lily. It's like the flowers are naming her. Another is red roses, like the first delivery, but they're not pretty. This time, the petals are withered and look like they've been crumpled in someone's hand."

"That's disturbing," Rodeo mumbles.

It's very disturbing, but there's more. Emily said there were three types of flowers today.

I'm afraid to ask, but we need to know. "What's the last flower?"

"Black Dahlias," Emily replies.

Jay's head snaps up. "That one means death."

"Emily, let me talk to Lily." Something greater than fear runs through me.

"She's not here."

Jay and Rodeo reach out to steady me.

"Where is she?" I demand.

Jack

"It's her lunch break, Jack. When you're not at the shop, she goes across the street to the market's deli or the sub shop. She's been to Angie's a few times, too." Emily's explanation isn't comfortable.

Dad snaps his fingers. "Nick, track her."

I don't know if Lily's flip phone can be tracked. We should have upgraded her phone by now. What am I thinking? There's probably a way to track every phone made nowadays. If not, I'm sure Nick created a way.

Nick clicks around on his laptop. In less than three minutes, he looks up. "She's at the library."

The library is halfway between the bakery and Angie's. I guess it's not a bad place for her to hang out on her lunch break.

"Books aren't bad," Worley Bird says.

"Emily, did you call Sandy?" This isn't a normal order. Sandy updated her online form to where customers have to fill out every question. An email address is now required to place the order.

"I called both flower shops in town. They didn't deliver this. We got really busy after Lily went to lunch. When it died down, the box was on the front counter."

"A personal delivery?" Dad rubs the back of his neck. He feels the same eerie feeling as I do.

"Jack." Nick taps the table to get my attention. "Libraries have computers too. If she used one..." He doesn't need to say anymore.

Jay's hand clamps around my wrist. "He's here."

I don't look back to see how many brothers follow me out. It's a lot. I run through the Den and straight out to my truck. If she's in danger, I'm not about to put her on the back of my bike. Besides, it's too cold today to ride with her. Rodeo jumps in the passenger seat. Jay follows us out of the parking lot in his truck. Bankz is riding with him.

In a way, I hope Joel Clark is here. I don't want him near Lily, but I'd love to get my hands on him. I haven't read the file Nick worked up on the scumbag or Lily's. Dad has. I know it. All I got was his name and photo. If he's here, I'll find him. First, I have to get to Lily. Once she's safely on club property, I'll hunt her ex down.

When the tires hit the pavement, I slam my foot to the floor. We'll be at the library in less than ten minutes.

Debbie Hyde

"I'm coming, angel," I whisper.
And I'm bringing an army of Warriors with me.

28
Lily

My lunch breaks are boring when Jack's not in town. They don't drag by. They're just boring. When Jack works at the garage, he picks up our lunch from one of the restaurants around town. Angie's seems to be his favorite. So far, I have to agree.

On nice days, we eat lunch outside in another area Emily overly DIYed behind the bakery. It's like a mini park back there with all the plants, decorations, and outdoor furniture. It's the perfect place to get some fresh air and relieve workday stress. Emily had a wooden privacy fence installed a year ago. Customers would see her from the parking lots and interrupt her breaks with their orders rather than going inside.

When Jack's not here, I walk to one of the nearby restaurants for lunch. As far as I go is Angie's. Today, I grabbed a rotisserie chicken sub at The Sub Shop. Yeah, that's its name. It's a bit chilly today, but I still sit on one of the benches outside the library and eat my lunch. I found the library the first time I walked the five blocks to Angie's. The Sub Shop is halfway between here and the bakery.

I finish eating and throw my trash away before walking into the library. My first stop is always the little gift shop. I've bought a couple of used books here. Book sales are always great. It's the coffee that pulls me in here. They even have pastries from the bakery. Since I work at The Cupcake Cottage, Mrs. Hammond gives me a little discount. She's a sweet little retired school teacher. She makes everyone feel special when they visit. Of course, she gives extra attention to the kids.

My lunch break is a little off schedule due to a midday rush of customers picking up special orders and extra sweets for Thanksgiving tomorrow. I still have forty minutes left. I aimlessly wander down a few rows of bookcases. I left the last book I borrowed at home and don't feel like starting another one. I can't call Jack. Another Church meeting was called before my lunch break started. I'm so bored.

The computers in the back area are free. I seem to be the only visitor at the moment. I slide into one of the little workstations. I'm not supposed to contact anyone from my old life. That included using my email addresses. I had one at the hospital and a personal one I used for just about everything.

Since I couldn't log into those, I created a new email with a fake name and birthday on a different site. My old ones had some part of my name in them. Now, I'm Gummybear. Nina and I ate them by the bags full. I sent her an email three weeks ago. The subject line and the body of the message just said hi. As of today, she still hasn't replied. I don't think she's even opened it. Wow. That stings.

The Google search bar taunts me. I should leave right now. I shouldn't look, but I do. No one tells me much of anything here, just the basics. Since curiosity kills the cat, it gets me, too. I type in Jack's sister's name and instantly regret it. Several news articles and the obituary for Ariel Magnolia McLeod pop up. She has a beautiful name.

I click on the first news article and stare at Ariel's photo. Like her name, she's beautiful. There's no doubt she's Jack's sister. Ariel, Nanny, Maci, Harley, and Everly all have the same facial features and brown wavy hair. Their shades are a little different. Ariel's hair has more red highlights than the others.

Her bright blue eyes sparkle and pull you in. Even from a computer screen, her eyes seem to talk to you. She's so happy in this photo that I can almost hear her laughter. She's playing with Logan and Everly. They were so small. The caption under the picture says they were three and four. My heart breaks for them. They were just babies. This is where I should've walked away.

Jack

The first paragraph says Ariel was killed by her boyfriend on January 18, 2011, almost fourteen years ago. A small photo of the evil man is included. Heartbreak turns to anger and hatred. I can't look at him. I should close the page out and leave. I read on.

Halfway through the third paragraph, I gasp and cover my mouth with both hands. My heart is broken. It's completely shattered.

A woman putting returned books away on the shelves nearby rushes over. I haven't seen this librarian before. She's younger than me, probably still in college.

"Did you lose what you were working on? Maybe I can get it back for you." She reaches for the computer mouse and freezes when she sees the article. "Oh."

"I shouldn't have looked." I sniffle and close my eyes.

"Probably not," the librarian agrees softly. "That was the worst thing to happen in Willow Creek. Ariel's death destroyed the McLeod family."

"She was pregnant." I cover my mouth again. No one has mentioned that part.

"She was." The librarian sits in the chair next to me. "About four months. They named the baby Angel."

Angel? Oh my gosh. Ariel's Angels isn't just for Jack's sister. It's for her and her daughter. I push back from the computer and shake my head. Even though the article is public record, I feel I've invaded the privacy of every member of Jack's family, and I didn't read it all. I can't. Ariel isn't my family, but I've never felt pain like this.

"Would you like me to close the screen?" She places her hand on the mouse and waits.

"Log me out, please. I'm sorry I looked." I quickly stand, letting her have my chair.

Somehow, I have to go back to work like this. I won't tell Emily or the others what I read. I'll never ask anyone questions about Ariel. I understand now why Jack's family only drops bits and pieces of their story. I have a couple hours left of my shift. Hopefully, I can get my emotions somewhat under control before I see Jack.

I'm so heartbroken and lost in my thoughts that I don't notice or sense everything around me. I'm moving on autopilot toward the front doors. I don't sense another presence nearby until a hand clamps over my mouth, and I'm pulled into the row of shelves along the back wall.

The hand over my mouth tightens as my back slams into the bookcase. He pins me against the shelves with his body. I don't have to look. I already know who he is. Just like the article, I look anyway. Piercing light blue eyes glare into mine. Eyes I thought were beautiful when I first saw them. Within six months, I learned that these eyes held more evil than the darkest night.

"Lily. Lily. Lily." Joel slowly shakes his head. "You've been a bad girl. You run away for nearly two months and crawl into bed with a dirty biker." The clicking of his tongue sends cold chills down my back. "When we get home, your punishment will be so bad you'll never think about acting out again."

His hand tightens when I try to scream. There weren't many visitors when I arrived, just someone returning a book. Everyone's busy today getting ready for Thanksgiving. As far as employees, I only saw three. Somehow, I have to get one of them to notice us.

"You're going to quietly walk out here with me like a good girl."

I shake my head wildly. My tears never fazed him. Crying makes matters worse, but I can't stop the tears today. If he takes me from this building, I won't survive. He won't just punish me this time. He'll kill me.

"You *will*." His hand around my arm tightens. His nails dig into my skin to the point I know there's blood. He lowers his head until his face is inches from mine. "You will, or the old bat in the gift shop won't make it home today."

I gasp into his palm. Mrs. Hammond. Oh, please don't let him hurt her. He would, though. I know he would. I shake my head wildly again. Sadly, his threats have just begun.

"And I'll lock those three in the bakery and burn it to the ground." His grin is pure evil. "I might even let you watch and listen to their screams."

I thought his laugh was evil before. This one belongs in a horror movie. His phone vibrates in his pocket. He doesn't reach for it.

"Time to go." He jerks me hard, causing my head to hit the books behind me. "Act up, and they all die today."

Jack

He peeks around the bookcase before pulling me toward the back door. The door and part of the wall on this side of the library are made of glass. There's a cute little garden area on the other side. I glance toward the desk on the side. The librarian I met earlier isn't there.

Hope builds when I see a biker hiding in the garden. At first, I thought I was being rescued. Hope dies when we get closer to the door. That's not a Viking Warrior. He was one of the bikers at the bakery when Jack took me to meet Emily. Oh no. He's signaling Joel through the glass with his hands. I can't go out this door. I just can't. But I also don't want four women to die because of me.

The sound of an object making contact with a body fills the quiet room. Joel grunts. His body slams into mine, pushing me into the glass door. He falls to the floor, taking me with him.

"Get away from her!" The librarian who helped me earlier holds a folded metal chair back, prepared to swing again.

"A chair won't stop me." Joel scrambles to his feet.

He doesn't take his eyes off the librarian as he reaches down and grabs a handful of my hair. With one swift jerk, he pulls me off the floor. I scream as loud as I can and shove against him. Hopefully, one of the other workers will hear and call for help.

The librarian takes a couple of steps forward and swings the chair at Joel again. With the wall behind us and the door on our right, she has us pinned into a corner. Joel has nowhere to go, and the chair makes contact again. He cries out and stumbles. The impact doesn't move him away from me like I think she was hoping. Instead, it knocks him into me.

"We're leaving now." He wraps an arm around my waist and pulls my back to his front. He uses me as a shield and tries for the door again.

The librarian can't swing now without hitting me, too. If hitting both of us will keep me in this building, she can swing away. She doesn't swing, though. I have to hand it to her. She's a resourceful woman. She turns the chair and uses its legs to jab Joel in the side. When he bends over, she runs to the wall and pulls the fire alarm. If this were a movie, it would be comical. As odd as this fight is, it's for my life.

Over the blaring of the fire alarm, the sound of loud engines and the roar of motorcycles fills the air. They're not all on motorcycles, but I know it's Jack and his brothers. The biker outside realizes they have no chance and takes off, leaving Joel behind.

"They're coming for you." The librarian holds the chair like a weapon as she glares at Joel. "There's no escaping them. You'll be the one who dies today."

I don't know who she is, but she has a lot of faith in the Viking Warriors. And whoever said librarians were sweet and timid had never met this one. She's proof you should never judge a book by its cover. No pun intended here at all.

Sirens blare in the distance, and tires screech to a halt. Joel weighs his options. The librarian realizes his intent. She screams and runs toward us, ready to swing the chair again. I don't see Joel's fist until blood spews from my nose, and I'm on the floor again. Before the librarian can hit him again, Joel opens the door.

He pauses long enough to issue one last threat. "I'll be back for both of you."

With him gone, I crumble all the way to the floor, still holding my bleeding nose. My sobs are uncontrollable now, so I don't even try to hold them back.

"Oh my gosh." The librarian drops to the floor next to me. She quickly takes her cream-colored cardigan off and holds it against my nose.

"I'll ruin it."

"It's just a sweater." She slowly helps me to my feet.

"Lily!" Jack bursts through the front doors and runs toward us.

Viking Warriors and firefighters run in behind him and quickly spread out around the building. The librarian steps away and motions for me to go. I listen and run into Jack's arms.

"Joel was here," I say between ragged breaths.

"I'm so sorry, angel. I won't ever leave you unprotected again." His arms wrap so tight around me it feels like he's trying to pull me into his chest.

"What happened?" Jay asks. He looks between me and the librarian.

"He was in the library. I didn't see him until he grabbed me." They can never know why I was so distracted.

"He tried to take her out the back door," the librarian tells them.

"This will help more than the sweater." Rodeo hands Jack an ice pack he got from one of the firefighters.

I lower the sweater, and Jack tries to hold the ice pack over my nose gently. The cold hurts, but it will help to reduce the swelling. I squeeze the bloody sweater tightly. I'd have been taken if it weren't for the woman who owns this sweater. She saved my life.

I turn my head just enough to face her. Tears run down my cheeks. I can never repay her for today.

"It's ruined." I slightly lift the sweater. "I can't give it back to you like this. I'll buy you a new one."

"It's just a sweater," she repeats.

"You saved my life." Whether she lets me or not, I will replace the sweater.

"Finley?" Jay narrows his eyes and moves closer to her.

Rodeo and Bankz surround her with stunned expressions on their faces.

"Angel?" Jack gently lifts my chin. "How did Finley save your life? What did she do?" He sounds concerned and surprised like the others are.

"She hit him with a chair." I point to it on the floor. "Several times."

Rodeo laughs. "Nick needs to pull the cameras. I wanna see this."

"Let's sort this out at the Den. I wanna get Lily home," Jack insists.

"Jack." I place my palm against his chest and wait for his eyes to meet mine. They're light brown now and haunted. He thinks he failed. He hasn't failed, but we can talk about that later. "Joel threatened to kill a lot of people here."

"Give me a list of names, and Jay will set up security details for them."

"He threatened everyone at the bakery and Mrs. Hammond." I look over my shoulder at her. "And Finley."

Jay growls and gives a firm nod. "I'm on it. They'll have guards within thirty minutes."

"Oh, that's not necessary. I'll be fine," Finley insists.

"It's not an option, Fin," Jay sternly informs her.

"But my family," she cries.

"Will have to deal with it." Jay pulls his phone out and storms out the front door to make the calls needed.

I look up at Jack. "Can we please go home now?"

"Absolutely, angel." He presses his lips to my forehead and lingers for a long moment.

Yeah, I know exactly what he's feeling. It's why I haven't tried to move out of his arms. I need to know he's here and real, too. I just want to go home and stay curled inside his protective arms all night, if he'll let me.

29
Jack

Every nerve in my body has exploded. I feel too much. I feel nothing at the same time. The darkness I try to suppress has crawled out of the corners and shadows. Lily's in shock and hasn't noticed. Even in her state of mind, her presence is all that keeps my darkness at bay.

Cloudy Daze and Big Papa, Bankz's dad, lead the way through the gate at the clubhouse. I didn't realize they were with me until they appointed themselves our escort home.

Dad wants another Church meeting. Worley Bird talked him into waiting a few hours. I need to get Lily settled at home first. Jay's arranging the security for the five women Lily's ex threatened. Hendrix and Bankz lead the search around Willow Creek for Joel Clark. Rodeo's in the backseat. He gave Worley Bird the rundown of what happened at the library since I had my hands full taking care of Lily. It took both Rodeo and Worley Bird to convince Dad to wait.

My brothers all head to the clubhouse. I take the private driveway to our houses. Lily's in no shape to handle the noise at the clubhouse. I drive past the guest house and take the left to my house. I promised her I wouldn't treat her like an Ariel's Angel anymore. I lied. Some of the aspects of the program training are ingrained into who I am now. Whether she's officially in the program or not, she's still a Domestic Violence victim. Our program gives battered women a safe home with stability and the start of a new life. When these women feel safe, they begin to heal and grow.

Lily's never been to my house. I've always gone to her. The guest house became her safe place. I couldn't take it from her. Mom noticed it the first night Lily was here when she and Everly stayed with her. It's why Mom let Lily remain in the guest house after she decided to stay in Willow Creek.

I pull up to the front and toss Rodeo my keys so he can unlock the house. As much as I hate to move the angel attached to my side, I need to get her inside.

The moment I was in the driver's seat at the library and closed the door, Lily tried to climb over the center console into my lap. It was all Rodeo and I could do to hold her back long enough for him to raise the console. She's been under my arm the entire way home.

"Come on, angel. Let's get you inside."

I open the door and try to slide out. Lily stays attached to my side. One of her hands clinches tightly to the front of my cut, and her other hand to the back hem. She's not going to let me go around and take her out the passenger door.

"Okay, angel. Hang on."

This will be tricky, but she's small enough that the steering wheel won't be too much of a problem for her. I keep my arm around her and pull her across the seat with me as I step out. Once my feet are on the ground, I slide my left arm under her knees and lift her out of the truck. Rodeo holds the front door open for us. He hurries down the steps to lock up the truck once I have Lily inside.

"Let me get you settled, and I'll make some coffee." I lower her to the couch.

"No. No." She claws her way up my cut until her arms circle around my neck.

Okay. New problem.

I sit and get as comfortable as I can. Lily immediately crawls onto my lap. Trust me. I'm not complaining. She can sit on my lap anytime, anywhere. Tonight, I give her whatever she needs. I need to protect her. I was slack in my responsibilities. I let her down. I failed her today.

Jack

From the stories I've heard and the things I've witnessed, Dad has always protected Mom fiercely. Jay's dad was just as protective of his mom. Dad's drilled into Jay and me for years that you never rest and never stop watching when there's even the possibility of a threat against the woman you love. After losing Ariel, Dad's protectiveness jumped up a thousand notches. He's unapologetic and has no remorse for the things he does to protect the women in our family. I didn't protect mine today.

Mine. Every thought and battle in my mind comes to a screeching halt. I look down at the sleeping woman in my arms. With trembling fingers, I move a few strands of her hair from her face. Her nose is swollen and bruised. Thank goodness the bleeding stopped on the way home.

Realization settles over me. Mine. This beautiful woman is mine. Dad's words shout the loudest in my head. *The women we love.* It's wrong for her. She deserves better than me. But there's not a force in the universe that can change it now. Lily Harman is the one woman I'll love for eternity. She may end up hating me for what happened today and for the things that come next because of it. But she's mine, and I do love her.

"I can make coffee." Rodeo walks through the living room and tosses my keys on the table by the kitchen door.

I glare at him until he disappears into the kitchen. I'm going to hurt my best friend for ruining my moment. I'm grateful he snapped me back to the present, too. Now that I know without a doubt who Lily is to me and admitted my feelings for her, I understand what Dad has been saying all along. I have an obligation and responsibility to the woman in my arms.

Rodeo quickly types a message when he walks back into the room. After sending it, he walks up behind me and glances down at Lily.

I gently run my fingers through her long hair. "She's my Queen."

Rodeo chuckles. "Glad you finally caught up with the rest of us, brother."

"Shut up."

"It's crazy out there right now. What do you want to do?" Rodeo leans back against the couch and crosses his arms. "Your dad still wants another Church tonight."

"Call Mom. See if she or one of the girls can come help out. I'll let Lily sleep for a little while. When she wakes, as much as I hate doing it tonight, I'll ask her to walk me through what happened. Let Dad know we can have Church then."

"He won't like it."

No, he won't. I lean my head back against the couch cushion. "I know. But she's the best person to describe what happened. She might have information that'll help us find Clark but might not realize it."

"Good point, but it's better to get Worley Bird on our side first. He and your mom are the only ones who can handle the Pres." Rodeo quickly scrolls through his contact list.

I point toward the kitchen. "Make the call in there or my office. I don't want her waking up and hearing us talk about all this."

"Right." Rodeo heads down the hall to my office. Good choice. Conversations in the kitchen can still be heard from the living room.

My Queen can sleep peacefully in my arms for now. We'll talk when she wakes up. Then, my family and brothers will help me figure out how to end the nightmare she lives in because of her ex. Once Joel Clark has been stopped and silenced in her mind, I'll show her how a man is supposed to love and care for his woman.

30
Jack

For over an hour Lily sleeps in my arms. I wish I could say it was a peaceful sleep, but it's not. The first half was fine. At times, she became restless. I was able to soothe her fears for a while. Her restlessness has increased. The nightmare will wake her soon. My gentle words aren't getting through this time, but I'll be here to banish her monsters when she wakes.

With a loud gasp, Lily bolts upright. Her breath comes in short, quick pants. Rodeo looks like he just lost ten years of his life. Hey, it scared me, too, but I don't show it. She's battling too much fear. She doesn't need to see mine.

"It's okay, angel. It was just a dream. I got you. You're safe." I slowly run my hand up and down her back.

"Jack?" Her eyes are lost, searching for recognition.

"Yeah, angel. I'm here."

She slowly looks around the living room. "Where's here?"

"My house."

"Rodeo?" She looks up at Coty. He's standing next to the arm of the couch. He dips his chin.

Rodeo lifts his phone and looks past Lily to me. "Your mom said someone's on the way."

"Who? What? Who's on the way?" Lily scrambles backward onto my lap again. She finally uncurled from a fetal position and stretched her legs across the couch before the restlessness began.

"It's okay." I lay my palm against her cheek and turn her to face me. "He means one of my sisters, or maybe Nana, is on the way."

"Why?"

"Dad's called for Church." I don't want to leave her, but I have to take care of this.

"About the library." She nods, not needing an answer. "Did you catch him?" she asks softly.

I drop my head. "Not yet."

It's been two hours with nothing. Joel Clark's trail disappeared. His dad's a cop. He has several big-name lawyer friends in LA. He has the connections to move quickly, but we should still have found something. Nick texted me a few highlights from Clark's file. I refused to take a call while Lily was sleeping.

Rodeo opens the door when someone knocks. Surprisingly, Kayla walks into the room. The two stare at each other for a moment. Neither speaks. Rodeo still likes her. I don't know what caused this rift between them.

"Kayla." Lily releases a shaky breath and smiles.

If a member of my family couldn't come to stay with her, Kayla or Emily would be my next choice. Kayla snaps out of the staring match with Rodeo and rushes across the room. Lily pulls her knees up so Kayla can sit on the last couch cushion.

"Hey. How are you feeling?" Kayla narrows her eyes and points to Lily's nose. "That looks broken. It definitely needs ice."

She jumps up and heads for the kitchen. Rodeo follows until she spins around and holds her hand out.

"I can get ice on my own," Kayla snaps.

"Rodeo." I shake my head.

He growls but thankfully listens. He leans his back against the wall and crosses his arms. From where he's standing, he has a clear view into the kitchen. I wish these two would sit down and talk.

Jack

"Angel." I lay my palm against the side of her neck and place a soft kiss next to her lips. I want to kiss her. I've kissed her every day since that afternoon by the river.

"You have to go," she whispers.

"I do, but I wanted to ask what you remember from the library first. What did he do and say? Any small detail could help us find him."

She drops her head and stares at her feet on the couch. "A hand covered my mouth. He pulled me between the bookcases. I knew it was him before I saw his face. He said my punishment would be bad this time. He threatened Mrs. Hammond. Said he'd burn the bakery down with Emily, Ava, and Melody inside. When he tried to take me out the back door, Finley hit him with the chair."

She gave me the basics. There's more, but I don't push for now. Nick will have the footage from the library's cameras by the time we have Church.

"Finley?" Kayla's mouth drops open. "Finley Rhodes hit your ex with a chair?"

Lily lightly laughs and sighs at the same time. "I take it the sweet little librarian doesn't do anything wrong or crazy."

Kayla sits at Lily's feet again and offers her an ice pack wrapped in a kitchen towel. "She doesn't, and I didn't realize she was still volunteering at the library. Wow. I should call her. Who knew Finley Rhodes had a dark side?"

"You like dark things now?" Rodeo huffs.

"Shut up, Coty. Shouldn't you two be leaving?" Kayla asks over her shoulder.

Lily turns and puts her feet on the floor. "We should go to the guest house."

"But..." Kayla's eyes meet mine over Lily's head.

Lily sits up straight and gives me a fake smile. "It's okay. Kayla's with me. I'll be fine at home."

This won't go over well. It doesn't matter, though. It's already done. If she freaks, she freaks.

"You are home." I'm already moving toward the front door.

"What? Jack? What's going on?" She's off the couch and right behind me.

I turn to face her. With my thumb and index finger, I lift her chin. "You live here now, angel. The prospects are packing up the last of your things at the guest house now." I press my lips to hers for a firm, quick kiss.

"Jack, no. We should talk about this."

"We can talk later, but my decision still stands." I ignore her further protests and look at Kayla. "Don't let the prospects in. They can leave the boxes on the porch. Two of them remain outside until I get back. If you need something, call Mom if I don't answer."

"Geez, Jack. I know what I'm doing." Kayla rolls her eyes.

"Jack."

I feel like a jerk for not answering her. I almost lost her today. She's not talking me out of this.

"Rodeo, let's go." I'm out the door and down the steps.

"You got a weapon?" Rodeo asks Kayla.

"Duh." Kayla pulls a handgun from behind her back and waves it at him. "You really are an idiot," she says before slamming the door in his face.

"Brother, if your woman breaks my door, and I have to replace it, guess who's paying for it?" I jab my finger toward him over the hood of my truck. "Now, get in."

Reluctantly, Rodeo stomps down the steps and gets into the passenger seat. We could walk to the clubhouse. The cool night air might help settle my nerves before Church. Driving's faster. It takes maybe five whole minutes.

The Viking Den is packed tonight. Two of our prospects are here, while the four closest to patching in pack up Lily's things. I ordered them not to touch her clothes or her stuff in the bathroom. Bankz's mother volunteered for the job. Around here, Darlene Banks is better known as Lil Mama. It makes sense since her husband, Jerry, is Big Papa. I call her Psycho Crazy. She is crazy, but in a good way. Most of the time, anyway. A better way of putting it is I'm glad she's on our side. I hear she's taken over supervising the prospects packing up the guest house, and she's already threatened to kill two of them. She's freaking amazing.

Jack

When Rodeo and I walk into the Den, our patched members start walking toward Church without being summoned. Pops and Granddad join us this time. Three bunnies hang out around the pool tables. Of course, Jenny would be one of them. The bunnies won't be here tomorrow. They aren't allowed at family events unless Nana says so. Nana doesn't say so with the group we have now.

Jay and I walk down front and sit with Granddad. Rodeo's sitting behind me. He'll stay at my house with us as an extra layer of protection until we find Lily's ex.

"Vikings! Time for Church!" Dad slams the gavel and gets straight to business. "Until we catch Joel Clark and figure out what the Mavericks are up to, I've ordered the club into the first stage of lockdown."

Whispers go around the room. I look over my shoulder to Rodeo. He shrugs and shakes his head. He didn't know about this, either. One look at Jay confirms he did.

Stage one means no one goes anywhere alone or stays by themselves. It's actually a good idea right now with two forces coming at us. The threat I thought would be the worst has turned out to be a joke.

"Nick has the footage from the library cameras. There's no sound, but we can clearly see what happens." Dad's eyes land on me, and his jaw tightens. He's already seen it. "Nick, if you will."

Nick clicks around on his laptop until a video pops up on the TV mounted on the wall behind the club officers.

Like Dad, Nick's eyes meet mine. "This might not be easy to watch."

I dip my chin. I understand, but I need to see it. Nick presses the play button. No one makes a sound as the video plays. When Clark's fist slams into Lily's face, I roar and spring from my chair.

"I'm going to kill him!" I fully intend to find him tonight.

I don't make it far, though. On Dad's order, Jay slams my body to the wall first before pinning me on the floor.

31
Lily

Jack ignores me and walks out. Unbelievable. Come to think of it, my life is unbelievable. Outside of the ladies I work with, Kayla's really the only friend I've made here. I toss my hands up and pace across Jack's living room while Kayla has some weird argument with Rodeo. When she slams the door shut, I whirl around on her.

"Did you know about this?"

"I guess I knew before you did, but not until after the decision was made. There's coffee. I'll make us a cup."

I follow her to the kitchen. I don't tell her that Rodeo made the coffee. "He can't do this."

She looks back, tilts her head, and smiles. "Actually, he can."

"What? That's insane. He can't go around telling people where they can live."

"Well, yes and no."

"That makes no sense." It doesn't explain anything. I don't tell her that, either.

"He can't go to town and tell the citizens of Willow Creek what to do unless they're a club member. That changes things. Granddad was one of the founding members of the Viking Warriors MC, and he was the first club President. Mack, Jack's dad, is the president now. Jack is expected to be the next one. If their last name is McLeod, they have a lot of say about everything that goes on in the club. The President's word and decisions are final. Oh, and all patched members have a say in what happens in their families."

Okay. She explained things a little better there. I understand the structure of it. I'm just having a hard time believing people actually live like this.

"What does that have to do with me? I was fine at the guest house." I've grown quite attached to that little house.

She sits across from me at the table and pushes a cup of coffee to me. "Because you're Jack's ole' lady."

I stop with the mug halfway to my lips. "What? That's not true."

She sighs and lifts her eyes toward the ceiling. "Come on, Lily. You're in love with him. You have to sense he loves you, too. Jack may not have officially claimed you yet and given you a property cut, but you're his."

I prop my elbow on the table and lay my forehead in my hand. This is too much for one day. One minute, I'm being kidnapped by my abusive ex-boyfriend. Now, I may end up claimed as a biker's ole' lady. I already learned that ole' ladies were patched members' wives or serious girlfriends. No one mentioned the men claimed them. And just what does *'property of'* actually mean? Kayla can explain that on another day. My brain can't handle any more today.

Tomorrow is Thanksgiving. I was looking forward to helping out in the clubhouse kitchen tonight. I'm not sure I have a job anymore since I didn't go back after lunch. Emily's cool and understands this club, so I probably do. I highly doubt I'll ever visit the library again. Oh, and we can't forget that another club is pulling one if not both, pranks around town. I hate the Midnight Mavericks, especially the one helping Joel today. Oh my gosh!"

I sit up straight and rapidly pat my hand on the table. "Kayla, can we get into that meeting?"

"Church?" She shakes her head. "No, women aren't allowed. Prospects can't even go. Just patched members."

"But Pops said women did go if they were part of the problem," I remind her.

She thinks about it for a minute and nods. "Yeah, that's true."

"*I'm* part of the problem this time."

"I know you're scared, but we can't rush in there."

"No. That's not it." I reach across the table and grab her wrist. "Joel wasn't alone today. He had help. I forgot to tell Jack."

"Oh. That *is* important." She quickly punches a few keys on her phone. "Let me try to call first."

My legs bounce while we wait. Jack's name lights up on the screen. He doesn't answer. She tries Worley Bird next. He doesn't answer. She groans loudly and drops her head.

"What?"

Kayla points and gives me a stern look. "I love you, or I wouldn't do this."

"Okay." But what's she doing?

She scrolls through her contacts. Her finger hovers over the phone for a long moment. Finally, she taps the contact. My eyes widen when Coty's name and an older photo of him on a horse pop up on the screen. She lays the phone on the table.

Coty answers on the fourth ring. "Kayla? You and Lily, alright?"

She puts the phone on speaker. "Yeah. Lily needs to talk to Jack. She just remembered something important."

He relays the message.

"Put it on speaker," Jack's dad yells.

"Angel? I'm here." Jack's voice sounds broken and strained. "Are you okay?"

"If I have to answer that right now, I won't be." I could lie if I had to answer, but telling the truth would rip me open again.

"Then don't answer it, love. What did you remember?"

Kayla mouths the words, *'I told you.'* Her smile is going to split her face.

"Joel wasn't alone today. I think he had help." No, I'm positive he had help. Time just makes it all feel weird and a little distorted.

"Okay. That's very important. Why do you think he had help?"

"A biker was hiding in the garden area. I thought it was one of you, but he talked to Joel with hand signals through the glass. He ran off when Finley pulled the fire alarm, and we heard you coming."

"Did you see his cut?" Jack's dad is closer to the phone now.

"No, sir, but he reminded me of one of the bikers Jack and I ran into at the bakery."

"Which one?" Jack asks.

"I'm not a hundred percent sure it was him, but the one with long blond hair."

"Okay, angel. That's good. We'll handle it from here. You and Kayla go watch a movie or something. I'll be home as soon as I can. Kayla, if Lil Mama is with the prospects, they can sit the boxes inside the door. That's as far as they go, though."

"Got it, Jack." Before Kayla ends the call, the screen goes black.

We sit quietly for so long that our coffee gets cold. Kayla warms them up in the microwave. So much happened today that I can't process it all. I jump when someone knocks on the front door.

"That's bound to be the prospects with your stuff. You can wait here if you want. If Lil Mama is with them, I'll open the door. If she's not, they can leave them on the porch."

"Who's Lil Mama?" I step into the living room but don't follow her to the door.

"Bankz's mom. She's insane. You'll love her. He has two sisters, but I don't think you've met them yet."

I haven't met half of the club members and their families. I don't know all the names of the ones I have seen. I expect that to change tomorrow during Thanksgiving dinner.

Kayla peeks through the blinds and grins over her shoulder. "Get ready."

Get ready for what? Do I need to run and hide? Call 911? Grab a kitchen knife? My friend needs to learn how to explain things better.

Kayla opens the door, and a little tornado rushes in. No, really. She's short, tiny, and a whirlwind of activity. She orders the four prospects around and stands guard while they put my stuff where she wants it. I've learned that prospects aren't patched members but are working to be. It sounds like some strange sorority initiation to me. I don't get it, but it's their life.

I study the little woman closely. Is this really Bankz's mom? He's six feet tall. He must get it from his dad. His mom can't be no more than five, two, or three at the most. She's a bossy little thing, though. She's already threatened to stab one of the prospects three times. His expression says he believes her. The others just laugh.

I slowly ease over to the couch and continue watching the little woman. She's finally still long enough for me to see the back of her cut. The patches say property of Big Papa. Well, of course, that's her husband's name. Makes all the sense in the world. Well, in their world, maybe. Once all the boxes are inside, she orders the men out. Now, I have another thing to process today. I doubt anything will explain this little woman.

Lil Mama locks the door before turning to us. "You ladies good? Need anything?"

"No, Lil Mama, we're good," Kayla replies.

"Oh, I smell coffee. I'll just grab a cup before I go." She hurries to the kitchen and comes back with a to-go mug.

I stand and walk with her and Kayla to the door. She's such a big ball of activity, I'm not sure what to say to her.

"Thank you for helping with my things." Nice and polite is definitely the way to go with her.

"Lily, this is Bankz's mom. Lil Mama, this is Jack's girl." Kayla sort of introduced us. She needs to work on that, too.

Lil Mama smiles up at me. "We'll talk tomorrow at dinner. You rest tonight. Kayla set her nose before it heals that way."

"Will do." Kayla snickers and holds up tissue for my nose.

Lil Mama spins around in the door. "Oh, Kayla. Pres ordered a level one lockdown. Nana assigned you with Lily. One of the guys will take you to get what you need after Church."

"Okay." Kayla locks the door behind her.

"Assigned to me?" I raise an eyebrow.

"It means we can't go anywhere alone. Looks like I'm staying here with you for a few nights."

Okay. That's not so bad. Having her here will make things easier for me. I'm really not happy about giving up the guest house. But this is Jack's house. Oh my. Jack and I are living together. Have I been claimed? Do I want to be? Oh, I can't answer that tonight, either.

32
Jack

Holiday parties at the Viking Den are great. Only family members and close friends are invited. It's good to see all the kids running around and playing. It's also nice not to have the stress of outsiders, excessive drinking, and fights. There's no live band today. We have music, but it's coming through speakers around the room and controlled behind the bar. The bartender decides on the music. Kayla's playing a mix of rock and country music. Most of my brothers hate country music. They loudly grumble and complain every time one starts. Kayla just laughs and dances along with the music. That little twig is doing this on purpose.

The food at our holiday celebrations is always the best, especially at Thanksgiving, Christmas, and Easter. The women in our club spend days preparing every dish you can imagine. Most of them are made from scratch. You can't beat southern home cooking.

With all the threats going on, everyone is on edge today. We've doubled security until all this is over. So far today, it's all quiet in Willow Creek. No emergency Church meeting has been called. I don't believe I can handle another one any time soon. The last one almost killed me. It's a bad night when your cousin, best friend, and father have to hold you down. Mark my words. I will find Joel Clark. He will pay for what he's done to Lily.

You know what else is trying to kill me? The universe. Yep, it's lining up tight against me. And to top it all off, my family is helping. Dad always pairs Coty with me in any level of lockdown. His dad is more than enough protection for their family. Since Hendrix lives next door, he gets paired with the Micheals family anyway. He ups their protection tenfold.

We don't just protect our families when trouble arises. Our protection extends to our friends around town. If someone lives alone and there's no one close by to pair them with, we bring them to the clubhouse. My grandmother pairing Lily with Kayla was fine. It would have been better if she still lived in the guest house. I'd even call it a blessing. With the day Lily had and it being her first club lockdown, she needed a friend with her. Having Kayla there last night wasn't good. It wasn't a blessing. It was a curse. It's proof the universe will never be on my side.

Having Rodeo and Kayla in my house last night was a disaster. After Church, I wanted to go home, help Lily come to terms with our new living arrangements, and hold her in my arms all night for the first time. It was a great plan. But NO! My best friend can't get along with the woman he's obviously in love with for five minutes. Okay. Maybe they didn't argue and bicker every five minutes. It was still enough to have a headache today because of them. I'm about ready to toss the two of them in the backyard of the clubhouse and demand they work it out within the fence. It's what we do when our brothers have disagreements. Vikings protect and love one another like family, whether we're blood-related or not. We also fight like family, too. Sometimes, it takes slugging it out.

"Hey, angel. You enjoying yourself?" I lean down to press my lips to her temple.

Lily's sitting with Mom and a few ole' ladies. The women in my family made it their mission today to introduce Lily to all the wives. Even Harley helped. We got to the clubhouse around two this afternoon. We ate Thanksgiving dinner around five. Now everyone is in little groups relaxing. Families with babies and small children have already gone home.

She turns and kisses my cheek. "I am."

"Go away, Jack," Mom orders.

I'd rather not, but I'm not about to ruin this day. I walk away, keeping their table in sight. Lily turns back to the conversation and laughs. She's been happy all afternoon. Some of the moments were fake. None of us can forget yesterday. Moments like now it's real and beautiful to watch. She's not even trying to hide her bruised nose. She belongs here. She doesn't realize it yet or understand our world, but this is her world, too.

Movement at the entrance of the hallway catches my attention. Jay's motioning me over. Rodeo's heading that way. I don't see Dad or Worley Bird. I walk toward my cousin at a pace that won't alarm our families. Maybe whatever is going on will be good news. Only, there's that thing with the universe not liking me.

"Your dad wants to see us in his office." Jay leads the way.

Dad, Worley Bird, and Nick are waiting for us. Nick looks exhausted. He won't rest while there's an active threat against us. When this is over, he'll hibernate for a few days.

"Nick has news." Dad motions to him.

"Joel Clark is back in LA," Nick says.

That makes no sense. No one says anything, not even Dad. I look between Jay and Rodeo.

"How's that possible?" Jay asks.

"He was here yesterday, right? We all saw him on the library footage." Rodeo's as shocked as I am.

It's good for Lily that he's not here anymore, but I wanted him. Every member of this club wanted to get their hands on him. My legs can't hold my weight anymore. I drop down into one of the chairs in front of Dad's desk.

"It was him in the library," Nick confirms.

The only way Clark could get out of here and back to LA that fast was to fly.

My eyes lift to meet Nick's. "You were watching the flights all night."

"I was." Nick nods once. "I watched every flight out of Tennessee from the time he left the library. Nothing. Clark wasn't on any of them."

Dad and Worley Bird are as disappointed as I am. Worley Bird watches Dad close. As an Ariel's Angel, Lily had the club's full protection and everything it offered. She's no longer a file on Dad's desk. She's not another case or rescue anymore. She's family. Lily has something more now, something greater. It comes with a price, though.

It doesn't matter how long ago we lost my sister. The pain never ends and will never go completely away. My family tries to function as normally as possible, as others think we should. Those people have no clue what dark hole we live in. When something happens within our immediate family, no matter how small or great that something is, Dad remembers losing Ariel like it was yesterday. We all do. The rest of us have gotten better at hiding our explosions than Dad has.

"How did he pull it off," Jay asks.

"I started checking the flights landing in LA just in case I missed something."

Nick is beyond exhausted if he's admitting to possibly missing something. He's never done that before. The club and Ariel's Angels have grown. We may need to look into getting Nick an assistant. We can't expect him to keep up with everything by himself.

"At 1:34 am Pacific Time this morning, a private jet landed in LA with a J. Clark on board. Joel lives in the same subdivision as his parents. I haven't gotten into those cameras yet." Nick taps a few keys on his laptop and turns the screen toward us. "But this is the last traffic camera before their fancy gated community."

Jay, Rodeo, and I get closer to the screen. Dad doesn't move. He's already seen it. I lean back against the chair and run a hand through my hair. Joel Clark is clearly the driver of the black Mercedes in the photo.

"So you forgot to check private flights." Rodeo releases a long breath and rubs the heel of his hand against his temple. Yeah, he's had a really long night.

"No. I checked every flight out of Tennessee, commercial and private." Nick points to his laptop screen. "The private plane he was on took off from Birmingham."

I sit up straight. We can't fault Nick for missing this. None of us thought anything about checking Alabama. There's nothing we can do about Clark right now.

"What about the Mavericks," I ask.

Nick pulled the camera from outside the back door of the library up again after Lily and Kayla called during Church. Joel ran out the door, through the sitting area, and off-screen. We only watched from the moment he ran out the door the first time around. No one else was there.

Backing the footage up a few minutes revealed a man hiding among the decorative bushes and trees in the garden. Zooming in distorted the image to the point that Nick couldn't get a positive ID. Lily wasn't wrong, though. Even from a distance, the man resembled Trace's buddy, Buck.

"Nothing around Willow Creek. Our sources in Chattanooga say the Mavericks are celebrating Thanksgiving at their clubhouse like we are," Dad replies.

"Should we call off the lockdown?" Worley Bird asks.

Dad stares at his desk, not looking at anything in particular. "No. It's getting late. Everyone expects it for the night. We'll end it in the morning if nothing happens."

"Okay, boys. You know the drill for the night," Worley Bird dismisses us.

My eyes land on Lily the moment I step into the Den. She's still with Mom and laughing. I wanna soak this up for a while, but without everyone else around.

I clamp my hand on Rodeo's shoulder. "I'm taking Lily home. Bring Kayla after things here get cleaned up. Don't you two break my house."

"No promises," Rodeo grumbles as he heads toward the bar. If he starts an argument with her now, it's Dad's and Worley Bird's problem.

I weave through the crowd, not letting anyone stop me to chat. These fools will talk for hours if I just say hello. I smile and toss my hand up when a brother calls out, but I don't stop.

I put a hand on the back of Lily's chair. I speak to all the women at her table. "Thank you, ladies, for dinner. It was amazing as always."

Mom knows we're leaving. She stands, and I wrap her in a hug.

"Don't mess this up," she whispers.

"Don't plan on it," I whisper back.

"You're your father's son. I'm no fool."

I lightly chuckle. "Okay, Mom. I'll try not to."

"That's better." She pats my arm. My mom's weird but in a good way.

I offer Lily my hand. "Let's go home, angel."

She stands and says goodbye to everyone. The sight of her hugging my mom makes me want to rub my chest. Some of Dad's off-the-wall decisions over the years don't seem so crazy anymore.

The ride back to the house is short, quiet, and peaceful. Like yesterday, Lily sits next to me with my arm around her. It's fine with me if the console never lowers when she's in my truck.

She looks down the driveway when I open the front door. "Where's Kayla and Rodeo?"

"They're going to help clean up. They'll be here after." Or they'll destroy the clubhouse when they start bickering.

"Oh, we can help."

"No, ma'am." I spin her back around and walk her further into the living room. "You and I are going to relax and take it easy."

She leans back against my chest and looks up at me over her shoulder. Something I've longed to see twinkles in her eyes. "How easy? How relaxed?"

I stop breathing for a moment. My angel is a seductress. The universe might not hate me after all.

"You're killing me, angel." I briefly close my eyes to break her spell. I'm an idiot. The biggest on the planet. "You wanna get a shower before we go to bed?"

Her pink lips part with a small gasp. It's cute and sweet. It's part of her seductress spell. I'm sure of it. She can have sweet for a moment. I press my lips to hers. Whatever she was about to say can wait. Her lips slowly move with mine. The tip of her tongue lightly brushes my bottom lip, activating her little spell again. When she tries to turn her body to fully face me, I lift my head, ending the kiss.

"Shower?" I ask again.

"A quick one."

"Nothing quick here, angel."

She sucks in a breath. I lead her up the stairs and walk her backward down the hall to my bedroom door without breaking eye contact. Our bedroom now. I push the door open and walk her one step inside.

"Go." I give her another quick kiss and nudge her toward the bathroom.

Jack

While she showers in the master bathroom, I grab a pair of sleep pants and quickly shower in the guest bathroom. I check the doors. Both are locked. Rodeo has a key to my house. He's crashed here so often at one point he might as well have moved in with me.

A quick call to Jay confirms everything's quiet and fine. I return to the bedroom and sit on the foot of the bed. Tonight, we're sleeping in this room, in this bed. There will be no girl sleepover party in the living room tonight. My back still hurts from sleeping in the recliner.

My eyes dart to the closed bathroom door. I'd love to be in there with her. One night in my house and not even in my bed is too soon to be taking showers with her. Or is it? The water shuts off before I can find out.

Her little seductress spell weaves around me the moment she steps into the bedroom. Last night, she wore pajama pants with a matching long-sleeve top. The shortie pajama set she's wearing now is designed to kill a man. She's a dream standing there barefoot, with long legs and thick thighs. Yep, I just might die tonight.

When one foot lifts and rubs over the top of the other, and her hands tremble, I'm on my feet.

"Come on, angel. Let's relax." I walk her to the side of the bed and pull back the covers.

"And take it easy," she adds as she slides between the sheets.

"As easy as you need." I slide in next to her.

Wrapping an arm around her, I pull her to my side. She curls into me and rests her head on my shoulder. Her fingertips gently trace over the tattoos on my chest. Both bedside lamps are on their lowest setting, allowing her to study the designs.

"I knew you had tattoos on your chest." She softly presses her lips to one.

Yep. I'm a dead man. "You been picturing me shirtless, angel?" This is the first time it's happened.

She grins and lifts one shoulder. "Maybe."

Oh, there's no maybe to it. From the gleam in her eyes, she's not only imagined, she's had fantasies, too. Good to know, cause so have I.

Her lips press against another tattoo. Light kisses follow the design up my chest. Before she reaches my neck, I raise up, pin her to the mattress, and claim those tempting lips with mine.

"Jack," she says my name with a ragged breath.

"Yeah, angel. I'll take care of that."

But first, wanna see my fantasy. Wrapping an arm around her waist, I lay back and flip her over me.

"Jack!" That gasp was all surprise.

"You look beautiful up there, angel."

"You're crazy."

"You like my crazy."

She does. Once she admits it to herself, she and I will explode like fireworks. The seductive gleam returns to her eyes. Oh, she's halfway there already. I crook my finger and motion her to me. Her grin widens. She lowers toward me.

And the world explodes.

33
Jack

And I mean literally explodes.
Shots fire.
Glass shatters.
Lily's eyes widen, and her mouth falls open.
More shots.
Blood drips.
Oh, please, no.

Before she falls forward against me, I grab her around the waist and flip us to the floor. Hard. All I had time to do was to keep her head from slamming against the floor. The weight of my body crushes her. Thank God I'm big enough to shield her completely. Bullets hit the walls and everything else in the room. From the floor, I slap my hand across the top of the nightstand until I feel my phone.

The covers bounce from the bullets. From this side, the bed shields us from the worst. Not true. The worst has already happened. My hands shake as I open my phone. Lily lays motionless under me. Her eyes are closed, her mouth slightly open. There's blood. Too much blood. It's not mine. I know I'm not hit. Why did I have to flip her on top of me?

"Lily? Angel? Stay with me."

She doesn't move or respond. I quickly go to the top contact on my phone. He answers before I hear it ring.

"Jay! My house is under fire!"

"Stay down!" Jay shouts back. "We're coming through the trees now! We'll get 'em, cuz!"

"Jay! Jay!"

He's already gone. I didn't get to tell him Lily was shot. She's dying. I know she's dying. I pull up the keypad on my phone and dial the three numbers I never wanted to dial again.

"911. Where's your emergency?"

"My house is under fire! My ole' lady's been shot. We need an ambulance!"

The dispatcher is quiet for a brief moment.

"Calls have already come from your location. Officers are arriving as we speak. The ambulance is three minutes out."

My location? I didn't give her my location. Her voice is familiar, but I don't have time to figure it out.

"Thanks." I end the call and let the phone drop to the floor.

I quickly lower my head over Lily's when another round of shots starts. These don't hit anything in my room.

"Lily, can you hear me?"

She doesn't answer. I lay my hand on her chest. I can't tell if the movement is her breathing or my hands shaking. I move my fingertips over her lips. Her breath is faint and too far apart, but she's breathing.

"Stay with me, Lily. Don't leave me, angel," I cry.

I haven't allowed tears to fall in years. I can't stop them tonight. I squeeze my eyes shut and press my lips next to her ear. "I love you, Lily. I can't lose you."

The gunshots stop. Sirens pierce the air. Something breaks through my front door. The sound of heavy boots run through the house and up the stairs. I raise my head as my cousin destroys what's left of my bedroom door. Jay's a wild man, completely unhinged tonight.

"Jack." Jay drops to the floor next to us.

"She's hit. It's bad, Jay."

Jay and Rodeo pull me out of the way so the Sheriff and two paramedics can get to Lily.

"Her pulse is weak."

"Blood pressure is dropping."

"Bullet in the back."

Jack

"We need to go now!"

I don't know who says what. I'm stuck in some weird tunnel. It's all faint and distant. A stretcher moves into the room, and my heart is lifted onto it. An oxygen mask covers Lily's mouth and nose. *Please, let it help.*

"Come on, Jack. We're following her to the hospital."

That's Jay. I'd know his voice anywhere. It's the voice I latch onto and follow. My cousin becomes my strength and keeps me on my feet.

The Sheriff steps in front of me, blocking my view of the paramedics taking Lily from the room. I find the strength to push him aside and follow the stretcher down the stairs. Even without legs, I'd find a way to follow her.

"Jack." The Sheriff catches up with me. "Are you hit, Jack? Do you need medical attention, too?"

He's doing his job. He's trying to help. I don't see it that way right now. I spin around on him and point to the stretcher, moving across the living room.

"No! She needs it! Nothing else matters!" I jab the Sheriff in the chest. "You do your job and find them!"

"Let's go, Jack. No time for this." Jay pulls me out the front door.

"We'll be at the hospital, Sheriff." Rodeo follows us down the steps.

"Jack! Jack!" Mom runs across the front yard and launches into my arms.

"She was shot, Mom. I gotta go." I watch the back doors of the ambulance close and lose my balance. Jay keeps me upright.

"Go, son. We'll meet you at the hospital." Dad pulls Mom back.

He points to the rest of our family clinging to each other across the yard. Firefighters hold everyone else back. They're all here. Safe. Unharmed. Logan dips his chin, letting me know he's taking care of them. Best nephew a man could ask for.

"Jack, get in." Rodeo holds the passenger door of Jay's truck open. It's exactly like mine. I glance over to mine. It's riddled with holes, and every window is shattered.

I get in. Rodeo gets in the backseat. Jays follows the ambulance out the gate. Lights flash. Sirens scream. The speed at which we travel isn't anywhere close to legal. Jay stays within two car lengths behind the ambulance all the way to the hospital.

I drop my head into my hands. My body shakes as I fall apart even more. I know exactly how Dad feels now. I can't lose her. I can't bury anyone else.

34
Jack

Everything about hospital waiting rooms is horrible. The chairs aren't comfortable, no matter how nice they look. So I don't sit. Can't. It's impossible. The room is too small. It has nothing to do with the fact my family, friends, and brothers fill every chair and empty spaces along the walls. Some even line the hallway outside the door.

More brothers and families are downstairs in the main waiting room. When we overfilled the main waiting room earlier, a nurse brought us up here. The entire room stood to follow her. The nurse said the immediate family only. Everyone still waited to follow her. Dad stepped forward and divided our group. My family and our closest friends are up here. We're Lily's immediate family for ever how long she has left, whether it's a few hours, minutes, or seconds. She's ours. If it's years or decades, she's ours. Mine. She's mine, and I failed her.

They shoved us into a corner to get us out of the way of other visitors. A sea of black leather with a double set of gold wings on the back apparently strikes fear into the hearts of regular people. Normal people? The faint of heart? Who knows what they're called? Others? That might be a better word. I don't know. Thinking about it hurts my brain. Shallow, they're definitely shallow. We're good people. We love deeply and fight hard for our own. If *'others'* can't look beyond the sea of black to realize it, that's on them, not us.

We're shut in here, out of their way, closed off from the rest of the world. It's suffocating. It's why I'm standing in this corner, leaning against the window sill. It's supposed to feel open here without the walls. It's not. The glass stops the air. Glass doesn't stop bullets, though. Glass shatters. I hear it now. It's deafening. I'll hear it for the rest of my life. I hate glass. I hate everything.

I glance toward the door. I can't move the rest of my body. My body's numb, yet it still hurts. My eyes drift back to the man less than two feet from me. Jay lifts an eyebrow and shakes his head. He doesn't have to worry. I'm not storming down the hall to the nurses' station to yell at them for the millionth time. I'm not supposed to move at all.

Hospital staff threatening to call security didn't stop me from yelling and screaming at them. Security threatening to throw me out and call the cops didn't stop me. The Sheriff's threats to arrest me didn't stop me. My club President ordering me into this corner tested my limits. Jay's words stopped me.

"Lily needs you here."

Lily.

My angel.

Needs me.

So, here I stand, numb, hurting, silenced, yet screaming into the darkness. Here, I wait.

The windows aren't floor-length. Jay leans back against the four-foot-high wall. His head sometimes rests against the glass. I wanna smack it away. Because glass breaks. I can't move, though. The numbness holds me in place.

My cousin is my strength and support tonight. I'm no fool, though. He's also Dad's muscle. Jay's strong. He's resilient. I've never seen anybody who can think through a fight like he can. Most men only think about swinging and swinging hard, so you come out the winner. Jay sees moves before they happen. Jay's dangerous. His help's needed tonight, for me, for Dad, and for everybody in this building.

Rodeo stands shoulder to shoulder with me on my right. Bankz and Hendrix are next down the line. There are no windows behind them. Worley Bird and Big Papa lean against each side of the doorway. Dad walks the room, comforting Mom, Nana, my sisters, niece, and nephew.

Jack

I'm not getting out of this room unless Dad says so. I'm outnumbered and outmuscled. I'm stuck in the corner. My head rests against glass that breaks. I'm numb and hurting. She's somewhere in this building, unconscious and fighting.

My eyes pop open when I feel the room shift. Everyone's on their feet, staring at the door. Jay taps my arm and motions to the door with his head. He and Rodeo take my arms and guide me toward the doctors and nurses. No one smiles. Not a good sign. My family surrounds me when I step in front of the lead doctor. Why are there so many doctors and nurses behind him?

"Mr. McLeod." My eyes snap to his. "I'm Doctor McCormick."

"Lily?"

"Miss Harman is out of surgery and in recovery." He still doesn't smile.

"She... she's okay?" The universe throws me some hope.

"She's stable and resting at the moment," Doctor McCormick replies. "After recovery, we'll move her to ICU."

"ICU?"

"Yes, Mr. McLeod. We need to monitor her very closely for the next twenty-four to forty-eight hours. We have Miss Harman in a medically induced coma," he explains.

"Coma?" I don't think I like this doctor. "You put her in a coma!" I roar.

I take a half step before arms wrap around mine. Dad moves Mom and our family back a few feet. I see red, and it covers Doctor McCormick. I want Lily awake and talking to me. This man put her in a coma? I'm going to put him in one, but it won't be medically induced. Jay can't stop me this time.

The small hand on my chest does stop me. Big blue eyes stare up at me. I know her. I think.

"Don't," Jay firmly orders. He leans close and speaks right into my ear. "Don't move. Don't hurt her."

The brave little woman stays between me and Doctor McCormick. She swallows hard but doesn't move.

"Jack." Her voice is familiar.

I blink, take a deep breath, and push my anger back into the darkness. Her face comes into focus.

"Finley?"

She drops her hand from my chest. "Yeah, Jack. It's me."

"You're here? How?"

Why does the preacher's daughter keep showing up in the darndest places?

"I'm a student at Staten Medical College. Most of us intern here." She steps to the side so I face the doctor again, not that I can't see him over the top of her head. "Doctor McCormick is a great doctor. Lily couldn't have asked for a better surgeon. Please don't hurt him."

"Lily? Is she going to be okay?" I don't have the praise she does for this doctor, but I trust Finley.

"I wasn't in there, Jack." Finley shakes her head. "But Doctor McCormick and his team are her best chance at pulling through."

"Okay." My eyes meet the doctor's again. "Is Lily going to be okay?"

"I can't promise that just yet. The next twenty-four to forty-eight hours are crucial," he replies.

"The coma? Why's she in a coma?" The word alone scares me.

The doctor behind him on the left answers, "The body heals while it rests. Miss Harman couldn't rest. Her body was fighting against us. We couldn't stabilize her. Putting her in a medically induced coma was our best chance at saving her."

This little doctor is better at explaining things. I might like her. Time will tell.

"The coma saves her?"

She sighs. Nope. I don't like her, either.

"It helps give Miss Harman…"

"Lily," I insist. I want them to say her name.

"Lily," she corrects. "It helps Lily's body fight how we need it to and not against us."

"Who are you?" I look at the people behind the two doctors. "Who are they?"

"This is Trudy Shaw. She's a medical student." Doctor McCormick has said enough.

"No. No students. She needs doctors who know what they're doing." I glare at the surgeon. "I wanna see Lily."

"Doctor McCormick, please forgive our son. What more can you tell us about Lily's condition?" Mom asks.

"She was shot once. Another bullet grazed her shoulder. We were able to remove the bullet. However, it did puncture her right lung. She's stable for now. We'll move her to ICU shortly. The ICU nurses will give your family the visitation times. These will be short and limited. Lily will need quiet." He glances at me and back to Mom. Yeah, she's his best bet to talk to right now. "Any disturbances and the visits will stop."

"We understand," Mom says.

I glare at Doctor McCormick's back as he and his medical team walk away. Finley and another nurse remain behind.

"I know you are scared. You probably don't understand all the medical terms or what Doctor McCormick is doing, but I promise they're fighting hard to save Lily," Finley assures me. She motions to the nurse with long brown hair. "This is Dana. She'll be Lily's nurse tonight."

"Are you a student, too?"

"No, Mr. McLeod. I graduated last spring," Dana replies.

That's about six months. Better than a student, I guess.

"I wanna see her," I demand.

"I can take you and one other person to see her for a few minutes once she's settled in ICU. You have to stay quiet, though. The more she rests right now, the better her chances are." Dana steps back and waits for me to follow her.

I take Mom's hand. "Go with me?"

"Of course I will." Mom wipes tears from her cheeks with her palm. She slides under my arm, and we follow Dana to ICU. To Lily.

35
Jack

It's been the longest thirty-six hours of my life. This waiting room grows smaller by the minute. Doctor McCormick has returned to see us twice. He talks to Mom, not me. His reports haven't changed much. Lily's still stable. Her vitals have gotten a little stronger. Other than that, it's all I know.

ICU is the best place for Lily right now. Their visiting schedule is nothing short of evil. This hospital's visiting hours are 8 am to 10 pm. No one left last night until Lily was out of surgery, regardless of their schedule. My family, brothers, and friends have been in and out of the hospital all day. I refuse to leave. At least a few of my brothers stay with me at all times. The hospital staff doesn't like it. The Sheriff allows it as long as we're quiet. Nathan has questions. I've answered a few. Dad's holding him off until we know Lily's okay. The doctor still won't confirm if she will be. ICU's visiting hours are for two people for fifteen minutes every even hour on the hour from 8 am to 8 pm. They don't deviate from it for anyone. I haven't missed one.

My alarm goes off, alerting me that my first visit with Lily is in fifteen minutes. I peel myself out of the uncomfortable chair and start toward the door. It's been too long since I've seen her. Jay follows me. My cousin won't leave me. We've taken up residence in the waiting room. Jay won't go inside the ICU. He always waits outside the doors for me to return.

Jack

Dana waits in the hallway outside the waiting room. She spent the first eight hours with Lily. I haven't seen her since her shift ended the next morning. The other nurses don't come get me like this.

"Good morning, Jack." Dana smiles up at me.

"Morning. You're happy today."

"It's a good day to smile." Dana walks beside me to the elevator.

"Glad you think so," I grumble.

"I know so." Dana pushes the number three button after the door closes.

Is she lost? "We need two." I reach to push the button for the ICU floor.

Dana grabs my hand. "Not today."

"What?" There's the universe throwing me a little hope again.

Even Jay feels it. He grabs my upper arms from behind and looks around me to Lily's nurse.

"She's not awake yet." Dana smiles. A real smile, not one just trying to be nice. More hope blooms. "But she doesn't need to be in ICU anymore. We're moving her to a regular room."

I never thought relief could be heavy. It pushes me down. I squat right here in the elevator. Jay's hands tighten and shake. He releases a long breath. When the doors open on the third floor, not the second, today, Jay helps me stand.

We follow Dana into a private room. A fancy private room, but it's empty. Lily's not here. Dana moves about the room, pushing buttons on several machines. The monitors blink to life.

"Where is she?"

Dana keeps working. "She'll be here in a few minutes. I thought you'd like to be here waiting for her."

This is the best nurse I've seen yet. Well, Lily's a nurse. If she's anything like Dana, I see why she misses it. Until an angel is settled in their new location, they can't have a job. They need a new name and ID first. Nick gets those made for us. Hopefully, Lily will soon be able to return to the job she loves.

"Yeah. Thanks, Dana."

She's right. I wanna be here when they bring Lily in.

"I'm glad she's going to be okay." Jay pats my shoulder and pulls out his phone. "I'll step out and let everyone know."

"Jack." Dana's smile fades.

I release a slow, long breath. Hope slips again.

"She's going to be okay, right?" I ask.

"She still has a long way to go. She's doing better, getting stronger. She doesn't need constant supervision anymore. She's fighting, Jack. Help her fight. You can be here in this room with her all the time. Whisper encouragement in her ear. Tell her you love her as often as you can. This is good. It's what we want for her. It means she's on the right track. Tell your family, but be honest with them about it."

Jay nods and steps out into the hall to make the calls.

It wasn't confirmation Lily would pull through, but it's the biggest hope anyone and the universe has given me. She's fighting. That's good. Great even. My angel's fighting. Nothing will stop me from helping her fight.

"It's good." Tears well up in my eyes. "I'll take it."

"I thought you might." Dana smiles again. "Once we have Lily settled in, I'll help you get set up to stay with her."

"You're not going back to ICU?" I'd rather she didn't.

"No. I'll be staying with Lily. Can I get you anything for now?"

"I don't know what I need," I admit. "Just make sure Lily has what she needs. I'll figure things out as I go."

"I'll see that she does. Right now, I think this room, and you are exactly what she needs."

"This room is fancy." I've never seen a private room this nice. It has a sitting area on one side with a couch.

"This room was requested for her," Dana says.

Requested? Did Dad do this for her? He had to.

"My dad?"

"Uh, no." Dana glances at the doorway.

"I requested that Lily have this room."

I turn to face the man standing in the doorway. My mouth drops open. Jay laughs behind him.

"Grayson Westbrook." I can't believe what I'm seeing.

Jack

"Hey, man." Grayson walks over and clasps my arm. I've tried to talk him into becoming a Viking Warrior. He chose a career in the music industry instead.

"Why?" I'm grateful for his help, but it makes no sense.

"I heard what happened and wanted to help. You're my friend. I can't ignore that. Dana couldn't give me any medical info, but she's really attached to Lily." Grayson winks at Dana.

"You two know each other?"

"Kinda obvious, cuz," Jay laughs.

"She's married to my band leader." Grayson glares at me. "And don't snap at my drummer's wife anymore."

"I've gone off on a lot of people in this hospital. How am I supposed to know who that is?" I'm really surprised security hasn't actually tossed me out.

"Tru was the student doctor with Doctor McCormick after surgery." Dana pushes Grayson and Jay out the door when two nurses arrive with Lily. "I need to get my patient settled in her room."

"Thanks, man." I wave to Grayson, but my eyes stay on the unconscious woman in the bed as it moves into the room.

Lily's here. It's time to help her fight through this stage. She's not out of the woods yet, but a path now leads toward the light.

36
Lily

Beep
Beep
Beep

"Wake up, angel."

Beep
Beep
Beep

"I need to see those pretty brown eyes of yours."

Beep
Beep
Beep

"Wake up, angel. When you're ready, I'll take you for a ride through the mountains on my bike."

Beep
Beep
Beep

Jack

"I love you, Lily."

Beep
Beep
Beep

37
Jack

"Jack."

I raise my head off the bed at the sound of Mom's voice. My eyes instantly go to Lily. Her eyes remain closed. She's still sleeping. I let go of her hand and run both of mine over the top of my head. This room is supposed to be better. I'm supposed to help her fight. I do. I whisper encouragement to her all day and into the night. Lily still sleeps.

Everly brought me a book with encouraging poems. I've read those. Maci showed up late yesterday with a romance novel. I refused to read that. My sister highlighted a few of the romantic lines for me. She thinks I need help in that department. I skimmed over a few of those. They're ridiculous. No way does a man talk like this. Somewhere around midnight, I read the highlighted lines. Lily still sleeps.

They're no longer keeping her in a medical coma. I don't understand why she doesn't wake up. Waiting for her eyes to open is as bad as waiting was when she was in surgery.

"Sweetie, I think the couch folds out into a bed." Mom's hand rubs back and forth across my shoulders.

It does, but I refuse to leave Lily's side. The couch is too far from where she sleeps. Jay's napped there a few times, not me.

"It's been two days, Mom. Why won't she wake up?"

Mom sighs. Her hand stops moving. "Her body will know when it's time. We have to talk her through it until then."

Jack

A throat clears from across the room. I raise my head all the way. Dad stands in the doorway.

"We need to talk."

"Jacob, can't it wait?" Mom asks.

"Afraid not," Dad replies. "Step into the hall with me, son. Your mom will sit with Lily."

Dad's jaw clinches. This isn't about Lily's medical condition. It's about what happened that night. Club business. Good. I need something to do.

I push to my feet and kiss Mom's forehead. "Talk to her, please."

"I will." Mom takes my place by the bed. She holds Lily's hand and presses the back to her cheek. "Hey, sweet girl."

Mom launches into a funny story about the kids of a few club members. They're probably the ones at Lily's table during Thanksgiving dinner. It's good. She needs to hear happy stories. I wish I could stay and listen, too.

Dad taps my arm. I turn away from the bed and follow him across the hall. Lily's room is at the end of the hallway. A small waiting room is just across the hall. It's perfect for when larger groups come to visit. It appears to be perfect for a club meeting, too. Not all of my brothers are here. A few have day jobs they can't easily get time off from. Most of the club officers and my closest friends fill the room. Their sad expressions already set the mood.

"Just go ahead and give me the bad news." I brace myself. The universe is about to run over me again.

"The Sheriff's Office wrapped up the investigation at your house this morning. They wanted to search the entire property, but our lawyers were able to keep the warrant at just your house and outbuildings," Dad says.

Of course, the Sheriff's Office got a search warrant. I knew they would. It's fine. There's nothing illegal at my house. As long as they stay out of Nick's office and lab, everything should be fine. Nick stores all the information for the club and Ariel's Angels. Our little rescue mission isn't exactly legal.

My parents tried to work with the cops to help women after my sister was killed. There was so much legal red tape to cut through. They weren't helping anybody. Cops have so many laws they have to respect that their hands are tied in most situations. Ours aren't.

I'm glad the cops are off of club property now. This isn't what I need to know today. Dad and my club brothers can handle this. They don't need me. Lily does.

I toss my hands up. "Just tell me y'all got 'em."

"I highly doubt we got them all," Hendrix says.

"Look, son." Dad put a hand on my shoulder. "Lily wasn't the only one shot that night."

No one has mentioned this. I quickly scan the room to see who's missing. This isn't half of our members.

"Who? How many?" I ask.

"Just Lily and Sandman," Worley Bird replies.

Sandman is our Sergeant At Arms. Some clubs call the position Enforcer. Sandman and Dad have been friends since middle school.

"Why didn't anyone tell me?" I lock eyes with my cousin. He's been with me the most.

"Sandman was shot in the shoulder. He's fine, already at home. Your priority was to Lily. So, we waited to tell you," Jay says.

He's right, and I appreciate it.

"Okay. How many were there? How many did we get? How many got away?" My eyes harden. "And who are they?"

Midnight Maverick did this. They can skip that part and tell me the rest.

"One was killed on property. It's why it's taken this long to get the cops out." Worley Bird stands on Dad's other side.

"A cop's bullet got him, not us," Rodeo adds.

"Captured two. Cops are holding them in Memphis for now," Dad says.

"Memphis? Why?" Memphis is about two hours away.

"So we don't storm the Sheriff's Office and take them," Cloudy says.

I swear, Cloudy comes up with some insane ideas. It's not like we live in the 1800s. But he could be right. Some people around here would think that's what we'd do.

"Mavericks?" I plainly ask since no one is going to say it.

Jack

"Not that we can prove. One is from Alabama. The one that was killed was from Georgia. The third one is from Murfreesboro. The two in custody aren't talking." Dad runs a hand over his mouth and beard.

"How many got away?"

"That we don't know. The only information the cops got from the two they have in custody is that it was just the three of them," Worley Bird says.

"That's a lie." There was too much gunfire for me to believe three men pulled it off.

"We all know that but can't prove it." Jay shakes his head.

"Cameras? Surely, Nick got on video how they got in. How many there were, and what they destroyed." I can't believe we have nothing.

"The cameras from your house to the side of the fence they cut and entered through went down two minutes before they opened fire on your house." Dad's words drop me into a nearby chair.

How could we just lose these guys? Nick's good, but can he find them with little or no info? How will we find the rest if the two in custody don't talk? Too many questions. Not enough answers. If they really wanted to cut us open and destroy us, why not open fire on the clubhouse during the party?

I look up at Dad. "How many more buildings and houses did they hit?"

He presses his lips together and shakes his head. "Just yours."

Mine. My house. My room. My woman. I spring to my feet and pace the room. I stop and lock eyes with Jay. My cousin won't lie. He might hide information for a while, but he won't lie.

"So I was the target." It's not a question. I feel it.

Jay dips his chin. "I think so."

Lily was shot because of me. I grab my head with both hands and squeeze as tight as I can. I'm gutted clean to my soul. My hands clench into fists, but I don't let go of my head. If I could apply enough pressure to shut my thoughts down, I would. I can't. I don't yell. I search the shadows inside for the darkness that's always clawing to consume me. I find it and make it my friend.

My eyes meet Jay's. "Guard her."

"Where you going, Ghost?" Jay, unlike the others, sees what I've unleashed.

"Chattanooga."

Dad steps in the doorway. "Son, that's not a good idea. We can't prove it was the Mavericks. We got nothing right now."

"That's not true!" Okay. I lied about yelling. "We've got plenty. We're just not connecting it yet. We know Trace was there when the first firecracker prank happened. He was in the bakery before that. Buck was helping Clark at the library. They. Were. There. It's them! We know it!

"They came for me. I don't know why I'm his target. They shot my ole' lady!" My voice rises with every sentence. "In my house! Our bedroom! In my bed! They shot her! I'm going to Chattanooga! You'll have to kill me to stop me! If it were one of your wives, you'd already be halfway there!"

"Okay, son." Dad slowly nods. "You're right. We would. I won't stop you. But I have to ask you an important question first."

"What's that?" I snap. Not a good idea on my part. Thankfully, Dad lets it slide.

"Son, are you officially claiming Lily as your ole' lady?"

My head jerks back slightly. Jay snickers. I guess I walked into that, didn't I? I wanted to talk to Lily about it first. Explain what it means. My world confuses her. It doesn't matter now. It's fine. If she never wakes up, she'll never know. But I will. For ever how long she has left in this world, and I do hope it's years, she's mine.

"Yeah, Dad. I am."

"Vikings, Church," Dad calls out.

My brothers stand and surround us. All our patched members aren't here. There's enough for it to be official, though.

"Jack, are you officially claiming Lily Harman as you're ole' lady? Are you granting her the rights, protection, and responsibilities of the title?"

"I am, Pres. I claim Lily as my ole' lady."

"All in favor?" Dad asks.

Ayes go up around the room.

"All opposed?"

Not a sound is made.

Jack

Dad places a hand on my shoulder. "Congratulations, son."

"I'll have her property cut made. We'll celebrate when Lily's home with us," Worley Bird says.

A path opens up between my brothers to the door. Rodeo, Bankz, and Hendrix wait by the doorway.

"We're going with you," Rodeo says.

"Not all the way. I'm going in for Buck alone." If I tell them to stay here, they won't. "Oh, Dad."

"We'll watch over Lily," he assures me.

I know he will. "You said one of the men in custody was from Murfreesboro."

"That's right," he confirms.

"Have Nick check to see if there's a connection between him and the owner of the stolen bike Jay found the camera on." It's weak, but it's a thought.

Dad and Jay grin at each other. They'll figure it out. I have a Maverick to hunt down tonight.

38
Lily

Beep
Beep
Beep

"Hey, angel. You're still sleeping."

Beep
Beep
Beep

"I have something to take care of."

Beep
Beep
Beep

"I love you, Lily. I'll be back as soon as I can."

Beep
Beep
Beep

Jack

"Jack, no."
"I gotta, Mom."
"Jay, stop him."
"Sorry, Aunt Ev. Not this time."

Beep
Beep
Beep

39
Jack

It took half the night to track Buck down. Nick sent me all the information he had on Randle White. For a while there, I thought I was going to be stuck in Chattanooga for a few days. Oddly enough, the same universe trying to kill me threw me a bone. Well, maybe two universes collided, and this is what fell out. Either way, it's turning out to be a good night. Morning? It's getting close to three am. That's definitely morning.

The Midnight Mavericks have gotten sloppy lately. What club declares war on another club and then lets its members roam around unprotected? Maybe after, what is it now? Four or five days? I shrug to absolutely nobody. Well, unless you count Buck. He's unconscious at the moment. So yeah, it's nobody.

The moron at my feet decided he was going to get a drink at a bar down the street from his house, all by his lonesome. *Thanks, universe.* I tap Buck's cheek. He doesn't wake. You know who else won't wake up? My ole' lady. She can't. Her body won't let her. She's trapped in a void somewhere, trying to heal because somebody came for me and missed their target.

I'm not a betting man, but I'd bet my left kidney that the unconscious man on the ground was part of it. Oh, I doubt he was one of the crew who shot up my house. This man is on camera helping a lowlife piece of dung try to kidnap my woman. He gets no sympathy from me.

Jack

The video of Joel Clark hitting Lily in the face plays on repeat in my head tonight. Seeing this man trying to communicate with Clark through the window pisses me off. I kick him in the side. Buck grunts. Oh, good. He's waking up. Sadly, he doesn't. This is taking too long. I need to get out of here. I grab two bottles of water from the van and twist the tops off.

"Wakey. Wakey." I nudge Buck with my foot again and pour the water over his face.

Buck coughs and rolls to his side. His body jerks and his legs kick out when he realizes his hands are tied behind his back. He looks like a fish out of water.

"Ah. We can't have that now. Can we? Let me help you up." It's not help. Trust me, it's not. I grab Buck's arm and pull him to his feet. I prefer a man on his feet when I face him.

"McLeod?" Buck frantically turns his head in every direction.

He won't find help. We're in a small field surrounded by forest on three sides and a small hill on the other. You can't really call it a mountain. City folk might. We're about fifty miles west of Chattanooga. I have no clue exactly where. I saw the dirt road going into the forest and decided to take it. The universe threw me another bone. This spot's perfect.

"What are you doing?" Buck asks.

"You've been a bad boy, Buck. You shot up my house and shot my ole' lady in the back."

"I did nothing."

I'm not convinced.

"You may not have done it yourself. You didn't step foot on Viking property. You didn't pull the trigger once, but you *did* send them."

He stares at me but doesn't speak. Good. We've come to an understanding. He doesn't deny it, so it's close enough to admitting it.

"You did, however, personally help Joel Clark try to kidnap my woman."

He sucks in a sharp breath through his nose.

"We have you on camera behind the library in Willow Creek. You don't belong in Willow Creek."

His eyes drop but don't close. He knows he links his club to crimes against mine if he says anything.

I grab him by his cut and jerk him forward hard. "Why? What does Trace Coombs want from me?"

"For you to die." Buck laughs like a maniac.

Well. Well. Well. He just linked the Mavericks.

Buck's eyes widen, and so do mine, when a knife lands in the side of his neck. We're not alone in this field. Buck gets one gasp for air. It's over. I release his cut, dropping his body to the ground.

I don't run. I don't pull a weapon to defend myself. There's no need. I know that knife.

"Blade!"

I whirl around as my psycho cousin walks out of the forest. Rodeo, Bankz, and Hendrix follow him out. Those three are supposed to be waiting for me a mile down the road at an abandoned country store.

"What are you doing? I was questioning him."

"You didn't come here to play around and ask questions. You don't need 'em. We have this man dead to rights on camera working with Clark. You came here for revenge. You know as well as the rest of us. You serve that hard, cold, and fast."

"You're supposed to be at the hospital," I snap.

"Which is where you need to be heading." Jay bends down, pulls the knife from Buck's neck, and wipes it on the man's shirt. He stands and shoves the knife into my hand. "Now, when we find the next one involved with hurting your ole' lady, don't talk. Use that."

"Head on to the hospital. We'll handle this," Bankz says.

"Is she awake?" I ask Jay.

"No, but you're needed. You and Rodeo take the van and go. My truck's at the end of the road. We got this."

"Why, Jay? Why am I needed? Don't keep something from me." I understand why they didn't tell me about Sandman and me being the target. But this is Lily.

"Flowers were delivered today." Jay's word drives a knife in my heart. "Don't worry. She's well-guarded."

I don't ask any more questions. I don't waste time. Rodeo and I jump into the van and rush back to Willow Creek.

40
Jack

Three hours later, Rodeo pulls into the hospital parking lot. Jay wasn't kidding. Lily is well-guarded. Viking Warriors walk the parking lot. Two are stationed at every door. Four more brothers guard the elevators and stairwell on Lily's floor. Cloudy Daze and Big Papa lean against the wall outside her room.

"Ghost." Big Papa clasps my arm. "It done?"

I nod. "Who's with her?"

"Your parents," Cloudy replies.

"I'll stay out here. Give you a minute." Rodeo pulls out his phone and goes into the waiting room.

I lightly tap on the door before pushing it open. Dad meets me at the door. I'm sure one of our brothers called and let him know I was on my way up. Mom closes the book she was reading to Lily and rushes to me.

"You okay?" Her voice shakes. Her hug is tighter than normal. I didn't mean to worry her.

"Yeah, Mom. I'm okay." I want to know about the flowers, but I need to see my angel first. "Give me a minute, Dad."

He pulls Mom into his arms and leads her to the couch.

I sit in the extremely uncomfortable chair by the bed and reach for Lily's hand. "Hey, angel." I press my lips to the back of her hand."

I slide closer and place my palm against her cheek. A quick glance at the monitors doesn't give me anything. I don't understand what all the numbers mean anyway. I focus on her instead and gently rub my thumb across her cheek.

"You look beautiful today, angel."

She's beautiful every day, even with black eyes and a bruised nose. Her skin is starting to get its color back. Just yesterday, she was too pale, ghostly white. I never want to see her like that again. Today, her cheeks are a little pink. That has to be a good sign. I want to stay with her, but I have business to take care of.

I stand and kiss her forehead. "I'll be back in a few minutes, angel. You rest."

I quietly follow Dad out the door. Surprisingly, Mom comes with us.

"Mom, I don't want to leave her alone. What if she wakes and no one's there?"

"I'll sit with her." Lil Mama rushes past us into Lily's room.

That might not be a good idea.

"It's fine, Jack." Mom walks into the waiting room like everything really is fine.

I motion between Big Papa and Lily's door. "You go in there and keep your ole' lady in line."

"Uh. Yeah, sure." Big Papa doesn't sound so sure, but he goes into Lily's room with his wife.

Worley Bird closes the door behind me. I'm the last to enter. Once again, it's just my family and brothers in the little waiting room. Jay, Bankz, and Hendrix are here. They must have been right behind us. I don't want to know how they cleaned that field up. It's probably best I don't.

"What kind of flowers were delivered this time?" If the flowers are messages, I don't think I wanna know what this one means.

"The same as the last delivery to the bakery." Mom opens a gold box like the long-stemmed roses were in from the first delivery.

White lilies and red roses with slightly wilted petals lay on red satin in the center of the box from the top to the bottom. Black dahlias lay over those. Emily was right. These flowers don't go together. They weren't meant to. They deliver a message. Lily's name. A lost love. Death.

Jack

Another message I get from this is that Joel Clark won't stop coming for Lily. He doesn't want her. He wants to destroy her and end her life. Not on my watch. I failed Lily twice already. It won't happen a third time. Jay's right, too. I don't need to play games and ask questions. Well, the right questions to the right people need to be asked. The men who came after me and hurt Lily deserve no mercy. Her abuser deserves nothing, not even the air surrounding him right now.

"Delivery details. What have we got? Can we link it to him? Is he in Willow Creek?" These are the only answers I need.

"No, son. He's in LA. Nick has him on traffic cameras outside his office today." Dad ends my biggest fear at the moment.

"These weren't a personal delivery this time," Worley Bird adds.

"Since he's not here, it was an online order." Mom puts the lid back on the box. She can't stand looking at them any more than I can.

"He used Blooms and Bows again. Sandy called us the moment she saw the order. The flowers never made it to Lily's room." Dad gives a firm nod.

I rub the back of my neck. He knows she's in the hospital. Great.

"So, Sandy got his email and credit card this time?" I really wanna get my hands on this man.

The other orders were paid with a prepaid Visa gift card. Hopefully, Nick had more to work with this time.

"He still used a Visa gift card to pay, but since he had to fill out the entire online form this time, he used a fake name and email address. He's a sick man, son. The email address used part of Lily's name." Dad presses his lips together and shakes his head.

"That is sick." It's beyond sick, and it turns my stomach. It proves he's obsessed with Lily, but how does it link to Clark if it was in Lily's name?

"Nick used the order form and the email to trace the IP address. It went to Joel Clark's office." Mom smiles. I swear she just read my mind.

"So we got him? The flower deliveries won't prove anything to the cops, so we haven't told the Sheriff about the flowers. But we know it's him. No doubts." Worley Bird offers me a black backpack.

"What's this?"

"A change of clothes and a little care package from Nick, in case you need it." Worley Bird hands a matching backpack to my brothers.

"Dobson is waiting for you and the boys at the county airstrip. It's a helicopter. It'll be a choppy ride, but he can get you in and out of California without your name being on a flight list." Dad drops a hand on my shoulder and leans in eye-to-eye with me. "It's LA, Jack. It's different. Listen to Drew. Do exactly as he says, and go stop this threat against our family."

" I don't like you sending my son off to get hurt," Mom pouts.

Dad pulls her under his arm. "*Our* son will be the next Viking Warrior President. He needs to know how to protect our family, no matter what it takes."

"He's not going alone, Aunt Ev." Jay kisses her cheek.

"I need to see her before we go." I point across the hall.

"Meet you downstairs." Rodeo leads the others to the elevators.

"Mom, destroy those flowers. I never want to see that bouquet again."

Separately, the lilies and roses might be okay. It'll take a while for me to see it, though. I'll burn an entire field of black dahlias down if I ever come across one.

"They're on the way to the hospital dumpsters now." Mom passes the box to Cloudy.

41
Lily

Beep
Beep
Beep

"I love you, angel."

Beep
Beep
Beep

"When I get back, I'm gonna need you to open those pretty brown eyes for me. Okay?"

Beep
Beep
Beep

"I won't give you up, Lily. I can't."

Beep
Beep
Beep

"Your world will be safe when you wake up. I promise, angel. I'll make sure of it."

Beep
Beep
Beep

42
Jack

Don't take a helicopter ride across the country. Just don't. Trust me. Choppy was putting it mildly. However, our plans didn't allow for a nice, sweet commercial flight. Flying coach is better than this.

Dobson's connections at our little county airstrip and all the private ones along the way were exactly what we needed to get into California quietly. Drew was waiting for us at a small airstrip outside the city. We could be in the desert for all I know. We rode for over an hour. Drew didn't take us to his clubhouse. We're hiding out in one of the safe houses his chapter brings angels to when they have a layover in LA.

Rodeo, Jay, Hendrix, and Bankz are with me. My brothers and I slept for about four hours this afternoon so we would be rested for tonight's hunt. It's hard to sleep when you're on a mission.

This one is going to be tricky. We're in a city with cameras everywhere. The moment LA rose in the distance, I knew this wasn't my territory. I understand why Dad said to listen to Drew. He has some odd requests and instructions. If we want to get out of here, we have to follow them to the letter.

"You do this a lot?" Rodeo asks. Drew just stares at him. "Hunt men through the city, I mean."

"Not really." Drew hands us a pair of black gloves. "We have roughed up a few abusers. My job mainly consists of transporting angels in and out." His eyes meet mine. "I hear you claimed one I carried out."

"Yeah," I admit. "Nina brought her to you."

"We'll talk about that later." Drew takes us to an underground garage and flips the light on.

Hendrix whistles when he sees all the bikes lined up on one side. Cars, vans, and trucks are on the other. Wow. Drew's chapter stocked a fleet of vehicles down here. He leads us over to the row of bikes. They're a mix of Harleys and crotch rockets.

"You know how you wanna handle this?" Drew asks me.

"Not like the last one." Jay walks over to one of the Harleys.

He's right. The last one was messy enough in the country. There's no way we could pull anything close to that here.

"I don't care how we do it. I just don't want him coming after Lily again." The last flower delivery is proof he won't stop until he kills her.

We had to use Lily's real name at the hospital. We should have gotten her a fake ID weeks ago. Once again, it's where I failed her. We didn't have her social security number. Somehow, the hospital found it in their system, maybe because she was a nurse. Nick thinks Clark's dad had Lily's name and social security number flagged, and that's how he knew she was in the hospital. Or the Mavericks could have told him since they were helping him.

"Leave it to me." Drew walks over to the first crotch rocket and takes the license plate off. "Leave the Harleys. Pick another ride."

Jay looks heartbroken. The way Bankz's eyes dance as he walks around a Ducati, he may ask it to marry him. After removing all the plates, we suit up head to toe in black. It's fine with Jay and me. It's what we wear nearly every day. It's weird turning our cuts inside out and wearing a plain black jacket over them, but we do it.

"All right, brothers. Joel Clark is a cocky douche who thinks nobody can touch him because his old man's a cop. His dad is a dirty cop, so that's close to being true. We can't get near him at his job or his house.

"Every Thursday night, Mr. Clark meets his friends at a bar for dinner and drinks. He leaves between eleven and one. We'll be waiting for him at the back of the parking lot. He doesn't like parking near the front. We'll have some fun with him first and wait for him to run. There are no mics in these helmets, so follow my lead." Drew starts up his bike and leads us out of the garage.

Jack

He's got some great intel on Clark. His plan concerns me. What does fun mean to him exactly? And why do we want Clark to run? This is going to be a disaster.

The ride through the city streets is a nightmare. Give me a country road, and me let go. Thankfully, we turn off the main streets and move to smaller neighborhoods. It's still too much traffic for me.

Sure enough, we find Joel Clark at a local bar with his friends. We watch and wait for an hour and a half. Most of his friends have left. Clark shows no sign of leaving any time soon.

"You sure about this?" I ask around 12:45 am.

"Just wait. He sets an alarm on his phone to ensure he leaves on time. After all, he has a big boy job and has to get to work in the morning. If this were Friday or Saturday night, we wouldn't be here."

"Uh, Drew." Rodeo turns his back to the building and points to his chest with his thumb. He's signaling at something behind him. I see nothing out of place. "There's a camera across from us."

I drop my head. As long as we've been waiting on the edge of the back parking lot, someone somewhere knows we're here. I'm surprised the cops haven't shown up already.

"That particular camera malfunctioned early this evening. The replacement won't be delivered until Monday." Drew grins.

As Drew predicted, at 12:50, Clark pulls out his phone for a moment. That must be the alarm. He says goodbye to the two friends still inside and walks to his car. It was so nice of him to park in the furthest row from the building, away from most of the cars. Guess he doesn't want anyone to scratch up his paint with their doors. It's happened three times since we've been here.

"Remember, hard, cold, and fast," Jay whispers.

"Here. You'll need this." Drew shoves something in my hand.

I glance down and freeze. "Why do I need this?" I don't even want to touch it.

"Trust me." Drew dips his chin and steps back.

Just as Clark gets his door unlocked, I grab him and slam his back against the side of his car. His eyes almost pop out of their sockets when he looks up at the dark figure looming over him.

"Joel Clark," I growl low and deep.

"Wh… What do you want?"

"I want you to pay for your crimes."

He bravely lifts his chin. "My father's a cop."

"Not a problem."

Fear flashes in his eyes. He just lost his biggest bargaining chip.

"I can pay you…whatever you want. Name your price."

Of course, this douche resorts to money. Money isn't a factor for me. It never will be.

A long whistle comes from behind me. *Okay, Jay. I hear ya.*

I hold up the Black Dahlia Drew handed me. "An eye for an eye."

The whites of Clark's eyes overtake the blue. I crush the offending flower into my fist, draw back my arm, and punch him dead center in the face. Blood splatter sure is pretty tonight. It's not enough for me.

Cold, hard, and fast. I beat this evil man to the ground. Before I slam my boot into his face, arms grab me and hold me back. Clark scrambles into the car and starts the engine.

"Let him run," Drew says in my ear. He pushes me toward the bike. My brothers are already on their rides. "Let's go, boys. Stay close. Follow my lead."

We chase after the Mercedes. Drew risks getting next to the driver's door several times and tosses something from his pocket onto the windshield. Each time he does it, Clark makes a right turn. If Drew's on the passenger side, Clark turns left. This is insane.

Somehow, we end up in a high-speed chase on the freeway. This is beyond dangerous. There are too many innocent people out here. As the first sirens pierce the night, my worst fear happens. A woman in a Toyota Camry panics and swerves into Clark's lane. He jerks the steering wheel to the right to avoid her. His car slams head-on into a concrete pillar near an exit ramp. The car shatters to pieces before our eyes. Drew motions us on. We hit the gas and leave Clark and the freaked-out lady behind. What in the world just happened?

We don't return to the safe house. Instead, Drew leads us out of the city, away from the traffic and sirens. We don't stop until we reach an abandoned building an hour later. A black van waits for us. We get off the bikes, and the five of us stare at Drew, speechless.

"Drew, I'm glad you're a brother and work with Ariel's Angels." I jab my finger in his face. "But, man, I'm never coming back here to work with you." I point back toward LA. "I don't know what that was, but you could have gotten us all killed."

"Nobody died." Drew shrugs. "We need to talk."

I toss my hands up. "Sure, brother. What would you like to talk about?"

"I have an angel I need you to move. No file, but I think your dad will make an exception this time." Drew opens the van's sliding door. A woman steps out with tears running down her face.

"Nina?" I haven't seen her in years, but it's her. "What's going on?"

"They found Lily through me." Nina wipes her tears away with her sleeve.

"How?" We've had suspicions about how Clark found Lily but couldn't confirm anything.

"Lily sent an email from a new address to my hospital email. I didn't open it, but I knew it was her when I saw the address. I deleted it, but Joel's dad's friends found it. He's a dirty cop with less than legal connections. They figured out where she sent it from."

"You sure about this?" Jay asks.

Nina nods and wipes more tears away.

"His dad's buddies have been threatening her for weeks. A few of them like to brag. They wanted her to know it was her fault they found Lily. I took Nina from the hospital garage just like I did Lily. They're hunting Nina. Figured sending her to your dad was best. We haven't been able to move her across the country yet. Thought you boys wouldn't mind escorting an angel tonight." Drew doesn't have to ask. He knows we will.

This woman saved Lily's life. If it weren't for her, Clark would still be hurting Lily. Without Nina, I wouldn't have my angel.

"We got her." I proudly shake Drew's hand, even though he tried to kill us an hour ago.

My brothers and I surround Nina and climb into the van. Dean, one of Drew's helpers in the area, drives us to the airstrip, where Dobson is waiting for us. Hearing the word angel, he asks no further questions. We've kept radio silence with our families on this trip. We couldn't risk being tracked. We'll deliver this angel to Dad. Hopefully, my angel will be awake when I get to the hospital.

43
Lily

Beep
Beep
Beep

Oh my gosh. Will somebody turn that beeping off? It's all I hear. Wait. No, that's not true. I hear faint voices at times. Other times, I think I forgot to turn an audiobook off. I can't seem to find the button to stop it, though.

"Morning, angel. You look beautiful today."

The voice is back. I could listen to his deep voice for hours. He could talk me into anything.

I sigh deeply and lean into the palm against my cheek. It's the first bit of warmth I've felt in a long time.

"Lily?" His voice is louder. It's no longer soft like a lullaby. "Come on, angel. Open your eyes."

I want to do as he asks. My eyelids feel so heavy. I try to blink, but my eyes feel glued shut.

"Oh, my gosh, Jack. She's waking up." A woman says.

Her voice seems familiar, but I can't place it. Jack? I've heard that name before. Who's waking up? Have they been asleep long?

"You can do it, Lily. Come back to me," his deep voice coaxes.

Me? My name is Lily. He's talking to me. My eyelids lift slightly. The first rays of light peek through. With each blink, more light comes and pushes the darkness away. Finally, the voice I've clung to in the dreams becomes a real person.

"Jack," my voice cracks. My throat hurts.

"Hey, angel. Welcome back." Jack presses his lips to the edge of mine.

The beeping grows louder.

"Shut that off, please." I can't take it anymore.

"Shut what off, love?"

"The beeps."

"I can't, but this lady probably can."

"Hello, Lily. I'm Dana. Let's get your vital signs, and I'll see what I can do about the monitor sounds." She's the familiar voice.

Monitors? I frantically look around. The beeping gets louder. Dana's a nurse. Oh my gosh.

"Jack."

"Shh. Easy, angel, easy."

"Where am I?" I know where I am.

"You're in the hospital. Do you remember anything?"

I close my eyes and immediately pop them open again. I don't want to see darkness anymore. Instead, I focus on each stroke his fingers make down the side of my face, sweet, gentle, loving.

"Do you know who you are?" Dana asks.

That's not a good sign. I don't yell at her or look at Dana like she's crazy. I'm a nurse. We usually ask that question when someone's been unconscious for a long time.

I lock eyes with the man looming over me. "I'm Lily Harman. You're Jack McLeod."

He grins. "That's right, angel. Good girl."

"We had Thanksgiving dinner at the clubhouse." I gasp. "Oh my gosh! You're a biker."

Jack, my nurse, and several more people laugh. Jack stands up straight so I can see the room full of people behind him. I know them. I know them all.

"You're Viking Warriors." I can't help but laugh with them. Only laughing hurts. I lay my hand against my throat.

"Here you go." Dana holds a straw to my lips.

The first sip of water hurts. The next soothes. I push the straw away when my throat is no longer dry.

My eyes find Jack's again. "I was shot."

His face drops. "Yeah. I'm sorry, angel."

"Not your fault." I turn to my nurse. "Am I going to be okay?"

"Yes, ma'am. You'll have some therapy, but you'll be fine. I hear you're a nurse, too. Maybe one day, I'll see you around here in scrubs." She looks across the bed to Jack. "I knew you could talk her back. Doctor McCormick will be by soon. We let him know she's awake." Dana waves to Jack's family and quietly leaves.

"Hey, sweet girl." Jack's mother moves to the side of the bed and squeezes my hand.

"Hey, Nanny." I smile up at her.

Her smile fades. "No, ma'am. I'm not Nanny to you anymore."

"Mom," Jack warns.

"What? Why? You're Nanny to everybody."

"Uncle Jack officially claimed you," Everly announces. "Nanny's Mom to you now."

I snap my eyes to Jack. "You did what?"

"You're his ole' lady. We've already ordered your cut." Everly claps and bounces on her toes.

"Did he now?"

"Yep. You're officially ours now. No takebacks." Everly giggles.

I raise my finger and motion for Jack to lean down. He lowers to loom over me again.

"No takebacks from you either," I whisper.

"It's sealed for eternity, angel," he vows before his lips claim mine.

Epilogue
Jack

I've always enjoyed Christmas with my family. The last two were through video calls. I was a fool for leaving and staying gone as long as I did. The roaming days are through for me. I'm not ready to be club President yet, but I'm settling down.

It's been three weeks since Lily woke up. Mom and Nana wouldn't let her do too much in the kitchen this year. It can take six to eight weeks for a punctured lung to heal completely. She says she's fine, but we're not taking any chances.

It's Christmas Day. Santa has come and gone. Kids run around playing with their new toys. It's just after two. Everybody's full and happy. I know I sure am. Everyone's here today, even the club bunnies. Yes, Jenny's pissed, but I don't rightly care. Every time she gets within ten feet of me, one of my brothers steers her in another direction. After today, she'll have no choice but to leave me alone.

"Vikings!" Dad calls out. He's in front of the doors to Church. We're not having Church today. This is where he stands when giving club news inside. It's too cold to use the stage in the backyard.

The Den quietens down except for the preschoolers. It's kinda hard to get a two-year-old to sit still. Worley Bird stands behind Dad with a beautiful piece of leather draped over his arm.

Jack

"We have an announcement to make. Jack?" Dad motions for me to join him. I happily walk across the Den. "Lily?" He calls her from the kitchen doorway.

She narrows her eyes at me. She knew this was coming. We just didn't tell her when. I smile and nod. What better time than Christmas? Her face explodes with happiness as she hurries through the crowd. I don't think she fully understands what this means yet, but she wants it.

"Slow down, angel. I'm not going anywhere."

She laughs and wraps her arms around my waist. I drop a kiss on top of her head.

"No takebacks," she reminds me.

My niece's words have become a joke with my family.

"Never," I promise.

"The rumors are true. Today, we're making it official. Three weeks ago, my son officially claimed Lily Harman as his ole' lady. It was a unanimous vote among our brothers. As of this moment, Lily holds the status of Jack McLeod's ole' lady. Every member of the Viking Warriors MC and their families will honor her and show her the respect she's rightly due." Dad hands me Lily's property of cut.

I turn the cut so she can see the club logo. "I love you, Lily. Nothing will ever change that. Never forget this." I tap the property of patch and my road name, Ghost.

"I won't."

I hold the cut open, and she slides it on. The smile on her face is beautiful. I turn her around so everyone can see the back and claim her lips with mine.

"Welcome to the family, Lily!" At Dad's shout, the room bursts into an uproar.

I end the kiss and hold my arm up. The room goes quiet again.

"Merry Christmas, Vikings. Enjoy your night. I'm taking my ole' lady home."

More shouts and cheers erupt as we walk across the Den. I don't look back. I know everyone is watching. I walk her to Dad's truck and drive around to the guest house. My house now sits empty. I can't live there anymore. I almost lost Lily inside those walls. We're staying here until our new house is built further back on the property. Security and the property fence are in the process of being upgraded. An enemy won't get through so easily again.

We haven't found all the men involved in the attack that night. We won't stop until we do. The two men in custody still aren't talking. A trial date hasn't been set yet. No one is stepping up to try and free them. They won't fare well in prison. The one from Murfreesboro is cousins with the owner of the stolen motorcycle Jay found the camera on. Nick's searching for more connections.

The freaked-out lady in the Toyota wasn't a random driver that night. She works with Ariel's Angels. She helped Drew move Nina around LA until the night we got her out. Nina's in Willow Creek, hiding until we figure out her next step. Lily doesn't know she's here yet. We should tell her soon.

Lily's nightmare has been silenced. She's considering talking to a counselor about the abuse she's been through. Joel Clark didn't die that night. He suffered a brain injury and will be in a vegetable state for the rest of his life. His parents moved him to a care facility. He's quiet. That's what matters.

"We didn't have to leave the party," Lily says as we walk into the house.

"Yes, ma'am, we did."

I pull her against me and walk her over to the Christmas tree. She loves Christmas lights. The more, the better. Her face lights up at every house with decorations we pass around town. Yes, we've taken long drives so that she can see them.

"Wait here." I grab the blanket and pillows from the couch.

"What are you doing?"

I spread the blanket on the floor and arrange the pillows. I turn off every light in the house except for the Christmas tree. With her wrapped in my arms again, I lower us to the blanket. What better way to spend Christmas with her under a tree?

She sits up, slides her cut off, and turns it over. Her fingers gently trace over the logo. "It's beautiful."

"Mom redesigned the club's logo." Maybe it's time she knows why.

"It's for your sister." Well, she's figured that part out.

"Yeah." I slide my finger along the design. "Ariel's favorite color was red. It's why there's red trim and a burgundy glow around the emblem. The two A's for Ariel's Angels are hidden in the ribbons." I point them out. "It has two sets of wings." I touch each one. "The larger set is for my sister. The smaller is for her little girl."

"Jack, I have to tell you something." She looks up at me with tears in her eyes.

"What's that, angel?"

"That day at the library, I Googled your sister's name. I'm sorry. I shouldn't have pried."

"You didn't," I assure her. "It's hard for my family to talk about it. Nick monitors what's online. Mostly, what's there now are just the case facts."

She runs a finger over the smallest set of wings. "She was pregnant."

I take a deep breath and try to control my emotions. She knows about the baby. She saw part of my sister's story. It's why she was so sad, crying, and unaware of her surroundings as she walked through the library. We all saw it on the video, but I never asked her about it.

"She was about four months." I can't tell her more tonight. There's more. A lot more. We didn't know the baby was a girl. When the coroner told Mom, she named the baby Angel Magnolia. She deserved to be called more than the unborn baby.

As if sensing I'm at my limits, she lets the subject drop and places her palm against my cheek.

"I love you, Jack."

"I love you too, angel." I lean down and kiss her neck. She shivers. I love it when that happens.

"Why do you still call me that?"

I raise my head and stare into her eyes. She has no idea how much she means to me or what she saves me from.

"I told you before, I carry darkness. I've found even more since that day."

"I love you, Jack. The darkness and all."

She might regret saying that someday.

"I thought I lost you. Don't ever leave me. If you go, you have to take me with you. I can't survive this world without you."

"Jack," she whispers softly.

"You're the only light in my darkness, angel. You're burned into my soul."

Her gasp turns into a moan against my lips. It's true. It's all true. I wouldn't make it without her. If I ever lose her, the darkness takes me completely.

Fighting for the Innocent

Thank you for reading Jack – Viking Warriors MC - Book 1.

This book and series carry a hidden meaning. Some of you may know, most don't. On January 18, 2011, we lost my daughter, Kacy Magnolia Roberson, and her unborn daughter, Angel Magnolia Roberson.

People have asked me for years to write a book about Kacy's story. They said I could help so many people. A few of those people were genuine in that request. Most, I fear, only wanted a play-by-play of what happened to her. I'll never write that. But I do want to tell parts of Kacy's story. I'm not sure if it'll help anyone. When I decided to write an MC series, I thought I could share bits and pieces of Kacy's story here. I'll never share it all. I can't. Writing this book ripped me open so many times. Seriously, my friends even called to check on me. It was hard.

In this series, Ariel's story is Kacy's story. Everything about Ariel's story is real. Some of the other scenes are, too. Everything else in the series may be different and changed; just know Ariel's part won't. It's as close as I could get to sharing it.

If you or someone you know are in an abusive relationship, I encourage you to leave. Nothing is more important than your life. It doesn't get better. It only gets worse. Sometimes, like with Kacy, there are no warning signs. Sometimes, it only happens once. We didn't have the warning signs.

If you need help, here's a place to start:

National Domestic Violence Hotline
CALL 1-800-799-SAFE (7233)
CHAT www.thehotline.org
TEXT "START" to 88788

And for love is respect for youth, focusing on healthy dating relationships:
CALL 1-866-331-9474
CHAT www.loveisrespect.org
TEXT "LOVEIS" to 22522

Follow Me

Sign up for my Newsletter:
https://linktr.ee/debbiehydeauthor

Facebook Page:
Debbie Hyde Author

Facebook Groups:
Debbie Hyde's Reader Group: This one is for all of my books. I hold giveaways in the group.
Debbie Hyde's Book Launch Team: I would love to have you on my book launch team! The team gets all my book news first. They get to participate in the writing process with me at times and even help with cover design ideas. Team members get first chance at Beta & ARC opportunities. Join me today!
For the Love of a Shaw: This group is dedicated to the series.
Hayden Falls series: This group is dedicated to the series.
The Dawson Boys series: This group is dedicated to the series.

The Fireside Book Café – This is a book community group with various Authors and books from every genre. We hold Giveaways here, too.

Instagram:
www.instagram.com/debbie_hyde_author

Twitter:
Debbie Hyde5

Acknowledgments

The manuscript for this book was not even halfway written around New Year's Day. When I decided to release this book on January 18th, an amazing tribe of women stepped up to help keep me encouraged and writing. Without them, I wouldn't have made it.

Nancie Blume, thank you so much for all you do for me, and not just in my author career. You've been my Alfa Reader long before we knew what it was called. This is my 21st novel, and you've been there for every one of them. You kept me on track with this one. You knew when scenes were hard and personal and that I wasn't okay. You called and messaged me every day and night. There were some really long nights, too. Thank you for the information you're giving about motorcycle clubs. I'm going to stop here because I could write a whole chapter for you. I love you, lil buddy.

Wendy Sizemore, thank you so much for being my friend and unbiological sister. You prefer the books when they're finished because you love getting the whole story at once. Thank you for all the calls and texts helping me come up with story ideas. You always read between the lines lol. Some of my books wouldn't be what they are without you. This past week, you messaged and asked if I was okay. You didn't know I just wrote a hard chapter and was broken. I replied, no. You called right away. I love you, Winnie.

To my beyond awesome Beta Readers, Victoria Trout, Tiffany Buras Parker, and Nancie Blume. You ladies are beyond amazing. You had less than a day to do this, and you came through brilliantly. I wouldn't have made the pre-order deadline without you. We had 11 minutes to spare.

To my amazing Admins and Mods of The Fireside Book Café group, thank you so so much for keeping the group going through the two medical issues my family had and while I buckled down and finished this book. I don't know everything you ladies did to pull it off, but thank you. We are definitely a tribe.

Thank you, Jenna Graceli Kaye for encouraging me and doing Writing Buddies with me at times, and for making the author takeover announcement, and I don't have a clue how much more. You helped while you were sick and writing your book. I can't wait to read it.

Thank you, Victoria Trout/Heidi Swift. I'm so grateful I met you. You have become family to me. I think we agreed on cousins. I think it's more. You have been so supportive through this book. Your messages and encouragement kept me going. I wish we didn't live in separate states.

Tiffany Buras Parker, thank you so much for being there when I need you. We don't get to talk every day, but girl, you know how to show up right on time. You're one of the best beta readers I could ever hope for. This book wouldn't have made it without your help. I'm so glad we got to meet at the Fair. I hope we can do more events together. I love your books. I can't wait to read your next one. Your shifter series is my favorite. And then there's always Sam. I love Sam.

To Ghostface_gulfcoast, thank you for being our Jack. I'm glad I found you on Instagram. Thank you so much for helping Indie authors. I don't think you get enough credit or thank yous for all you do. And thank you for the sacrifices you make for our country. We'll have you back when it's Jay's turn to share his story.

Thank you to Coty and Kayla Pearson. I'm so glad I met you two. Thank you for the motorcycle club information you give me. I had no idea where to start with this. I'd look stupid without you, lol. I can't wait to see you two on Coty's book. It's coming real soon. Your photo shoot was awesome. You're both natural models!

Thank you, Darin Worley. Hey, cuz. Thank you for being our Worley Bird in this series, and real life lol. You were the first person I contacted when I decided to write an MC series. Hope my guys don't step on too many toes for you.

To Frank Thompson. Dude, you are so so missed. There was no way I could write an MC series and not have Cloudy Daze in there. Fly high my friend.

Big Papa, aka, Jerry Blume. Thanks dude for allowing me to keep your wife on the phone and text messages all the time. Thank you for being in my series. We can't have Lil Mama in here without you. You're also a bartender in the *For the Love of a Shaw* series. Take care of my best friend, dude.

To Joe Milam, thank you for talking to me in a Walmart parking lot in middle Tennessee. I hope you see this. I gave you a character and helped you out with a road name. Hopefully, we'll meet again sometime. Meeting you on New Year's Day gave me a new purpose. I drove away, hearing in my head, *Meet them all.* Now, I'm on a mission to meet as many bikers as I can. In fact, I'm getting a journal and hoping they'll sign it. I'm saving the first spot for you.

To Chrystal Harman, the BEST PA and Sissi I could ever hope for, want, and need. Thank you for all you do for my books, but I thank you more for becoming part of my found family. We met through T. L. Drake when I found her book *Wren* from the *Road Demons* series in a contest and tagged her. Y'all didn't know it was there. We helped her win that! Over the next couple of years, you became more than a friend. We have so much in common it was scary. Thank you for becoming my PA last year. Three years, Sissi, and eternity to go. You can't get rid of me. For this book and series, you gave me the name Lily for our female lead. You gave me Willow Creek for the town. You gave me Shepherd as an Enforcer. He's in the Texas chapter. Thank you, girl, for everything. Mainly for listening when I needed you.

The Dawson Boys

Holding Her ~ Book One
Harrison & Tru
　　Losing her destroyed me. One letter gave me hope. Like a man on a mission, I went after her.

I Do It For You ~ Book Two
Bryan & Dana
　　Sometimes, slow, steady, and sweet are not the best way to go. Did I wait too long? Did my plan fail? I don't know, but I'd do anything for her.

Everything I Ever Wanted ~ Book Three
Calen & Daisy
　　"Get out!" I've shouted those words every day. Does she listen? Not a chance.　She challenges me. She tests me. How did she become everything I ever wanted?

Book Four ~ Coming Soon!

Hayden Falls

Forever Mine ~ Book One
Aiden and E
   Today, I'm going home to a town that wrote me off years ago. Home to watch the woman I love marry someone else. I'm not going to survive this.

Only With You ~ Book Two
Miles and Katie
   My career was strong and sure. My personal life was a mess. My only regret was keeping her a secret. Winning her back won't be easy, but I have to try.

Giving Her My Heart ~ Book Three
Jasper and Hannah
   The dance teacher annoys me at every turn until she twirls her way into my heart and my daughter's. Now, I need to find a way to get her to stay.

Finding Home ~ Book Four
Luke and Riley
   I was the fun brother until my twin almost died in a fire. Now, I'm a mess. Then she came along. I'm charming, but am I enough for her to stay?

Listening to My Heart ~ Book Five
Phillip and Tara
   My family took the biggest part of my heart from me. A piece I didn't know existed. After nine years, the woman who holds every piece of my heart returns, bringing a huge secret with her. This time, no one will keep me from her.

A Hayden Falls Christmas
Spend Christmas in Hayden Falls. Enjoy a short story about the five couples we've met, plus two of the town's beloved families.

Falling for You ~ Book Six
Lucas and Hadley
I'm a career-minded deputy. I wasn't looking for love. Until my little brother butted into my love life, I never even noticed the woman right in front of me.

Finally Home ~ Book Seven
Aaron and Kennedy
If I had known joining the Army would have cost me her, I never would have enlisted.

Protecting You ~ Book Eight
Leo and Kyleigh
I'm the quiet brother. Nothing gets under my skin. Well, not until a little brunette swings her way into my life and changes everything.

A Hayden Falls Christmas ~ Two
Spend Christmas in Hayden Falls. Enjoy a short story about the three couples we've met since the last Christmas book, plus updates on a few of the town's beloved families.

Book Nine ~ Coming Soon!

For the Love of a Shaw

When A Knight Falls ~ Book One
Gavin & Abby
The future Earl will battle his long-time enemy more than once when he falls for his nursemaid. Will Abby marry the wrong man to save an innocent girl?

Falling for the Enemy ~ Book Two
Nate & Olivia
Nathaniel Shaw takes a job to prove his worth to his father. He loses his heart to the mysterious woman in his crew only to discover she isn't who she claims to be.

A Knight's Destiny ~ Book Three
Nick & Elizabeth
Nicholas Shaw is a Knight without a title, but he's loved the Duke's sister for years. When Elizabeth needs protection and runs away, Nick goes with her rather than sending her to her brother.

Capturing A Knight's Heart ~ Book Four
Jax & Nancie
The rules of society don't bind Jackson Shaw. He's free to roam as he pleases until he stumbles across a well-kept secret of Miss Nancie's. Will Nancie guard her heart and push him away? Or has she truly captured this Knight's heart?

A Duke's Treasure ~ Book Five
Sam & Dani
The Duke of Greyham, Samuel Dawson, has loved Lady Danielle Shaw for years. Dani stumbles into his darkest secret, leaving Sam no choice but to steal her away.

A Knight's Passion ~ Book Six
Caleb & Briley
Caleb Shaw feels lost, alone, and misunderstood. His mind is haunted by his past. While running for his life, he devises a plan to save Briley. The bluff is called, trapping them together forever.

A Mysterious Knight ~ Book Seven
Alex & Emily
Alexander Shaw had no light, peace, or love if he didn't have her. The day she sent him away almost destroyed him. Emily's trapped in her father's secrets and can't break free no matter how much she wants to. Alex will risk his life to free hers.

About the Author

Debbie Hyde is a Contemporary & Historical Romance Author. Her series include, at this time, For the Love of a Shaw, The Dawson Boys, Hayden Falls, and Viking Warriors MC. More series are planned. Another will be released in 2025.

Debbie loves helping readers, authors, and narrators connect. She created the Facebook group, The Fireside Book Café, for that purpose.

She's a seamstress and a cake decorator. When she's not reading and writing, or running around for her children and grandchildren, they keep her VERY busy, she loves creating book covers and graphics.

Debbie Hyde

www.ingramcontent.com/pod-product-compliance
Lightning Source LLC
LaVergne TN
LVHW041701060526
838201LV00043B/513